Killer Series Book 3

KILLER WITH BLACK BLOOD

KILLER WITH BLACK BLOOD

J L HILL

To P.C. for all the rides we shared.

'Do not be amazed at this, for a time is coming when all who are in their graves will hear his voice and come out– those who have done what is good will rise to live, and those who have done what is evil will rise to be condemned.' John 5:28-29

CONTENTS

A HOME IN HELL

Nicky exits the Long Island mansion and quickly turns his collar up against the harsh March wind. A scowl carves his face but not from the cold outside, it's the bitterness that is eating through his soul this morning. He pulls the door to the Cadillac with enough force to almost unhinge it and dives into the back seat to the cheerful voice of his driver Rocky,

"Good morning, Boss. Looks like plenty of sunshine today, a great day for a ride. Don't ya think?"

"Who the fuck asked for a fucking weather report?" snarls Nicky. "Drive the Goddamn fucking car. I want to get Sal and get this Goddamn thing over with. Fucking great day for a Mother Fucking drive. Are you shitting me?"

"Well, I'd say you just found out somebody been kicking your dog. But I know you don't have a dog, not as a pet anyway. So, what got your nuts all twisted this morning, you miserable fuck," Pauley says, shifting in the back seat next to Nicky. He gives a nod and wink to the young driver through the rear-view mirror and the car speeds up the driveway.

"I just got the final bill on the thing," Nicky throws his hands up, "fucking crooks, every goddamn one of them. Three fucking mil, can you believe that?"

"I've seen it," Pauley says in a serene voice. He opens the bar built into the back of the driver's seat, shuffles the two .45s automatic to the side, and takes out two glasses. "Here, hold these."

"I don't want a drink!"

"Well, I do. It's fucking early. So, hold the fucking glasses and stop being a prick."

"Look, Uncle Pauley, stop trying to treat me like a kid. I ain't no kid anymore!"

"Then stop acting like one," Pauley's face is hard now. His snow-white hair barely covers his head, which is why he always has his fedora on, except in the car. He pours two stiff drinks and takes back one glass. He has put on weight in all the wrong places, his daily regimen of boxing three rounds obviously a losing battle. Strong hands and arms don't make up for a bulging mid-section. Still, he commands respect. "Look, you did a good thing. Italian marble all the way, not that cheap crushed façade stuff. It is going to make Sal happy. You know he's fucking miserable in that fucking nut house."

"I know." Nicky shoots down the drink and opens the compartment behind the passenger's seat. A mirrored tray extends, and he pulls out a glass medicine vial and a silver straw. Removing the glass stopper from the vial, he dumps a pile of white powder on the mirror. With one finger, he closes the left nostril and snorts the powder through the silver straw into his right. Then he holds his glass up for another pour of Absolut. "But what am I supposed to do with him now? It's been six months and not a word about it. Somebody got to him…"

"You know that's crazy," Pauley sips his drink like a gentleman, "I've known you boys all your lives, nobody could talk to Sal but you and your father. And Sal never left the farmhouse except for his doctor's visits. And I was with him for most of those. And your father or mother, it's just impossible…" He pours a drink for Nicky and takes the silver straw. He inhales a good amount of the powder from the mirror and shoots back in his seat. "Is this stuff pure?"

"Only the best!"

"You know your father wouldn't approve of you doing drugs like this."

"Such hypocrisy," Nicky fakes, "youse guys drink ninety percent of the time and you're not alcoholics. I take a little bump as an eye-opener and I'm a drug addict."

"Hey, it's nothing like that. Just take it easy with the drugs. I've seen, and you have too, it can take people to some dark places." Pauley snorts again into the other nostril, a little less enthusiastically, and passes the straw back to Nicky who finishes off the pile of cocaine. "Back to Sal, whatever happened at the farm is locked inside his head."

"That's why he's at St. Joseph Hospital. And let me tell you, those fucking guys…" Nicky shoots down his second drink like he forgot he was holding it. He shudders and blows hard as this shot burns more than the first. "…no one can spend the money like the Catholics. I'll give you that."

"I did like you asked and checked out the doctor. He was handpicked by your father, and you know how thorough he was about things like this," Pauley sounds apologetic. He wants to tell Nicky something good, but this is not going to make him feel better. "The doctor is clean. He has more money than God, so no one could have paid him off. No evidence of coercion either. He said it could have been the medication. Maybe they gave him too much, or Sal stopped taking it. You remember the chickens… There is just no way of knowing what was going on inside Sal's head."

The rest of the short drive out to St. Joseph was quiet.

THE HOSPITAL COMPLEX was about ten miles from Angelo's mansion, which Nicky now occupied fulltime since Elizabeth and Maria had moved to the Greek Islands with MoJo. It had always been the seat of power for the Family, even when his father ran things they would meet out on the Island, not at the farm Upstate. When he took over from his dad, everyone knew he would run things from there.

The car turned up the driveway of St. Joseph, each of the white brick buildings separated by immaculate green lawns the size of a football field. They passed three edifices before turning down another driveway towards the biggest one. It was five stories, made from massive granite stones, and the only building in the complex surrounded by a six-foot tall iron fence. The black rods came straight up and out of the ground too close together to even get an arm through. Every window had the same black iron rods. The place looked more like a prison than a hospital.

It had been a military prison during the Civil War. In the mid-nineteen-hundreds the Jesuits bought it from the state and added two more buildings. And now, there were five, thanks to Nicky's generosity.

Nicky laughs. "Is it just me or does this place gets bigger each time we come here?"

"We haven't been here in what… a month? But I would say so. You want I should come in with you?"

"No, I'm gonna talk to the fucking priest for a minute before Sal comes down."

The gate rolls back slowly as something that size does and then the black caddy with blacked-out windows drives straight to the front door. A very old priest, Fr. Sheridan, steps out of a crack in the huge oak doors.

Rocky, the driver, says, "you think the old guy has the cojones to open that door? Or are there like a dozen old guys back there with him?"

They laugh. As Nicky exits the car, Pauley grabs his arm, "I have to tell you something later. Don't let me forget. It's important."

"Tell me now."

"No, it can wait. Just don't let me forget. You know how us old guys are," Pauley looks into the rear-view with a twisted grin.

"I wasn't talking about you, Mr. Pauley," Rocky says with a slight shrill. He is less than half Pauley's size no matter how you measure him. And is probably not much in the ring either, "I know you got the balls for anything."

"Relax, kid. Maybe one day, when you're ready to become a man, I'll let you borrow them."

Nicky laughs, "You should be thankful your momma sucks good head, Marrone!"

Nicky takes the stairs quickly, shakes the priest's hand, and disappears into the hospital. They walk down the marbled hall, their footsteps echoing loudly in the spacious interior. It's dark with drapes and tapestries, pictures of Jesuits hang everywhere, a few are smiling, very few. Nicky hates this place. From the prison look outside to the austerity of the atmosphere within, it embodies everything he hates about his religion. Putting Sal in here was a bad idea, but he felt if anyone could get through to him, these priests would.

They reach the office, and he takes a seat. "So, tell me, Father, has he said anything about what happened? You know… has he made his confession?"

"Confession?" the old priest leans back in his high back chair covered in plush red velvet. "He was very agitated this month.

With you not coming for your weekly outing. He does not confess to anything per se, but he does... and again, he got extremely emotional when you didn't show for the second weekend in a row. He started talking about killing bananas and Old Joe. Ah, I don't know how to put this, so here's the thing. Was he involved in any other killings? A witness or a..."

"Hey, I'm not interested in any other killings!" Nicky explodes. "I brought him to you, so you can get the truth out of him about one thing and that's it. Youse guys have been taking my money for years and now you want to get all holier than thou on me?"

"Mr. Rocci, this place may look like a medieval castle," Fr. Sheridan, his slim body almost invisible enveloped in the black robes of his order, says firmly but calmly, "but we don't practice any inquisition tactics here. We do not preform exorcisms or cast any magical spells. The priests here are trained psychologist and psychiatrist, not mind readers. Let me give you a little advice."

Nicky squirms in his plush chair and sinks a little deeper. He has hated the clergy for as long as he can remember and almost feels the sting of his mother's slap on the back of his neck just as when they used to be called into the office for something or other. He pretends to listen.

"There are three people you should never lie to," cautions the priest. "Your lawyer because he holds your freedom. Your doctor because he holds your life. And your priest because he holds you for eternity. We might be better able to help your brother and get the answers you seek if we knew more about what went on at the farm. What Sal was exposed to and what was kept hidden. And as a doctor, like a confession, anything you tell me is confidential information. Think about it. Meanwhile, I'll have Sal brought down."

SAL SITS between Nicky and Pauley and every five minutes asks where they are going, but Nicky hasn't said a word since leaving St. Joseph.

As they cross the Throgs Neck Bridge into the Bronx, Sal squeals, "You are taking me home to Mommy and Daddy!"

Pauley looks at Nicky and shrugs.

Nicky shakes his head slowly, "Sal, you know where we're going. But I have a big surprise. I built Mom and Dad a house just like the farmhouse."

The car pulls into St. Peter Cemetery. Sal starts rocking and bouncing in the back of the car. As the car turns up a winding road, Sal's arms flail wildly. Nicky, who daily gets in the ring with Pauley, grabs Sal's wrists with one hand and pins them to his lap.

"No. No. No. Nicky, you are supposed to take me to Mommy and Daddy. Not here. Mommy and Daddy are in Heaven. Daddy said you will take me to Heaven with them. I've been good. I've been a good boy, Nicky. I promise." He starts to cry.

"Well, there go three million dollars down the drain," Nicky says angrily. "Get the fuck out the car, Sal. Let's go look at this fucking mausoleum I built for you."

They walk up the hill—a hard climb as the path is steep—to reach the marble farmhouse at the top. Nicky had to buy all the gravesites around his family plot to build the mausoleum. He recalls the picture on the office wall of St. Peter, maybe a hundred years or more in the past, the view from the cemetery was of apple blossoms, white trees, and quaint little homes spread out across the valley. Now, the view is blocked on three sides by high-rises fifteen stories and more, the only clear view a sliver of the river to the north.

Although no one had been buried in the graves around his family plot in more than a century, they still charged him over a million dollars to acquire the land. And of course, he could not move the graves, there had to be a small plaque in the ground alongside the mausoleum with the names of those it covered up, state law. It covered thirty-two gravesites. The farmhouse replica was built to scale, 25 feet long, ten feet wide, and seven feet in height. It had rose-colored marble insets for the windows and black marble for the roof. The main doors in the center were hung on gold hinges, guaranteed not to rust.

I must have been pretty stoned when I okayed this monstrosity. I got to tell Pauley to send some boys over to that contractor to break his arms and legs. The last time he had been here, it was to bury some aunt he barely knew, fifteen years before he had to lay his mother and father to rest last winter.

"NO. NO. NO. I DON'T WANT TO BE HERE. DADDY SAID I WOULD GO TO HEAVEN WITH HIM AND MOMMY. HE PROMISED ME. I'VE BEEN A GOOD BOY."

Sal was becoming hyper, turning in circles, not knowing where to go. Nicky grabs his arm and gives him a yank. Sal is both taller and huskier than Nicky, but meek and submissive.

Nicky places both hands on his shoulders, "I don't know what you're talking about, Sal. You can't go to heaven if you're still alive. And even when you do, God knows you'll be the only one in this family to make it in, I sure as hell won't bet on Papa being there. Mom, yeah, she'll be there. But if you see Dad, you took the wrong elevator."

Sal pulls away, standing in front of the marble structure mumbling incoherently.

"What are you saying? Look, why don't we go inside? You can see Mom's and Dad's urns. I got them those real nice gold vases you said you liked. And their wedding picture is in there too. Maybe say a little prayer. Tell them YOU ARE SORRY FOR SMOTHERING THEM... YOU FUCKING RETARD."

"Mommy said you are not supposed to call me that," Sal

says. "Father Sheridan said God knows everything. The why and the how, He forgives all that we do."

Well, thank you Father Sheridan. At least you are not just taking my money and fucking me up the ass.

Sal drops to his knees in front of the mausoleum door.

Nicky yells, "If you are crying, I am gonna kick your ass!"

Sal falls face down on the mount. Nicky sees a wide blood spot on the back of his head. Then, nothing.

"So, what do you think?"

Pauley lights a cigar, "What do I think about what, Rocky?"

"Do you think Nicky is going to off his brother? I mean… the word is Sal killed his parents," Rocky remarks. He puffs on a cigarette and tries to blow smoke rings in the air. He leans one elbow on the front fender of the caddy, "I mean, if it were my mother and father, I'd off him. Even if he is my own brother. Nicky must want to whack him. Maybe not personally but get someone to take care of him. Nicky seems to be on the edge of crazy."

"Shut the fuck up! Are you fucking crazy? If Nicky hears you talking like that… fuck it! Nobody touches Sal, understand me. NOBODY. If you ever say anything like that again I'll…" Pauley is about to take a swing at him when he notices Sal and Nicky lying in front of the marble farmhouse. He starts running up the hill, dodging headstones as he goes.

Rocky takes the path and being younger beat him to Sal's side.

Pauley arrives a second later and quickly accesses the situation, "Leave him! Sal is dead. Help me get Nicky to the car."

Rocky had Nicky under the arms and carefully pulls him into the back seat.

Pauley takes off his jacket and then his shirt. "Here! Use my shirt and keep pressure on the wound. I'll drive."

Pauley floors the gas pedal and the caddy roars through the cemetery. He hits the street, heading for Our Lady of Mercy Hospital not far in the northern section of the Bronx. The car weaves in and out of traffic. The vehicle swings across the double yellow lines, dodges oncoming cars before swinging back to the right lane, then blows through red lights. His experience as a get-away driver kicks in; never hitting the breaks, he races through the streets. Four police cars fail to stop him until he's at the hospital's emergency entrance. The police look in the back seat and run inside to get help.

A doctor throws up his hand and stops Pauley from entering, "Sir, you have to ditch the cigar."

Pauley looks at his right hand, the fat stogie is lodged between his index and pointer fingers still smoldering. He tosses the cigar into the street and follows the doctors, Rocky, and Nicky on a gurney with his fedora neatly on his head, but bare chested.

Two police officers, one on each side of him, shout questions at him.

SITTING at the pool under the hot and high sun, Yana looks out from under her wide brim straw hat at the servant's legs approaching. *What the hell does she want now?*

The young Greek girl bends over her, "Miss Yana, there is a long distance call for you. From America."

"Why didn't you bring the extension with you?"

"It is on the line in the study." The girl steps back to give her room to stand then leaves her, having done her job.

Yana stretches lazily, swings her feet from the lounge chair, and stretches again. *More gossip from the girls. I don't care what Nicky Nails is up to, I'm not telling Morris. He is not running off to America on some wild adventure Nicky has cooked up.*

Before she can say a word after hello, Cherry Bomb is frantically telling her Nicky is near death. She tries to console her between the sobbing and crying that pours out of the receiver. An eternity passes before Rosalina is calm enough to comprehend what Yana is saying. "It's going to be okay. I don't know where Morris is right now, probably in town, so I'm sending someone to get him. We will be there by tomorrow. It's going to be okay."

MORRIS RUSHES into the bedroom and sees Yana, Elizabeth, and Gisella packing bags. "What's all this?" he asks.

"We are going to New York with you," Yana says, acting as the spokeswoman for the group. It has been her role since Morris returned to her life.

"No, you're not," he replies. "Elizabeth, you have to look after Maria. Or did you just forget about her?"

"The servants can get her off to school like they do every day."

Morris casts her an angry eye and she shrinks away from the baggage. "This is probably nothing," he says. "Just another crazy scheme of Nicky's. Besides, I'll be flying on a military jet, can't exactly bring along three hotties, can I?"

"If this is nothing, why the military jet?" Questions Gisella.

"You know I'm not exactly welcomed in the U.S.," Morris laughs, "but if this turns out to be anything at all, I need to travel incognito. I can't be seen arriving in New York every time a mobster bites one, even if he is my friend. And a NATO jet will have me there in half the time."

"Well, I'm coming with you," demands Yana.

"Oh, yeah, like you wouldn't be recognized. A movie star, known worldwide, travelling on a military jet wouldn't raise anyone's suspicions?"

"Okay, then I'm going," Gisella insists, "I'll be your military aide. No one knows me."

Morris studies the three women, trying to figure a way out of this situation.

They stare back, ready for his next argument.

"If Nicky's been shot what makes you think I would let you three get mixed up in this mess? And since when do I need a babysitter?"

"You probably always needed a babysitter," Gisella tells him, and slams shut her suitcase as if to say the matter is settled.

"Military aides don't travel with Gucci," Morris admits defeat as graciously as he can. "I have my bugout bag ready, go get a duffle bag from the storage room and meet me at the car. You have five minutes and then I leave without you."

GISELLA WAS AMAZED when Morris produced fake ID badges for her, because for a spur of the moment trip, he had planned an unwelcome inconvenience well in advance. She had now been living with him for two years and he still managed to surprise her every day.

Morris appeared at the base in full uniform, presenting credentials that the guard at the gate took one look at and waved him ahead. He played the part well, saluting on cue, barking orders to the grounds crew, even putting one man on report when he queried about Gisella.

The flight crew got the plane ready quickly, none wanting to spend more time than they had to with the surly officer. He was having a bad day, and no one wanted to make it worse. Gisella would have chalked it up to an act, but she saw beneath the façade. Morris was having a bad day. She was right to insist on going. More than once she felt he was close to killing someone, for nothing more than a poorly chosen word.

The sleek jet, a cross between a military and luxury aircraft with wings long and tapered thin, took off from the NATO base in Thessaloniki. She had never seen such a craft.

Seeing her interest, he told her. "It's an updated model of the U2 spy plane. Built for high altitude, high speed flights. It will get us to New York in a third of the time any conventional plane would. But I had all the spy gear ripped out, so it's really nice inside."

When they entered the plane, she noticed a spacious although narrow cabin. There were four lounge chairs that swiveled and reclined all the way to a bed. A small bar ran along one wall and a small bathroom with a shower was at the back of the plane. "This can't be a military plane, can it?"

"What? You didn't know this day would come. I told you, in my world, I have to be ready for everything all the time. The U.S. military has the best aircraft in all sorts of configurations."

"Is the pilot in the Air Force?"

Morris filled her glass with champagne, "He is in the Greek Air Force and as far as he knows I'm Major Nelson, Anthony Nelson." Morris laughed, knowing she didn't get the reference to the popular TV show. The pilot didn't connect the name either. "Before we land, you will have to put on the uniform in the back.

And no matter what, you don't say a word. You just carry the bags, OK?"

"Why a Major? Why not a General?"

"Too many questions," he said, "a Major is high enough not to be stopped by some Airman at the base we are going to. Don't worry, I'm sure this is going to turn out to be a whole lot of nothing. I know Nicky."

"I don't know, Morris. Yana said Rosalina was hysterical on the phone. This may be more than what you think."

It was more than a year after they had left Argentina before Morris reappeared in her life and she didn't know much about him other than that he was involved in crime. His name never came up in news stories, but the way he acted, including back then, definitely pointed to him being a crime boss. She should have told him to keep going, but he was true to his word and come back for her. She had already fallen in love with him back in the jungle, so she followed her heart and him to Greece.

It was somewhat of an idyllic situation, even if he had two other wives already, but she felt like she was the only one that mattered when he was with her. She could see the pain he was in now and wanted to ease his burden, but as soon as the plane took off, he withdrew to a place she could not reach.

Morris didn't want to say it, but he was concerned this time. Last time he got a call about Nicky being shot, he had rushed to New York from Aruba, been much closer then, only a couple of hours. This trip would take six hours at supersonic speed.

Way too much time, Nails could be dead by the time I land.

2

YOU KNOW HE'S CRAZY

I am on my way to Manhattan General Hospital at 5:00 a.m., having just stepped off the plane at LaGuardia Airport fifteen minutes ago. Naturally, there is no traffic this early in the morning, just a few garbage trucks rumbling through the streets. The night crew, hustlers, hoes, cops, and drunks have found their way back to their little holes. Mounds of homeless dot the sidewalks and tuck into corners, but they are quiet at this time. The city is preparing for the onslaught of daytime life. Businesspeople will soon storm the streets and create their own brand of mayhem. This is the time of day I like best, the in-between time when I feel I'm the only one in the city.

"So, tell me again, how do you know it's Nicky Nails who was gunned down?"

"It was all over the news last night," Byron George tells me while driving up the West Side Highway. "They went on for hours. How he's a suspected member of a mob family. His girlfriend, Angela Lucas, was killed in the attack. She's the daughter of Peter Lucas, he's a crime boss in Brooklyn."

"I know who Peter Lucas is," I snap, "I've only been in

15

Aruba for the past three years, I didn't fall off the face of the earth. How did it happen? What's the word on the street?"

"I can't tell you, boss," Byron looks up to the rear-view mirror, "it just happened, out of the blue. You know how crazy those Italian boys are. One day everything is fine, business as usual, then BAM! Bodies are popping up all over the place."

I know that's the truth. Things are getting hot in Colombia; the cocaine business is new and untamed. New players every day trying to make a name for themselves or trying to make a big score and get out quick. Well, if someone thinks they can pop Nicky and get away with it, they are sorely mistaken. "When you drop me off at the hospital, put the word out, everybody gets locked and loaded. We are hunting bear. If someone looks at you cross-eyed take them out."

"Boss, this may not have anything to do with us," Byron offers.

"If it hits the Roccis, it hits us. We can't afford to be caught sleeping, or second-guessing. If the Rocci Family is going to war they are going to need our soldiers on the front lines too. Capisce?"

"You got it, Boss." Byron stops the car at a side entrance to the hospital.

I get out and start towards the door.

Byron yells, "You want I should send some guys over for you. You know, just to be on the safe side?"

Reaching inside my jacket, I feel for my gun in its shoulder holster, then the one in my right pocket. I even strapped a third into a leg holster when Byron picked me up at the airport. "No need, I'll be fine. I'll page you later."

The halls are sterile white, and the low hum of medical equipment fill the chilled air. *Why do they always keep these places so cold? People are going to die of pneumonia if whatever they came in with doesn't get them.* I go up a back stairwell to reach the third floor while avoiding the usual gathering of cops and come out beyond the nurses' station and another group of cops.

I see Nicolas and Lucille sitting in the hall outside of Nicky's room. Pauley is with them and so is Vincent, Nicolas' two closest friends and confidants. Before I can say hello, Lucille gets up and gives me a hug. The men pat me on the back.

Nicolas says, "You didn't need to come."

"What are you talking about? Of course I'd be here. Nicky is my closest friend. Maybe my only friend."

"Well, OK then, go on in and see him," Nicolas pushes the door open.

Nicky is lying on his back, wires and tubes running from under the sheets to various machines beeping and humming along. His eyes are shut, and I watch for a second, studying the monitors. I stare back at his face. The door silently clicks shut.

Standing by Nicky's bedside, I put a hand to his forehead. "My old friend, your mother and father are out there suffering. It's better that I end this quick. I know you would thank me if you could." I pull my .45 from the shoulder holster and pull the slide back. I let it go and the gun chambers a round, loudly.

Nicky bolts upright in the bed. "What the fuck are you doing? Are you crazy?"

"Thanks be to God," I cry out, "Nicky, you are healed… You cock-sucking son of a bitch!"

"What? You were just going to shoot me. That's how you treat a wounded friend?"

"You… Fucking… Bastard," I yell at him. "No offense to your parents. There's not a thing wrong with you. I flew all the way from Aruba because I heard you'd been shot. And this is what I find. You could get out of that bed and run a marathon; you prick."

"Don't blame me, I didn't tell anyone to call you."

"It's all over the news, stupid. Of course, I'm gonna hear about it."

"Oh, yeah," Nicky gets out of the bed. The tubes for medicine are taped to his body. "Well, as you can see, I'm fine, so you can go back home."

"I should still shoot you. Just because. What the fuck have you got going on this time?"

Nicky hesitates to tell me, but he knows I'm already pissed, "OK, sit down. This is gonna take a while."

NICKY ARRIVED at the farmhouse late in the evening and Sal was happy to see him. As he always did when he went home, he teased Sal, calling him a momma's boy, then told him he had a secret mission for him. "Go to the kitchen and get me some Prosciutto. Don't you get caught."

His father had called him for dinner, but afterwards admitted to the real reason for the invitation.

Nicolas says, "Come to the wine cellar, we have to discuss a very important business deal. I have a proposal for you to consider."

Nicky follows his father into the barn and down into the wine cellar.

Nicolas uncorks a bottle and pours two glasses of red wine. "Salute!"

"Salute," responds Nicky and drinks. The horrid beverage twists his face into a mask of death. "This stuff is truly poison. Why do you keep trying to make wine? You stink at it."

Nicolas chuckles. "Your great grandfather and his two brothers came to this country with ten dollars between them and a couple of pots of grape vines. Back in the old country they were wine makers, but so bad, they got run out of town. And were told to take their grapes with them."

"Maybe, instead of making wine, you should make vinegar." Nicky laughs.

"Your Great Uncle Piero suggested that," Nicolas says with a boyish grin, "and your great grandfather shot him where he stood. So, we take one drink of wine and no more." Nicolas got serious again.

Nicky felt the change and sat down across the little table.

"Nicky, our family is in trouble. I must ask you to do something, not as your father, but as your Godfather. You understand the difference?"

He did. "You want me to take a bid for someone. I can do it. How many years are we talking about?"

"No, it's not that, but it is a life sentence. Nicky, our businesses are strong, and since Banoa and Lucerella are gone, we have thrived. Thanks to you of course, but we have not grown. There are those in the other family who will try to push us out."

Nicky laughs, "You're kidding, right? You want me to get married and make you some babies. You are losing it, old man."

"I'm not talking about you giving me grandchildren, moron," yells Nicolas, wonderings how his son never comprehends the immediate situation. "You only see past the end of your nose. That is going to get you in more trouble than you can handle one day. I'm talking about our family not having enough muscle on the street to defend what we have."

"Are you kidding? You know MoJo has our back. He has… I don't know… hundreds of guys across the country and in South America. I got the Irish on our side, and the PRs."

Nicolas pounds the table, "that's exactly what I'm talking about. They are not Italians. Morris is a great guy, but he's not Italian. Neither is your friend, Jesus. The other families don't respect us, and they are planning on making a move. I hear talk…"

"Let them try and pull some shit, I will hand them their balls," Nicky explodes. He gets up from the table and starts for the steps.

"Come back here," demands Nicolas, fire in his voice. "I'm not done here. I am trying to avoid a war; one we cannot win no matter how many outsiders you bring in. If we have others spill Italian blood, the war will never end until we are dead." He walks over to Nicky and grabs his son by the back of his neck. He shakes him a little roughly and points to the chair. Nicky sits back down, and Nicolas continues, "you marry either the Della Russo girl or Lucas' daughter. Both are good looking and more important, it will tie their family to ours."

Nicky softly says, "You are crazy, old man. What do you think this is, the middle ages?"

"It has been the way powerful families maintain their power. By building alliances," Nicolas tells his son. He speaks with fatherly tenderness knowing the great weight his son must shoulder. "Look, it will strictly be a marriage of convenience. You can keep your whores and whatever you like to do with your time. Just treat the girl right in public… Maybe knock her up right away to seal the deal. As I said before, I am asking this as your Godfather. You do this for the family." He stands behind Nicky, his hand resting heavily on his shoulder, waiting for a favorable answer.

Nicky shakes away the grip. "I tell you what, I'll go out with them. You know, see what they're like. In the meantime, I'll put some of my guys on the street to see if there is anything to worry about. Now let's go back to the house and get some real wine."

NICKY SAT on the bed smoking a joint I had rolled. He was deep into his story, but I wanted to know how he ended up getting shot. He showed me the bullet wound on his chest, it wasn't impressive.

"OK, so, my boys tell me Lucas is pushing on my territory in the Bronx." Nicky continues. "He got some of his guys running football sheets. You know, you pick the winners of the games each week and get paid if you get twelve or more right. Only with the points spread and such, very few people win. It's a really good money-making deal."

"Get to the point, will ya."

"Yeah, Lucas is trying to muscle in on my gambling operation, and his daughter Angela is a real slut. To say she's been around the block a few times is like saying a bus is just a big car. Yeah, I nailed her, but marry that bitch? No fucking way." Nicky passes me the joint. "Anyway, the funny thing is, she's down with the whole marriage deal. Her father's been riding her ass and she thought she could get out of the house and be able to do as she pleased."

"Nicky, I'm dying over here," I plead with him. "How did you get shot?"

"Ok, you fucking kill-joy." Nicky takes another hit off the joint and continues, "I go out with Carmella Della Russo. She's not ok with marrying me. She has a boyfriend and all, but here's the thing, she wants to head up her own crew. Being married to me is the same as being the boss' daughter, no chance she'll get to run a crew. So, I make her an offer."

NICKY AND ANGELA are sitting at Carmine's in Little Italy. It's a small place, an intimate bar outside of either of their territories. Nicky picked the spot for their third date for that exact reason, telling her they need to get away from both their families. She was more than willing to go, the thought of her father not knowing her location for a few hours all she needed. They had dinner and a bottle of wine.

"I have an apartment around the corner." Nicky says. "No one knows me here. In this neighborhood, I'm just a regular guy."

"This wouldn't be where you take your Russian hoes?"

"What? What the fuck are you talking about?"

Angela smiles and rubs his arm from across the table. "Oh, don't play dumb with me, Nicky Nails!" She purposely says his name a little louder. She watches him squirm, his eyes scanning the room without moving his head. "Oh, you are good. Yes, I know all about your Russian prostitutes. I know you have one or two on the side as your favorites. Tell me, what are the Russian girls like? Because no matter what stories you heard about me, there's a bunch of stuff I'm not going to do."

"Oh, yeah, Angela Lucas," this time, I call out her name. "I heard them call you the Soul Sucker, because you can suck a man's dick so hard, he nearly dies when he cums."

"Hahaha," she laughs loudly, tossing and letting her blonde locks fall around her face her dark roots show. Her sparkling blue eyes accent the suppleness of her smile. She has a devilish look that is highlighted by the candle glow and Merlo. "That's not why they call me that. It's because I gave a blow job to a black guy in high school. He was the captain of the basketball team. Big, six-two, strong, with the biggest cock I ever seen. My father had him shot… After he had the guys burn his genitals off."

"Well, we're not in high school anymore," Nicky says, not knowing if she's just messing with his head. *My little cunt, I'm fucking the shit out of you tonight. And if your father doesn't like it, I'll have someone burn his dick off.* "That's why we're here. And don't worry about my dick size, the Russians exercise it regularly. Not here though, I don't need to hide my activities with them. However, he's quite healthy."

"We will see," she laughs again, freely, "I might be in the mood to give you a little head if it measures up. But no ass stuff, I hear those Russian whores love to take it up the ass. I tell you right now, that shit is out."

"You're thinking of the Greeks. And I'll be the one deciding the ins and outs, and the wheres." He says as they come to the end of their meal.

Nicky opens the door to the second-floor apartment, revealing a dark interior bathed by light from the streetlamp a bit down the block streaming through a large double window.

Angela walks into the middle of the room and pulls the ties on her shoulder straps. Her dress falls to the floor and she is totally naked, bathed in the white light.

What a slut, who doesn't wear underwear to dinner? Nice tight little ass though, I'm definitely hitting that thing tonight. She wouldn't have brought it up if she didn't want to give it up.

Angela turns around to look at him. "You can shut the door, unless you're expecting more company to help you handle all of this. And I see you are already thinking about it. This way to the bedroom then." She turns back around and shakes her ass before heading into the other room.

Oh, that freak wants me to tap that ass, as the niggers say. Probably been worked over before. Nice tits too. There isn't an inch of her that hasn't seen some action, I'll bet. But she keeps it in good shape. This is going to be one fucking good night.

"Are you coming in?" Angela yells from the bedroom, "or are you cumming in your pants out there?"

Nicky starts undoing his belt as he walks, his pants landing on the floor next to her dress. He throws his shirt in her face as he enters the room. "I may have to stuff that in your mouth before the night is over. The walls are thin, and the neighbors are nosey."

"I'd rather you stuff that in my mouth right now," she says and grabs his dick. She digs her black nails into his ass and swallows him.

He feels her nails going deeper into his buttocks, then her teeth sink sharply into the base of his shaft. Blue eyes look up innocently at his face, not lovingly, but looking for signs of pain. Then she lets him slide back.

I may have to marry you, but you won't be thinking of your little Russian cunts anymore.

Nicky grabs the back of her head, entwining his fingers in her hair down to the black roots she leaves for effect. He tilts her head up at an acute angle, forcing her mouth to open wider. *Ok, so this is the game you want to play. Let's see who cries first.* He shoves his dick hard into her mouth, her teeth bang against his groin. With her head pulled back she can't clamp down. He repeatedly humps her mouth violently until he feels trickles of blood from her lips and his groin.

He pushes her back on the bed and grabs her legs underneath her knees. He spreads her open. She licks her lips and smiles that wicked smile from the restaurant. *Ok, Daddy's little girl likes to be punished. Figures.* He begins pumping her as hard and as fast as he can. This isn't love making, it is naked combat. Within seconds, his chest is pounding and sweat is streaming down his body. His pace slows.

Oh no, you don't! I'm not done with you yet, Nicky Nails. I've only just begun to play. Angela kicks her legs up and free, wraps them around his hips, and in a move, that can only mean she's an accomplished trapeze artist or professional wrestler, rises up on him and flips him onto the bed. "Oh, dear boy, you are about to get the ride of your life from the Soul Sucker."

Driving her hips down, she rocks back and forth with

increasing speed and force, then slams her hands down on his chest, digging into his hair, covering her tips in blood. Her small stiff breasts barely move as she rides him. He grabs her nipples, one between each of his thumbs and index fingers, and pinches them hard, causing their color to flush to a bright pink then a darker red. She smiles wider. Her blue eyes turning darker as she works him over.

Nicky slides his hands down to her waist and bench press her body off his dick. It is swollen and throbbing, it wants more. Her body is gyrating in midair. He slams her face down ninety degrees onto the bed. She is now stretched out lengthwise and he rolls on top of her. This time it is Nicky whose fingers dig into ass flesh. He pulls her cheeks apart and admires the tiny red hole between the small mounds of soft white flesh. She flexes her knees and raises up slightly. Nicky slowly and deliberately pushes his engorged head through her anus. She coos. Then a slight shriek escapes her lips before she can bite down on his shirt.

Nicky rams her as hard as he can. Over and over, sending his dick fully into her tight little hole. His grip on her hips keeps him from slipping all the way out of her. She is slamming her ass into him on every down stoke. *Yeah, there's some Greek in you, girl.* Nicky screams loud as he rips his cock from her anus a second before he shoots his load. Like a machine gun he fires multiple streaks of cum up her back. His body jerks in rhythmic spasms. He laughs as the last two shots land on the back of her head.

"I hope your fucking shower works!"

"Who said anything about a shower," Nicky says then laughs at the shocked look on her face. "Yeah, the shower works. It's through that door. So, are you staying the night? Maybe have another go at biting my dick off, you crazy bitch."

"No, I got to go home," she tells him from the bathroom, "my father gives me hell if I stay out all night. Can you believe it? I am twenty-fucking-four years old and he still treats me like I'm in high school."

"Well, maybe you shouldn't go around fucking niggers…"

"Oh, fuck you, Nicky Nails! You fuck anything with a hole," she yells over the sound of the shower. Then dries quickly and puts on her dress.

Nicky turns on the lamp by the living room double windows.

Angela asks, "what are you doing?"

"I'm going to stay here tonight. But I'll walk you down the block and get you a cab."

"Why don't you just call for a cab? We can wait here until it arrives." She gives him that smile and flashes her blue eyes at him.

"Uh, remember, nobody knows about this place," Nicky says.

"Yeah, so who's gonna know?" Angela starts unbuckling his pants. "I know how we can pass the time…"

"Ok. But no teeth this time. I'm gonna have to get rabies shots."

When the cab blows its horn, Angela gets off her knees. They walk down the stairs, Nicky still trying to adjust the hard-on in his pants. As they stroll between the parked cars, the doors to one on the left opens.

Two men get out and say, "Nicky Nails, you are dead man!"

The first man fires, hits Angela in the head, then the chest and back, and she falls to the ground. The second shooter fires once, hitting Nicky dead center in his chest. They jump back in their car and peel out of the parking space.

The shocked cab driver calls his dispatch for help even as a police car turns the corner at the same time. They forego going after the shooters instead calling for an ambulance, which arrives in a couple of minutes. Too late for Angela, who was killed by the first shot, but they rush Nicky to the hospital where it will be reported he slipped into a coma due to shock and loss of blood.

"ARE YOU FUCKING SHITTING ME," I say in utter disbelief.

"Nope."

"You'd rather take a bullet than get married? Are you sure you're not gay? You know, like a little juice in the caboose."

"Fuck you, Morris!"

"That! That right there. That's what I'm talking about."

Nicky purposely finishes the joint. "I got Carmella to kill Angela, and her guys hit me with a powderpuff. Plus, I was wearing a vest just to be sure. At least Carmella was a virgin. I made it look like I fucked her then dumped her… while making sure Angela knew about it, and she spread it around. So, it looks like Carmella's people put out a hit on me. Lucas is going to war with the Della Russo's, and I'm going to help Carmella win. I'll be on Lucas' side because she tried to have me killed, but I'll feed her information, so she can thin the herd. You know what I mean."

"I know you're fucking crazy. I thought you said mob wars were bad for business."

Nicky gets that crazy look on his face. The one that announces another mad scheme is brewing. "They are, unless you're the one calling all the shots. And none of them are aimed at you."

"Well, one of them was," I point at his bandaged chest. "And what about when your future, now grieving, father-in-law to be discovers you're not really hurt? He'll know you set up his daughter… then the war will really be on."

"Hey, I'm in a coma for a while," Nicky says with confidence. "No one gets to see me. All those cops out there are on the payroll. Lucas will never know what hit him."

"Uh, I got in," I point out. "Your cops don't even know I'm here. Are you sure they're on your side? I'll bet they don't give a damn if you live or die. Besides, Lucas doesn't have to come himself. He can pay off a doctor, a nurse… hell, an orderly can tell you're faking. You are a sick individual, but you're not dying or comatose. Your plan needs some work. I'll go think about it and come by later." I walk out the room.

Lucille Rocci shakes her head.

I give her a hug, then I say to the four of them, "you know he's crazy."

Nicolas smiles, "He says the same thing about you."

"Yeah, but I'm not the one to get myself shot to prove it."

"You'd be surprised what someone would do for love."

"Love?"

"Yes," Nicolas confirms. "He loves this family so much he risked a bullet to save it. That girl could have had the shooters put one in his head. God protects babies, drunks, and fools. Walk with me." He leads me to the end of the corridor and looks out of the window.

There is nothing to see this early in the morning, so I get it, he doesn't want his wife to hear what he has to say next. I can see it's hard for him to say.

"I don't know what Nicky told you in there. I'm not really sure what his plans are, but this is a family matter. You know I think of you like a son. Hell, you make a better son than the idiot I have lying in that bed, but this thing must be strictly between the families. Capisce?"

I do.

He walks me back to the rest of the group. "Stick around a while, I think he's going to need more than God's help in this."

I leave the hospital and stop at a payphone on the corner, "Byron, tell the boys to stand down… I know what I said, but this is what I'm saying now. They are to protect what is ours, what's on our turf. Make sure the boys in Brooklyn get the message. Tell our Jamaican cousins to keep their dicks in their pants. Those boys are the Italians of the west, always going off half-cocked for no reason… Don't worry, I'll handle everything else myself."

CARMELLA SAT on the grass in Bryant Park behind the library at 42nd street. At lunchtime, the park fills with businesspeople and the jobless. Except for the ties, it's hard to tell who's who, as people sprawl out across the lawn. She watches a drug deal go down and the police stroll through pretending not to notice. It's a Friday afternoon, a nice sunny day in May, no one wants more work to do.

Nicky approaches from the white granite library steps. "You look comfortable."

"I'm not," Carmella growls, "and you don't look like a man who's in the hospital, comatose. How come? Are you trying to fuck me over, or are you just crazy?"

"Neither. Although the fucking part sounds good to me," Nicky slowly rolls his eyes up and down her body.

She tugs at her tie-dye skirt that is already down to her ankles.

"Relax. I'm still in the hospital, still in a coma, that part of the plan is still good. I told you to meet me here today because we have other…" Nicky looks around then sits beside her on the grass. He resumes his statement, "…problems with the plan that was recently brought to my attention."

"You are going to fuck me over," her voice jumps an octave. She calms herself and continues, "Nicky Nails, if you think you can hang me out to dry on this murder thing, I swear to GOD…"

"Will you just listen for a moment. Jesus, grow a pair." Nicky chuckles at the absurdity of his statement. "My friend MoJo came to see me in the hospital a few days ago and pointed out a couple of flaws. Let's call them that, flaws in our original plan. He has taken care of the whole I'm not in a coma problem."

"Yeah, how?"

"He swapped me out for someone who is in a coma."

Carmella squints her eyes as the images cross her mind, "Where did he find someone who looks like you in a coma?"

"Don't really know," Nicky shrugs, "for all I know he could have beat someone in the head with a hammer. Did I tell you he's fucking crazy? No matter. The other problem with the program, as MoJo sees it, once we go forward with clearing your name, Lucas will be looking hard for his daughter's killer."

"Yeah, I know that. No, wait… You didn't have anybody in mind when I had that girl wacked?"

"OK, I admit, I forgot that little detail. But here's the good thing, everybody knows MoJo is in town. He's like a bulldog and he won't stop going after the assassins until they are dead. The two shooters were from your friends in Colombia, right?"

"You can't go after Jimenez's men, he'll think I set them up, and it will start a war between his family and mine. Besides, he's my coke connection, you'd be killing my business." Carmella face twists even more. She runs her hands through her short golden-brown hair.

Nicky remembers running his hands through her hair the same way a few weeks ago and savors the moment.

His father approached her for a date with him, her father made her accept. She told Nicky straight she wasn't interested in him, wanted to marry her boyfriend Christopher, a soldier in her father's family. Her father didn't know about them and she hoped he would just leave her alone.

Nicky saw the opportunity and took full advantage, black-mailing her into sleeping with him to keep his silence. After all, her father would kill Christopher if he found out. She gave up her virginity to save the man she loved. Nicky's mind had jumped two twisted plans ahead of hers. By sleeping with him and then letting it out that he jilted her, her family would be the natural suspect in Angela's killing. He convinced her there could be no doubt by her father or his doctors that she was indeed taken advantage of. A war was sure to follow. But she also knew what kind of man Nicky was, who ran an unconventional family, so she demanded something in return; making him promised to make her head of a crew, something unheard of in the Mafia.

She bit her lip, lost virginity was a small price to pay for a seat at the family table, but now, he was going back on his deal? "You promised if I killed that girl, I'd get my bones. That if I'd helped you knock off Lucas' people, you'd get rid of the old crows in my family who have been holding me down. Now you want to take away my only business? My cocaine connection? What gives?"

"Look, this is really a simple deal," Nicky rubs his hand up her back and across her shoulder. "When the time is right, MoJo will kill Jimenez's whole family, so no need to worry it will come back on you. He'll say he tracked the killers to a retaliation hit on me over cocaine and territories. You'll be in the clear, Lucas will have his daughter's killer, and as part of the settlement to restore your good name, you'll get my cocaine business in Florida. It's already three times the value of yours and once Jimenez is out of the picture it will be worth even more. Plus, you get whatever we can bleed out of Lucas for his part in the war. See, nothing really changed, we are just tossing the old man a bone." Nicky strokes her shoulder again.

She shudders. "I told you, don't touch me, and I'm going to marry Christopher. That night meant nothing. Touch me again and I will tell my father what happened."

"Doesn't your father already know what happened? Isn't that the reason for the hitmen?" Nicky smirks. *Her mouth says no but her body screams 'do me again, Nicky. I need your hard salami in me.'*

"I told him you tried to force yourself on me, but I got away. That's when he called Jimenez to send up two of his boys. Of course, I told them who the real target was that night and gave them the dummy bullet. Shit, I should have let them blow you away, you fucking pig." Her words are coming fast and sharp. Then she bolts to her feet, wants to run away.

Nicky grabs her hand, then lets go as she shoots him a look while he still sits on the grass. "Relax, everything is gonna be ok. You can go marry your douchebag boyfriend; I don't care. We all get what we want out of this deal. But just for the record, if those guys did kill me, MoJo would be all over them, and eventually you. He's like a bulldog, never knows when to stop."

Carmella hurries out of the park.

Oh yeah, she wants another ride on the big boy. She just doesn't know how to get it. Not to worry, your time is coming.

3

THE DOUBLE CROSS

The park crowd thins out as lunch hour turns to mid-afternoon. Businessmen toss their jackets over their shoulders and head back into the canyons of midtown offices. Office girls smooth and adjust skirts and dresses, packing small blankets into oversized totes. The dealers huddle together, passing money and what's left of their stash to the runner; the one who has to make it past the police at the exits. It's an interesting game Nicky remembers all too well. The trick his crew played to perfection was to make the nervous guy the decoy and let the nonchalant person who looked like he handed off the wares the courier. After the decoy headed to one exit, the true courier would leave from another exit. The cops would converge on the wrong guy. It worked for his guys every time back in the day.

He watched as Carmella reached the exit of the park, turned back and saw him locked in on her. She hurried down the steps and practically ran up the block, the huge granite blocks of the library's retaining wall dwarfing her frail body. He figured she had just turned twenty, but like most people who grew up in a mob family was more mature for her age. They had to be,

33

because either the family business was out in the open, usually for the boys, or you grew up with whispers and closed doors, but always knowing at any moment your world could be ripped apart.

She was a strange little girl, and an only child.

Della Russo wanted a boy but his first was a girl, then, a bullet in an alley made a second an impossibility. He wanted to get Carmella out of the family business, but by the age of thirteen she was doing his books. By eighteen she knew more about the business than he did. Fat Tony should have been proud of his daughter who was a better mobster than he was at her age and given her a seat at the table, or at the very least, made her his advisor. But she had no voice, having to tell her father what he needed to do in private, and he conveyed it to his men. It was a shameful and humiliating charade, but she had to keep it up, for his sake.

Her family was on the decline. Her father's most trusted men were getting busted and jailtime. There was a coordinated effort in the New York District Attorney's office and the FBI to break the back of the New York Mafia. The old boys had held power for so long that when they went to jail it left a vacuum, and the younger guys were not ready to step up. Seemed like every day someone was getting arrested, either young or old. Then, her father introduced her to Nicolas Rocci.

He was a charming old man, hair dyed black, of course, but very soft-spoken, with kind eyes. She had never met him, merely heard his name mentioned numerous times in the past few years and knew he was well respected. Then the conversation turned to Nicky Nails. Nicolas saw the smile fade and the bright rosy cheeks turn sour. She knew his son, or at least knew of him. And from the look of her, it was not good. Regardless, she was forced into agreeing to a meeting with Nicky.

His reputation was that of a snake, quiet, sneaky, and quick to strike. He was dangerous. She agreed to meet him with their fathers' present. The Della Russos invited the Roccis to a cousin's wedding. It was loud, and a lot of people were there. She didn't know this part of the family much, they stayed away, but a couple of the boys got low level jobs from her father, drivers and that sort of thing. It was a good setting to meet Nicky. To her surprise he acted much like his father.

Nicky listened to her intently, empathizing over the plight of their families. He was smart, knew exactly what he wanted, and somehow, knew what she wanted too. She knew he liked her, but more than that, he respected her. He was quiet and soft-spoken, not the boisterous thug he was reputed to be. By the end of the night, she agreed to see him again.

Nicky did like her, a lot; she was a natural boss with a great body. Five-five, big breast and hips, just the type of woman he had to have. *Maybe my father isn't off base with this marriage thing. She'd be great for the business and good to have in bed. I can keep Cherry on the side, she wouldn't mind.*

He took her to dinner at his house. Her driver and bodyguard stayed in the car. The night started off ok, a little wine and cheese, some clams, and crackers. But as the wine got to her, she started talking more and more about her boyfriend Chris; getting him moved up in the family so she could marry him. Nicky smiled and listened. Gave her more wine and agreed she could run a crew. And finally hatched a plan.

Maybe it was the wine, maybe it was his charm, maybe it was the hypnotic effect of the serpent in the garden. Whatever it was, she agreed to the hit on Angela. To seal the deal, and guarantee she didn't tell anyone, not her father or his, she would spend the night in his bed. She left the next morning, knowing she had made a deal with the devil.

DOMINICK DELLA RUSSO sent Nicolas a request for a meeting to discuss affairs between their children. Nicolas showed up at the Royal Crown on Fifth Avenue with Pauley and Vinny, meeting Dominick and his two capos in a small dining room off the main restaurant. Dominick didn't stand to greet them, and Nicolas knew they were not there to discuss wedding plans.

"Dom, old friend, what is troubling you?" Nicolas took the chair across from him. The other four men stepped away from the table, standing by the door, their eyes locked on their bosses.

"Nicky. Nicolas, I know you're a respectful man, an honorable man. So, when you propose a union between our families, I was happy to indulge your wishes." Dom spoke very distinctly, softly, but then his voice rose slightly with his next words, "I thought your son was the same type of man! I know he's… a little rough in business… this is a good thing. But I expected him to treat my daughter, MY ONLY CHILD, with more respect the other night."

"What are you talking about, Dominick? Nicky told me they had a great time. A nice dinner and conversation, he was a gentleman. I raised him right!" Nicolas became defensive and concerned as to where this conversation was leading. *God damnit, Nicky, what did you do now?* "What did Carmella tell you? I'm sure it's just a silly misunderstanding between kids."

"No! I'm sure she understood what Nicky Rocci wanted," Dominick was now in full throat, "He tried to get her drunk. Then he told her he wanted a sample of what he'd be getting!"

"That's absurd," countered Nicolas, "even if he was drunk, he would never act like that with your daughter."

"So, you call my daughter a liar?" exploded Dominick. "She locked herself in another room and snuck out in the morning. She was humiliated. I raised her to be a good and proper lady. Not to be treated like one of your son's common whores."

"Let me talk to Nicky. We get the kids together and straighten this out."

"No need. My daughter and my family will have nothing to do with your… son."

"So, now you call my son a liar!"

Dominick's face turned red, snorting like a bull about to charge, his little round body swelling up in his chair. Flushed to the top of his balding head, sweat ran down his face, the white wisp of hair on his head melting like snow. The four men at the door moved away from one another slowly, positioning themselves for what was to come.

Dominick took a drink of water and said calmly, "If he had been anyone other than your son, Franco would have delivered a corpse to his family. I'm sorry, Nicolas, but it's best you leave me now."

Nicolas Rocci rose slowly from the table, his eyes locked on his old friend. He started away from the table, then turned back quickly. All four men's hands immediately went into their jackets, reaching for their guns. He threw his right hand up, freezing everyone in the room. "We have a long history," he said unapologetically, "if anyone else had accused my son as you did, he'd be dead where you sit."

Getting into the back of his limo with Vinny and Pauley, Nicolas was in a silent rage. As the car pulled into traffic, he yelled, "PAULEY, VINNY, GET OUT! FIND MY ASSHOLE SON AND BRING HIM TO THE FARM."

Pauley and Vinny stood on a corner, a block from the Royal Crown Hotel.

As the car resumed its travels, the young driver stared ahead at the road, carefully avoiding any eye contact with his boss in the rear-view mirror.

IT WAS late night before Nicky, Pauley, and Vinny arrived at the farmhouse. They picked up Nicky from Long Island hours ago and drove around for a good long time before heading Upstate. Everybody had gone to bed hours ago, everybody except Nicolas. Pauley thought it would be a good plan to give Nicolas a chance to cool off. His plan backfired. Nicolas was madder than ever at his son when they arrived.

He had to keep his voice down because Lucille and Sal were sleeping, but his anger was just as clear. "What the fuck, Nicky? I told you to marry one of these two girls. And you go behind my back and act like some kind of asshole jerkoff."

"Take it easy, Pops. You're going to give yourself a stroke. It's not what you think."

"Really?" Nicolas came at his son and stopped within striking distance. "Because I think you intentionally fucked up your date with Carmella, so she would refuse to marry you. In fact, Della Russo is breaking all ties with our family. The complete opposite of what I wanted you to do. Maybe I should have picked Sal for this, at least he knows how to do what his father tells him to do."

Nicky laughed but stopped quickly as his father's eyes became blood red. He pleaded, "Dad, please listen. I told you I'd come up with a better plan, and I did."

"I didn't want you to come up with a better plan, I wanted you to marry one of the two girls. Preferably her."

"Well, Dad, this isn't the old days, or the old country, or the old anything. I do rather like her, and if I had to marry anyone, it would have been her, but she doesn't want to marry me. You see, there's one little problem with your plan, she has a boyfriend. And she wants to marry him."

"OH," says Pauley then raises his hands for forgiveness.

"Oh, is right, Pauley," Nicky agrees. "But I did make a deal with her. And it's better I don't tell you, because I know you're going to hate it."

"If it's like any of your other plans, I probably will. But go ahead, fill me in."

Nicky motioned everyone to the kitchen table, knowing that if his father is sitting down, he's less likely to catch one in the mouth. And when his father does hear the plan, he is going to want to punch him even more. "I know you reached out to Peter Lucas already. But besides his daughter being the biggest hoe in Brooklyn, Lucas will be running this family before we can cut the wedding cake. He's already trying to make moves on us."

"So, you plan to insult his daughter too?" Nicolas asks sarcastically.

"No. I plan to marry her."

The three men look at Nicky, then each other. Nicolas is bewildered, "You don't make any sense at all. What are you talking about?"

"Well, I'm going to say I will marry her, but I'm not. That's where Carmella comes in. She's gonna help me out and I am going to help her out. Kinda like one hand washing the other. She has done the first part, got her dad to turn on us. I can't tell you anything else because I need you to be surprised when things happen. Like you were today. Don't worry, Dad, I got this all worked out."

The next month, Nicky was in the hospital dying from a gunshot wound to the chest.

Franco Androletti was on top of Carmella's list of men who had to go. He was her father's second in command and had been undermining him for years. He was one of those old-time mobsters who came up hard on the Lower East Side and had the scars to prove his toughness.

He had half a right ear left from a bullet that grazed his head when he was a teen pulling a robbery. A "J" below his left eye he got during a knife fight in a prison yard in his late twenties; a fight he won with the aid of a shiv he made from a toothbrush and a razor blade, shredding the inmate's jugular vein with four rapid strikes in a matter of seconds.

He would have escaped the fight without a mark had not another man distracted him, allowing the assailant to get the first slash in. Unfortunately for that man, he was found hanged by his pants' legs tied to his cell bars a week later, both legs broken. Franco was in solitary at the time.

Carmella had heard rumors of other wounds, not readily visible, that confirmed he was not a man one should cross, or chance getting into a fight with. She gave Nicky four other names: Caesar Durbin, Sal Pepperino, James Zuccanni, and Marty the Madman. She didn't know Marty's real name, it was Martin something hard to pronounce, even for Italians, but for as long as she could remember he was known as Marty the Madman or Mad Marty, the family's exterminator.

The five were the Della Russo's high command; ran the businesses, recruited new people, paid off those who could be bought, and killed the ones couldn't when necessary. With them out of the way, Christopher Carmine, her future husband, would rise quickly to fill the void. She would make sure of it.

It was Androletti who was the most troublesome. He kept a keen eye on her and blocked her every chance he got. He was also aware of her backroom influence on her father and did not like it. If he wanted to take control of the family, he had to isolate her first, and did he try. He insisted on accompanying her to the meeting and subsequent dates with Nicky, and not because he cared. He figured that if she married Nicky, she would be too busy with the Roccis to be a thorn in his side. He also imagined getting Nicolas Rocci to help him take control of the Della Russo family. Especially if he proved instrumental in getting his son married to Carmella.

When the marriage plan failed, Franco pushed Dominick into the meeting with Nicolas, having no idea he was playing Carmella and Nicky's game. After the meeting, word on the street spread about the two families being at odds. Nicky further flamed tensions by talking openly about the night he had sex with Carmella. He joked with his boys about licking the hotspot just below her right nipple, a burn mark on her chest she had gotten as a child. Something only a few close family members would know about, like Franco.

He pushed Dominick hard to take action against Nicky. A tearful Carmella denied having sex with Nicky but admitted to him trying to violate her. Franco wanted to send Mad Marty after him. In the end, a war with the Roccis could prove just as fruitful as the marriage would have been. However, Carmella pleaded with her father not to, it would lead to a war they could not win, she argued. Instead, she convinced him to send a hit team from outside the family, her Colombian connection.

Because her name was being thrown around as the reason someone would try to kill Nicky, Peter Lucas sent a hit team after her father. He too knew the chain of command. A pair of hitmen waited for Sal Pepperino at his girlfriend's house. It was his third girlfriend, and the one who left him the most vulnerable. She didn't know what business he was in, even if working for him in a loan and saving bank in Manhattan. He loaned money to those who could not get it from other banks, for purposes that no legitimate bank would lend money for, especially gambling debts. He also took bets from the same gamblers he lent the money to.

Sal hired and fired girls from there on a regular basis. Besides being a loan shark spot, it was also his private sex shop. Sal's overtime hours involved driving home any of the girls at night and staying for a little dick-tation.

After leaving his latest twenty-year-old's apartment in the Gun Hill Road section of the Bronx, Sal found himself in a shooting gallery. Two men with .45s emptied their guns into him and a third with a pump-action shotgun, unleashed three blasts, obliterating his identity.

THE DELLA RUSSO – Lucas war got off to a great start. It wasn't long before I, now healed from my ordeal, was reaching out to Peter Lucas to seek revenge. Understandably, he was not so accepting. He blamed me for his daughter's death, not directly, but placed her demise squarely on my head. I was half expecting a visit from one of his hitmen too.

"Let me do what I can to make it right," I console him, "I only knew Angela for a brief time, but she was a wonderful woman. A joy to be with, and I'll do anything to get the people behind her murder."

"You can start by killing that bitch you bragged about," Peter lashes out.

"I'm telling you, that girl was a mignotta. Played all innocent and goody two shoes to her old man, but she was a straight up whore." *You know, like your daughter.* "We have some mutual contacts with the Della Russos, I'll get them to get me close to her. I may need to take down some of the people around her first, though."

"You know that whole thing with the Banoas and the niggers, I had my doubts about you… But my Angela said you were a standup guy. Don't prove her wrong. Get it done."

With Sal Pepperino gone, Carmella was eager to have Franco eliminated next. I had to convince her the way to take down a house of cards was from the bottom up. I had to take out a lesser player to prove to Lucas he could trust me. If I took out Franco, it would seem too easy, make him suspicious. She had to give me one of the other guys.

"I can get you information on Marty the Madman, my father keeps tabs on him all the time."

"Not him either," I say, "we definitely need to keep him around for a while, to take out Lucas' men. How about Caesar Durbin or James Zuccanni? Can you get me a location on one of them?"

"I know exactly where Little Caesar will be." She called him 'little' because he was shorter than her, although he claimed to be five-two. He was her father's muscle, always working out at the gym on the Lower East Side. After Sal's killing, he became her bodyguard. "Gorgio is my driver and Little Caesar is my shadow. I'm going to my ballet lesson tomorrow; he hates to wait for me there. I can send him on an errand. Can you get something done so soon?"

"Pick out a black dress."

Nicky hung up the phone on Brentwood Road. It was a few miles from the house, which was perfect. He did not want anyone tracing the calls directly back to him. He had told Carmella to make her calls from a public phone, not her house. They set up a rolling schedule, speaking at different times and on different days, both keenly aware of the dangers they faced, from the Mafia, and the law. As the killings continued, there was ever increasing pressure from the NYPD and the FBI. Starting a mob war during this volatile period could backfire and get them both killed by their own families.

The crackdown on the Mafia was into its fifth year and it was believed the FBI had infiltrated at least one family. The Godfather of the Carlucci family had been arrested and others had flipped, turned state evidence, and gone into witness protection. Suspicions ran rampant, people got killed just because they looked like they couldn't be trusted, and whereas Carmella was worried this atmosphere would hamper her plans, Nicky was delighted by the chaos. It took the focus off them and spread suspicion far and wide. He had become quite skilled at moving people and events from the safety of the shadows.

Nicky dialed another number, this one in Brooklyn, "Stephanie, I have a job for you two."

"The usual trash collection and disposal?" she asks.

Her thick Mexican accent sounds exotic and Nicky can picture her long wavy golden brown hair wrapping around her neck and down one shoulder. He gets a hard-on just talking to her.

"Do you want us to do the usual job, boss?"

"Oh, no. This time the bodies are to be left in place. Stay close to the phone, I'll call back with the details."

CARMELLA LOOKS at the clock on the wall, it's ten minutes to four. She would have thought her father would have called or sent someone to get her by now. *I hope Nicky didn't fail. But what if his people got caught? Surely, he wouldn't let them know the information came from me. But who else would have known I sent them to that mall?*

"Carmella, is there something wrong? Why are you not doing the relevé with the rest of us?"

"Uh, sorry Miss Sophia," Carmella begins the rises again.

"It's ok. Class, we are fini for today."

Carmella looks out the window and sees her car pull up. Gorgio is driving and Little Caesar is in the passenger seat. They look normal, like nothing at all happened. *Damn Nicky. He failed.* She stuffs her things into her gym bag and hurries downstairs ahead of the class. Just as she pushes the heavy iron and thick glass baroque style door to the dance studio on 57th street open there is a huge fireball in the street. The door slams shut, knocking her to the floor. She hears a loud continuous ringing like a high-pitched siren. She looks out through the ornate iron work to see her car engulfed in flames.

Amazingly, the door is intact and the reason she was not killed outright by the blast that threw pieces of the car everywhere. The glass however, has two big newly formed spiderweb cracks in it, one at head level, the other near where her waist was. If whatever hit the glass and caused the cracks had made it through, she would surely be dead now. The other girls reached her and helped her up. One girl screams when she sees a severed hand wedged between the glass and iron bars of the door.

IT WAS a week before Carmella could slip away from her four bodyguards. She found a telephone in the lounge area of the women's bathroom at a health club on Manhattan Upper Eastside. Dominick got her an apartment in the neighborhood under an alias. One of her bodyguards, Antonio Roman, pretended to be her husband. The first four days she was not allowed to leave the apartment. She was the prisoner of the 18th floor.

After many sweeps of the area, it was deemed safe for her to go out, but never alone, always accompanied by her husband and in the presence of his bodyguard and driver. The three of them stayed in the apartment, and the driver, from what she could tell, lived in the car. She was only alone going to the ladies' room, after it had been checked.

"What the hell was that about? You nearly killed me," she spoke softly because she didn't know how close to the door Antonio or the others might be.

"You were never in any danger," Nicky assured her. "The door was more than sufficient to shield you from the explosion."

"Why did you have to blow up the car right in front of the dance studio? I told you precisely where and when they would be at the mall. You should have killed Caesar there. Now, my father thinks the car bomb was meant for me."

"That is exactly what we want him to think," Nicky briefly explains, "it had to look like you were the target, or else he would know the bomb was meant for Caesar. And the only one who knew where Caesar would be—"

"Was me."

"Yes, you. It's the little details that make a plan work. And Lucas doesn't want Caesar dead… Well, he probably does, along with the rest of your family. But he wants me to kill you. And now that I tried and failed, he will offer me help. Which I will turn down."

"What? Wait. Why won't you accept his help?"

"Oh, I will. Maybe after I knock off another one of your guys on the list," he tells her. "Then when he insists on helping me, I will coordinate our efforts. I'll be in deep and able to pass you names and places of his key people to take down. Instead of them killing you, we'll be killing them. Now, don't forget to flush and wash your hands."

"What? You know where I am?" Carmella asks.

"Of course, I do. I haven't let you out of my sights since our first date," Nicky says softly and hangs up.

Carmella goes into the bathroom, flushes a toilet, and runs the water in the sink. She stares in the mirror, splashes water on her face, and stares again at her reflection. *What have I gotten myself into? Nicky is only interested in taking down Lucas, right? He can't be after me. I'm not his type. He knows I love Chris and I'm doing this for us. I will just make sure I set him straight. There is no us. Never was. Never will be.* She splashes more water on her face, like she is trying to wake herself up, then pats her face dry with a paper towel from the wall dispenser and exits the bathroom.

"Are you ok?" Antonio asks.

She doesn't answer.

NICKY SAT at the bar in the Sons of Italy social club, his place. Cherry Bomb and Honey are on either side of him. Pauley and Vinny are at the card table, each playing solitaire. It's eight in the morning and the place is otherwise empty.

Peter Lucas walks in with two men; one stops at the door, the other goes to the far end of the club and checks out the bathroom. When he comes out, he nods. Peter Lucas walks over to

Nicky and stands behind him, his hands folded across his chest, and stares at him in the mirror behind the bar.

Vinny pushes his chair back, making a loud scraping noise on the floor as his two hundred pounds of muscles weighs down on the chair. Pauley's hands disappear under the card table.

Nicky raises his hand and says, "Cherry, get these boys some vino. The best we got."

"Isn't it a little early for wine?" asks Lucas.

"Not if you've been drinking since last night." Nicky holds up his whiskey glass to the mirror and rattles the ice. "Honey, go in the back and start a fresh pot of coffee. Mr. Lucas, please take a seat."

"I won't be here that long," he replies.

"I don't like people in the rear-view. Sit down! Or leave now," commands Nicky. He's not intimidated by Peter Lucas and wants him to know it.

Lucas takes Honey's seat and Cherry places a glass of wine in front of each of them.

Nicky raises his glass, "salute."

"What are we toasting?" Lucas asks in an acid tone. He's not here for a friendly chat.

"I always welcome first-timers to my establishment. We can all use a little civility in these troubling times," Nicky informs him, still waiting for him to raise his glass.

Finally, Peter Lucas acknowledges the gesture.

Nicky places the glass on the bar after a light sip. "What brings you to the Bronx so early this morning?"

Lucas just puts his glass down. "You failed. The girl… she went home to a warm bed the other night. I'm not sure you know how badly my heart has been torn apart. I bleed every night I go home, and my Angel is not there to give her old man a kiss and a warm embrace. If you had any idea the pain I feel right now, you wouldn't be sitting here… so unprotected."

Nicky turns to Lucas and places a hand on his. "I understand your loss. But sometimes, things go off prematurely." *You know, like the premature ejaculation you have when your little hoe kisses you.* "I have two of my best people working the case. They will not fail again. I guarantee it."

"Really!" Lucas pounds his fist on the bar, knowing Nicky is toying with him. "Her father has sent her into hiding. When do you think your experts will get a second chance?"

Nicky drinks his wine then takes a cup of coffee from Honey's tray as she passes behind the bar. She puts the second cup in front of Lucas. Nicky sips lightly on the coffee, watching Lucas fume in the mirror.

Vinny inched his way to within arm's reach of Lucas. He could body-slam him with one hand if the need arose. He has been known to pick up cash registers, the old kind, with the rows of keys and bell that goes ding. Did once, a hundred-pound beauty, which he slammed onto a man's hand who was always short with his protection payments. Both cash register and guy's hand went through the wooden counter, left a huge hole, and blood everywhere. The man lost his hand in the 'accident' but paid on time from then on.

Nicky glanced at Vinny, knowing he could count on him to get things done; could take out Lucas and still shoot his other man across the barroom. But he was sure Pauley had a pair of pistols trained on the men as well. "She's in mid-Manhattan, upper eastside, four bodyguards," he blurts out as if the coffee has burnt his tongue. "It will take a little time to pick the next spot, but I'm on it."

"Give me an address," Lucas demands, "I'll send a couple of guys with guns. This thing is not all that complicated."

"Maybe not for you," Nicky asserts, "but I'm the one who took a bullet in the chest and laid in a coma for a month. I want a little flair for my trouble."

"And my daughter took a bullet in the head because of you," he announces to the bar, "I won't forget." Lucas kicks the chair from under him as he gets up to leave. It clamors to the floor.

Everyone holds their position, especially Vinny.

When he gets to the door, he turns back to Nicky who is sipping his coffee unconcerned, "I'm sending a couple of my best guys over. They will coordinate things with you. I expect you to get this thing done quickly... so my Angel can rest in peace."

True to his word, Lucas sent four men to the Sons of Italy that afternoon.

THOMAS, the son of one of Lucas' capos, was running the operation, or so he thought.

Nicky conned him into meeting at a different place in Brooklyn each time to discuss the latest development. Thomas thought he was keeping tabs on Nicky, but unwittingly, he was in fact exposing Lucas' operation. Within a couple of weeks, Nicky knew where all of Lucas' banks, stash houses, gambling dens, and holdups were located.

He fed Carmella the location of three of the biggest; a high-roller casino in Manhattan, a drug processing house in Queens, and a car chop shop in the Bronx. Each one personally managed by one of Lucas' capos.

They were the three places Nicky did not go to, managing to divert the meetings at the last minute to a neutral locale. Only Thomas knew Nicky was aware of the locations and before Carmella could move on them, he told her he need to eliminate Thomas.

"My team is ready to make a move," he tells her. "And I'll

take out Zuccanni at the same time. That will give your father more than enough reason to let Madman Marty off his leash."

"OK. I have Chris feeding Franco the information," she shifts her tone to show how happy she is, "My father is starting to take notice of him, sees how protective he is of me… He'll be please when this plan of your bears fruit. I think he will be able to step up. Thanks."

"You can thank me later. When this is all over." Nicky hangs up abruptly. *Maybe I should give the team Chris' name too. Get him out of the way early. But with him gone, she might lose interest in the whole deal, blow the whole fucking thing up! Better stick to the plan.*

STEPHANIE WALKS into a bar on Coney Island Avenue. It's a small place on the ground floor of a three-story house on the busy street. She steps up on the footrail and leans over the bar. "Are you Tony?"

The bartender turns around and throws a dish towel over his shoulder. "There is no Tony. Haven't been a Tony here in twenty years. I guess you're not from around here."

"No, not really," she says and sits on the stool.

The bartender comes over and flips a glass right side up in front of her.

"Oh, I'm not here for a drink. I'm here about the 'waitress needed' sign in the window." She swings herself around towards the door.

"That sign's been in the window for as long as the name Tony's Bar been above the door. I don't need a waitress, as you can see, we ain't very busy."

"Then why do you keep the sign in the window?"

"For the same reason, the place is still called Tony's. No one ever bothered to take it down."

Stephanie wiggles her bottom on the stool and her black and red plaid skirt rides up her legs a little. Her thick tan thighs are inviting to the old man. She adjusts her white button-down shirt over her black halter top. Her breasts are average but perky as a young woman's in the blossoming years of her life should be. She rolls her hair and lets it flop down her left shoulder. "Please, just a couple hours, a few nights a week while I go to school. I just moved here and I'm almost out of money. I didn't know New York was so expensive."

Johnny, at sixty and half Italian half Irish, knew the game she was trying to pull, and was not buying. "Yeah, well, it is. Where you from, Puerto Rico? You look and sound Spanish."

"I'm Mexican," she grabs her hair, gives it a twist, then lets it fall over her shoulder again. "Well, my family is from Mexico originally, I was born and raised in Texas. I waited tables before and bartended some too. Please Mister… Um…"

"The name's Johnny, just Johnny. Ok, I tell you what. You can work eight 'til closing on Friday and Saturday nights. And you work for tips, I can't afford to pay you."

"Thank you. Thank you. Thank you. Can I have a glass of water? It is kind of hot out there." She smiled.

He smiled back. "Hey, for your first job, go grab that sign out the window. I don't need any more of you college kids looking for a handout. I can barely afford to keep the lights on as it is." He watches her walk to the front of the bar, grab the sign adhered to the window by a thick layer of grime, and walk back. He likes her thick shapely legs and plump round ass. *If I was five years younger.* "You better wear more than that when you come in here Friday night. I don't know if you know Italian boys, they get really handsies. You understand."

"Yes… Johnny." She let his name roll off her tongue adding to her seductive look.

"Here," he tosses her a wet dish towel. "Now, that window looks really dirty."

Stephanie pulls a chair over to the window and spends the next half hour washing years of life off the glass. Johnny spends the time watching her ass swing and sway.

STEPHANIE SHOWS up Friday night in tight blue jean and a tee shirt. She is modestly built on top but there is nothing she can do to tone down the bottom. Johnny figures whatever she wears is going to be sexy. It's a warm night and Flatbush's Italian Stallions are out in force. Word spreads quickly because by ten o'clock, Tony's Bar is packed.

Stephanie has already caused two fights, as boyfriends have looked too long, or smiled too happily in her direction. The girls pulled their guys outside and demanded to be taken home with a good deal of animated cursing for her to witness. Stephanie takes it in stride. She's making good tips, and only dislocated one guy's wrist when he tried to put his hand in her back pocket. She knew word would spread quickly of the new meat on the street.

After midnight, the wise guys and wannabes started rolling in from the gambling houses around the neighborhood. The older guys took their turns slapping her bottom, and Johnny gave her a look not to retaliate. The younger ones were trying to throw an arm around her neck and steer her away from her duties. Johnny finally had to put an end to the shenanigans and placed her safely behind the bar for the remainder of the night. He brought the drinks to the tables and she could talk to the guys without being pawed to death.

She caught the attention of Thomas Fortunelli and all the others fell away. She kept returning to his corner of the bar, twisting her hair and flashing those dangerously golden brown eyes.

On one trip to the other end of the bar, Johnny whispered, "be extra careful with that one. He's not as innocent as he looks."

SATURDAY NIGHT STEPHANIE didn't show up for work. Johnny wasn't too surprised, she was a nice girl, and he figured people were more polite in Texas. Johnny noticed a couple of Thomas' so-called friends hanging around for a couple of hours then leaving disappointed. Most of the Saturday night crowd left dissatisfied… well, the guys did. The girls were quite happy the vixen had enough. They would all have been shocked to learn what the little sexpot was doing Saturday night.

She had spent a lot of time making eyes at Thomas the previous night, eventually gave him her address, and told him to pick her up at seven. She did not have to tell him to come alone.

He showed up at the single-family house on Ocean Drive ready for a little action.

She was waiting for him in a white knee-length dress with spaghetti straps. He was hoping to get a quickie before taking her to the bar. Then she introduced him to her brother Elie. Thomas was unhappy to meet him.

Elie was a curly-top, tall and slim soft-spoken guy, with a slight accent. Other than the brownish hair color they didn't resemble each other at all. He had a light tan that did not look like he came from Mexico, or any part of South America. Their accent did not match either, hers was definitely Spanish, but his was Mediterranean or possibly Middle Eastern. Thomas got the feeling that maybe he was her boyfriend, or, he hoped, her pimp. Of course, he was not going to pay for her. He tipped her generously the night before. She left the two of them alone while she finished getting ready for work.

Elie made small talk for a few minutes then offered to make them some drinks. They had a small bar in the living room. He carefully poured a half a tumbler of vodka over ice, then measured in some lime juice, turning the solution slightly cloudy. Lastly, he opened a bottle of ginger beer, adding enough to top off the glasses.

Elie tapped their glasses together and drank half.

Thomas sipped his before taking a big drink. "This is really good. Are you a bartender?" Thomas smiled. "What do you call it?"

"It's a Moscow Mule. I love it. It has a hard kick at the end," Elie smiled as he drifted away.

The room started getting longer too. Thomas got up and stumbled to the side and fell back onto the sofa. "Stefnie, get your ass out here, gurl."

"Oh my, looks like that mule has started kicking you in the head," Elie grabs him by the jaw and starts shaking his head.

"What the hell did you do?" Thomas asks clearly. Then he calls out again, "Sta, I fust you… me laving… now gerl."

"He's ready," Stephanie says, standing over Thomas sprawled out on the floor. She's wearing a plastic see-through raincoat and nothing else. Thomas' eyes are watery and glazed over but he must like what he sees because a twisted droopy smile spreads over his face. "Ah, good to know you are still in there, my friend. This wouldn't be as much fun if you were totally out of it. Elie, go get ready."

Elie comes out in the same raincoat and nothing else.

Stephanie has already started undressing Thomas but is having trouble turning him over to get his shirt over his head. "How much Quelicin did you give him? He's like a rubber chicken."

"I only put one succinylcholine cube in his drink. It's the alcohol that is boosting the effects. But that's good, it took effect immediately." Elie pulls Thomas' shirt over his head and lets him fall back to the floor. He grabs his pants and in a single move rips his pants and underwear off. Thomas is naked on the living room floor.

"I'll take his arms and you grab his legs."

"Why?" Elie grabs Thomas by the ankles and drags him out of the living room towards the bathroom. "Bring me the other meat cleaver and the hatchet, then start putting his things in the plastic bag. We must be out in three hours before the woman who lives here gets off work. Chop. Chop."

Stephanie gets to the bathroom just in time to see Elie hack off Thomas' head. She holds open the garbage bag and Elie drop the head in. There is warm water running in the tub from the shower. He turns the body on its side and takes three hard swings to take off Thomas' arm. He flips him over on the other side and severs the left arm at the shoulder with one swing. Blood spatters everywhere. Stephanie is quick to wipe down the walls.

In ten minutes, Elie dismembered, bagged, and packed Thomas in two large suitcases. He and Stephanie remove their raincoats in the shower and in their final act of the evening, make love. Slowly caressing and kissing, he cradles her breast, sucking the wet nipples as the warm water washes the blood away.

She massages his tired arms and rubs the stiffness from his shoulders. And when he's fully erect, she climbs up on the edge of the tub with one leg and wraps the other around his waist. Then she lowers herself onto him. He pins her to the wall and awkwardly humps her under the softness of falling water.

On a late spring evening, at nine o'clock, dressed and ready to go, Elie and Stephanie load the two suitcases into the trunk of their car and drive away. The neighborhood is quiet. They came, murdered, and leave the middle-class neighborhood as they found it. Their next stop will be eight hours away, a toxic waste facility where the suitcases will be sealed in a drum marked 'Radioactive Medical Waste. Do Not Open.' From there, Thomas Fortunelli will be loaded on a truck and driven deep underground. The hit team from San Diego is extremely efficient.

SIXTY-EIGHTH STREET and Park Avenue was on the east side of Central Park and known for its turn of the century three to five-story brick and white granite townhouses that lined the extra wide thoroughfare. Lush flowerbeds split the street down the middle.

It was the part of the city where affluent New Yorkers enjoyed the good life. Taxi cabs and Lincoln Town Cars patrolled the streets. It was also the perfect spot for a little casino, a place the mob could run a nice clean game for those who didn't want to trek all the way out to Atlantic City or pay taxes on their winnings; the true reason the Mafia still ran gambling houses after the casinos opened in New Jersey.

Lucas had operated the casino on the top floor of 88 Park Avenue for decades. He boasted of dignitaries from all over the world. But of course, New York's own elites from the Mayor to Congressmen to High Court Judges also tried their luck at the crap tables, thousand-dollar poker tables, and roulette wheels. The third floor was a wide-open gambling parlor, the floor below a rather pricey brothel, and below that some nicely appointed apartments guests could sleep off a bad streak.

The building had a tuxedoed doorman slash guard with a camera/buzzer system to get in. The servers on the floors did little in the way of security, as everyone who entered was by invitation or the guest of the invited. Lucas kept a small band of men in the basement for the occasional sore loser who needed to be escorted to a hospitality suite to recover from his losses. Lucas joked to his thirty-five clientele, "That fortress down the street is the Park Avenue Armory, if anything bad happens, they will send tanks."

If only that was the truth and not just a clever quip for a Saturday night. Marty the Madman arrived with two of his associates and a judge who owed him a favor. The judge ran up a large drug tab, which Marty would settle with Della Russo if he got him into the casino. The four men were dressed to kill in Brooks Brothers suits, Marty and his two associates with carefully concealed pistols, the judge with just his reputation.

When the metal detector went off, the judge opened his briefcase to display a collection of fine Swiss watches, collateral for the night's action. He was well-known there and also a very bad gambler. The tuxedoed doorman didn't bother to check his friends, was too busy picking out which watch he would wear home that night.

The four men took the little elevator to the third floor, where it opened to the noise and excitement of a Vegas casino. Girls scantily dressed in feathers and string bikinis flowed through the rooms with full trays of colorful drinks. Wheels spun and rattled, sucking in money as the patrons sucked down potent concoctions. A few men stood quietly in the corners, giving the impression of security.

Marty accompanied the judge to the back, to the money cage where he could exchange his watches, family heirlooms, for poker chips. After the trade was made, Marty released him to his addiction. All the Judge knew was Marty wanted in, he had no idea why.

One of Marty's men found his way down a back stairwell to the basement and waited there. The other associate positioned himself by the elevator. All was set.

Two minutes after the judge handed over the briefcase of watches, Marty pressed the detonator in his jacket pocket. The case exploded inside the money room and the noise panicked New York's elite. They rushed for the elevator only to be blocked by Marty's sawed-off shotgun-toting accomplice. He ordered everyone on the floor, facedown. The hundred plus people in suits, tuxes, and fine evening gowns cowered before the robber. The security guards threw their guns on the craps table as ordered, before dropping to the floor.

The explosion alerted the five-man security team in the basement who raced into action. In the dimly lit basement hallway, they ran into the second man of the robbery team. He opened fire with two revolvers and killed them all. Gunshots echoed up the stairway and could be heard in the hush floor of the casino.

The girls of the second floor heard the commotion above and below and convinced their customers it was safer to stay in the rooms. Whatever was happening outside need not concern or involve them. There would be a time when their customers could slip away into the night unnoticed. That was what they really were paying for.

The explosion wasn't strong enough to breach the money room's two-inch steel door, merely meant to disarm anyone inside. To gain access to the cash within, Marty grabbed the Pit Boss, the man with the keys, by his necktie and demanded. "Unlock the cage."

"Do you know whose place this is? Do you know what he will do to me if I open this door?"

Marty put his .45 to the man's neatly trimmed temple, "You own sixty percent as his Caporegime, don't you? You can either open the door and live one more day, or I blow your brains across the room and open the door myself with your key. If it makes you feel any better, I will leave his forty percent."

The man pulled a key on a chain, popping it from around his neck and handed it to Marty, who then shot him in the head and threw him out the way. He turned to the stunned gamblers on the floor, "No one else has to die tonight if you all stay where you are and leave me and my men to our business."

The man from the basement arrived on the elevator, walked over, and stepped over the bodies on the floor in the caged room. Money bags lay strewn across the floor, which the two men filled, then tossed towards the elevator, some landing on the prostrate people, causing them a great deal of pain, but no one got off the floor.

Marty found several of the watches and dropped them into one of the bags as well.

The three men carried a half dozen bag out of the build and into a waiting Town Car. Because of the thick brick walls and extra soundproofing done to the building, no one in the posh neighborhood knew a crime had just been committed. In a few scant minutes, Marty walked out with millions of Lucas' cash and dealt him a crippling blow. It was to be the first of three.

They headed to Queens to a cocaine processing house; another 'grab the loot and shoot the boss', but first, they would stop in the Bronx and burn down the chop shop. Marty was sure that on a Saturday night the place would be filled with expensive cars and parts. This night would cost the Lucas Family millions in revenue and manpower. Three of his Capos and dozens of soldiers were dead.

NICKY WAS a few blocks away in a high rise on Seventy-second street, dressed in the light-brown overall of the building's maintenance crew. He held the door for a heavy-set man in his early fifties; the short jaunt from the front door to the elevator had him breathing hard.

"What floor?" Nicky asked, staring at his feet.

The man reached past him and pressed 18. The door closed.

Nicky looked at the man, "I hope I'm not going to your apartment?"

"I doubt it," responded James Zuccanni, "No one's home now. Don't see what the trouble could be there. Hey, shouldn't you be carrying tools?"

"I got a complaint about a running toilet. Usually, I just giggle the handle. You think the tenants would be smart enough to do that themselves."

"Hey, for the rent we pay in this place, if the handle needs jiggling, you need to come and jiggle it."

"Well, I'm not complaining," Nicky says, "for what they are paying me, if you need your handle jiggled, I'm your man."

The elevator door opened. Nicky quickly looked down again, avoiding the camera inside the hallway. He waited for James Zuccanni to exit, as a good worker would, then followed him a few feet until they were out of view of the camera. He stuck a .22 in his back.

He fired three times, the gun pointing up his back, the shots muffled by Zuccanni's layers of fat. He stumbled along the hallway, trying to get to the next apartment, but fell about halfway there. Nicky lifted the man's head, stuck the gun all the way in, pressed the barrel against the roof of his mouth, and blew a hole through the top of his head.

He dropped the gun, which was wrapped in sticky black cloth electrical tape to prevent it from picking up fingerprints, alongside James Zuccanni's body. Nicky hurried to the stairs at the end of the hall, stripped off his overall, descended, and left the building.

PETER LUCAS CALLED the Sons of Italy again, looking for Nicky. Every time he got the same response, Nicky was nowhere to be found. Then he received a call to go out to Long Island. He was not happy but arrived at the appointed time.

Nicolas greeted him first, "I'm glad you came. We have some important things to discuss."

"Where's your son? He has been avoiding me."

"Not at all," Nicky said as he joined them in the den overlooking the garden. "I have been out of town the last two weeks."

"You picked a hell of a time to take a vacation," Lucas blasted the younger Rocci.

"You'll understand soon. But first, where's your man, Thomas Fortunelli? As you wished, I gave him information on Franco Androletti, one of two men who may have been hiding Carmella. I went after Jimmy Z, and he was supposed to take out Franco."

"I haven't heard from him in weeks," admitted Peter Lucas. "Did you kill the girl?"

"No. I had information that Jimmy was keeping a girl who matched Carmella's description. It turned out to be his side chick."

"Jimmy Z was shot dead uptown, was that you?"

"Of course! But I found out just before the hit that he wasn't protecting Carmella."

"Then why did you kill him?" questioned Lucas.

"Why not?" was the answer. "Anyway, Franco has disappeared. We believe he may have turned state's evidence." Nicky spread a dozen polaroid pictures in front of Lucas. "This is why I called you here."

He studies the pictures of a family, unable to recognize any of the stabbed victims. The last picture is of a teenage girl, unlike the others, she is laid out in a field, a single, neat stab wound to her heart. "Who the hell are these people?"

"They are Juan Jimenez and his family. My guy in Colombia executed them," Nicky told him. "I found out Juan Jimenez was behind the hit on me and the death of your daughter. Seems Juan had a problem with our trafficking business in Colombia. Maybe we misjudged Dominick. I'm pulling out of this war with Della Russo, I suggest you do the same."

"Are you kidding me? Dominick has just hit a number of my businesses. I'm not pulling back."

"He was reacting to the attacks on his family," Nicolas added. "You were wrong in going after his family. You have your revenge for your daughter. Let us negotiates an end to this war."

"An end to the war? This is bullshit!" Lucas was out of his seat and flailing about the room. "If you wanted an end to this war you should have brought that piece of shit to me. And his daughter too."

"For what?" Nicky asked. "Do you know how hard it was to make the hit on this guy?"

"I wanted to see him suffer as I have suffered. For him to know the pain of his daughter's death. I wanted…"

"Yeah, I get it," Nicky cut in, "so I made sure he died last. Watched his daughter die before his eyes, his whole family. Remember, it was me he tried to kill. I laid in that hospital bed for a month. I can still feel the pain in my chest. Believe me, he suffered plenty. That's what happens when you cross Nicky Nails!" He was making a declaration as well as a warning to Peter Lucas.

It took all afternoon to get Peter Lucas to agree to a cease fire.

Nicolas was very persuasive and offered to broker the deal himself, even though it was a risk to his life too.

A few days later, Nicolas, Peter, and Dominick sat down in his restaurant in the same posh hotel Dominick had called Nicolas to months ago. This time, Carmella and Nicky were in attendance, at Dominick's insistence. He wanted an apology from Nicky, first and foremost.

Nicky started the meeting by saying, "I regret things didn't go as planned with us, Carmella. I am sorry if anything I said or did was misconstrued in any way."

Carmella turned up her face and mumbled something that did not sound complimentary.

Nicolas quickly interjected, "we are all saddened by the unfortunate misunderstandings of the past few months. Let us bury the past and work towards a profitable future for all. We have all sustained losses during this time of unrest."

The meeting lasted all night. The bar and restaurant were closed, as all the guests were in for the night. Loud talk and fist-pounding emanated from the little dining room. Peter Lucas was adamant about paying any kind of restitution to Della Russo. He considered the loss of men and profits a wash. Della Russo claimed, and rightfully so, that his organization suffered from Lucas' hasty actions. Compensations should match his losses, not Lucas'.

As godfather, Nicolas Rocci had the final say. Although, if he did not speak authoritatively, the two families would be back at war in the morning. Without admitting to any involvement, but acquiescence to a little guilt over his son's actions and words, he gave Della Russo the family drug trade to add to Lucas' sports gambling and city casinos.

Nicky immediately objected, "What? No way. I built that business from nothing."

"And now you know the cost of empty words spoken in bad company," Nicolas scolded.

"My sources say you pull down half a billion or more through your Florida channel," Dominick smiles, "that should compensate for my losses. My second-in-command has gone missing, you gentlemen wouldn't have anything to say about it?"

"One of my most trusted men has also not been heard from in days," accuses Lucas.

"These days, people who disappear," offers Nicky, "turn up on the witness stand. Let's hope we all fare better than that."

4

THE WINE CELLAR

Morris' plane calls in to the Stewart Air National Guard Base in Newburgh, New York. The sole person on duty in the tower this night is Airman First Class Houssier. He checks his logs then radios the plane for confirmation, "This is Stewart Air Base, calling NATO175, please confirm your designation."

The plane does not answer.

AFC Houssier picks up the phone and starts dialing the base security officer. He is three numbers in when Colonel Johnson enters the tower and commands, "hang up that phone, Airman."

"Sir, I have an unauthorized flight about to violate our airspace any minute. Protocol requires that I alert the Chief Master Sergeant in charge of security."

Colonel Johnson asks, "Son, how long have you been in the ANG?"

"Three years, Sir." Houssier snaps out his answer.

"Do you think in your three years, you have been privy to all that the Air Force does?"

"No, sir," AFC Houssier admits.

"There are situations that are well above your pay grade," Colonel Johnson informs him, "no offense, but this is one of

66

those situations. As of 2200 you were relieved of duty by AFC Charles. That is what the duty log will reflect, understood?"

"Yes, Sir!" Houssier snaps a crisp solute and leaves the tower. His curiosity gets the better of him and he sits in his car off runway 22N. It takes about ten minutes for the plane to land and taxi to the terminal. A Major and a Captain, a man and woman respectively, exit the craft. They are met by a black limo and head off the base. It is the strangest occurrence Houssier will experience in his military career.

The limo heads down the New York State Throughway to eventually end up at the mansion in Long Island.

Morris is greeted by Rozalina, whom he calls Cherry Bomb. She asks. "Who is this? Where's Yana? I thought you would bring her with you."

"I had no intentions of bringing anyone with me, but you women are constantly undermining my authority. Gisella ultimately won out."

"So, you are the Venezuelan," Cherry looks her up and down. She has a few inches on her and more than a couple of pounds, although her curves hold it all beautifully. "Well, you certainly are his type. Very pretty, but at a time like this I really needed my friend with me. You understand?"

Gisella sees the hurt and disappointment in the other woman's eyes, "Of course I do. And I was not trying to keep Yana from seeing you, Cherry… Bomb?"

"It's a long story," Rozalina smiles faintly.

"Hey, it's not like you girls don't get together whenever one of you needs advice on a new nail polish color. You all fly off any time you like. But we are not here for that now. Where is Nicky? What hospital is he in?" asks Morris.

"He is not in any hospital," Cherry tells him, "he's upstairs."

"WHAT? I knew it. I fly halfway around the world and this is another crazy scheme by Nails." Morris only called Nicky by his street name when he was mad at him. This time he was livid.

"No, this is no scheme," Cherry breaks down. "The boys had him moved from Our Lady of Mercy as soon as he was stable. The second floor has been turned into a medical unit. He is still fighting for his life."

Pauley entered the room, thinner and grayer than Morris recalled. Putting a hand on Morris' shoulder, he gave him a shake. "It's still touch and go. But he's fighting for every breath. That's a good thing."

"What the fuck happened?"

"Don't really know," Pauley shakes his head, "we took Nicky and Sal to the gravesite. They are up there a few minutes, paying their respects, the next thing I know they are both on the ground. I never heard a shot. Must have been a sniper from one of the high risers around the cemetery. Goddamnit, is nothing sacred anymore?"

Morris sank into a chair in the lounge, "How is Sal?"

"Dead. The bullet went through the back of the head. Must have killed him… instantly. Poor bastard."

Morris sat in the chair a long time, Gisella standing beside him and cradling his head against her hip. She stroked his cheek over and over as he sat staring into space. She did not know what he was thinking but she could feel the darkness rising within. Now, she wished she hadn't come.

Their escape from Venezuela had been like something out of a James Bond movie. But after that, when he came and took her to Greece, life became mundane. He made a few calls every day and a couple of trips a month into town. She only recalled him going on a 'business trip' twice in the past three years. Life with a billionaire criminal was kind of boring. But this had her head swimming.

It started with the four men with high-powered assault rifles at the gate. And everywhere she looked was a man or two with huge guns hanging from their shoulders and rifles slung across their backs. This was a scene straight out of a thirty's gangster film. She had been lulled into thinking Morris lived a normal life.

Pauley broke her ruminations. "You must be tired. The women will take you two up the back stairs to a room. Most of the east side of the house has been sealed off, we are trying to keep the place sterile."

"Of course," replied Morris.

"I'm a doctor," Gisella added, "if you need my help, please call on me."

"I'll take them up," Cherry volunteered, and led them through the different rooms toward the back of the house. She waited until they were in the bedroom and gave Morris a look.

He knew what that meant, "What is it?"

She looked at Gisella and twitched.

"It's ok, you can talk to me in front of her."

Cherry did not say anything. Instead, she took the chain and locket from around her neck, opened it, and then another compartment behind Nicky's picture. She dropped a small key into his hand. "Here, I was told to give you this when the time came."

"Hey, I recognize this key!"

"I don't know what it is for, I was just told to keep it safe and give it to you when he died."

"Then you should hold on to it, Nicky's not dead."

"Not when Nicky is dead," Cherry said sadly. She felt relived as if a great weight had been hanging around her neck. "Nicolas said to give it to you when Sal is dead."

Morris took the key, but it would have to wait until tomorrow. He was spent.

I AWOKE BEFORE EVERYONE ELSE. It was still the middle of the night for them, but I was on European time, and that key kept invading my dreams until I could not take it no longer. I dressed, slipped out of the house, and took one of the Caddies in the garage. Four different men were at the front gate. They looked in the vehicle and asked if I needed a weapon. I showed them my Sig 45 and one pressed the button in the guardhouse to start the gate rolling back. As soon as I had enough clearance, I floored the gas pedal.

It is a six-hour drive from the mansion to the farmhouse.

I held onto the little brass key like it was made of gold. I felt a little queasy, I have not been to the farmhouse in years. Probably about two years before Sal killed his parents. *There will be ghosts in that house.*

The morning sun caught up to me about an hour out, even as I worked on my fourth beer. I passed a state trooper's car parked off the shoulder and kept glancing in the rear-view mirror for flashing lights, hoping he was sleep when I roared past him. *I'm really not in the mood to kill anyone today. I wasn't going that fast, officer. Besides, who else is on the road but me and you. Those beers, no they are left over from another party.* I ran more conversations in my head until I was a good five miles past his spot.

I turned off the highway and onto an unnamed two-lane paved road, driving on automatic. How many times did Nicolas call Nicky and me out here? Always to chastise some wild plan Nicky was working on. Right after Angelo's death, Nicolas took control of the family. The other bosses did not contest his claim because it was better than having Nicky on the loose with no one to control him. All the bosses knew Nicky would kill anyone to get to the top, anyone except his father. And only his father could curb his crazy ideas. As I told him many times, he was a mastermind of a criminal, but utterly reckless.

"Scared money doesn't make money," Nicky used to tell me.

And I'd reply, "there's no banks in Hell."

"Yes, there is, I've been there," he'd laugh, referring to Hell, Grand Cayman.

I turned onto a dirt road; two miles of bumps and dips, so I had to slow down. I asked Nicolas once why he didn't have it paved or at least put down gravel.

He said, "I don't want people coming down that road too fast."

I reached gate to the property, there was a padlock and chain on it. I took out my Sig 45, backed up a few feet, and took three shots before the lock fell to the ground. *Fucking good lock.* I drove up to the farmhouse. The place looked nice. Empty of course, but nice. I was not going in there, the key which had made an impression in my hand was for the barn. More accurately, for the wine cellar in the barn. I unlocked the door and started down the steps. The flashlight lit up the stairway well enough but was less than adequate in the large room beneath the barn floor. I shone the light around from the foot of the staircase. *What the fuck am I looking for? Nicolas, you could have told Cherry Bomb more. Just giving her a key isn't very helpful. And why when Sal was killed? What the fuck, old man?*

I walked up and down the racks of wine bottles. Row after row of what we called, "badly labeled vinegar." I was about to give up when I spotted one bottle's butt in, instead of head down like the rest. Nicolas told me that wine is always stored with the cork down, so it stays moist and doesn't let air into the bottle. I pulled the odd one out from the rack; it could have been a mistake. It did not have a label. I drew several others around it, they all had labels, names, and years on them, hand written.

As I walked to the little round café table at the front of the wine cellar, I heard a rattling coming from the bottle. I held the flashlight up to it and saw a key inside. *Your wine is already near poisonous without adding whatever kind of metal you put in there, Nicolas.* I found a corkscrew, opened the bottle, and poured the contents on the floor. It was thick and greasy. *Oh, olive oil. Smart, Nicolas, your family's wine would have dissolved the key in minutes.*

The key was for a safe deposit box, stamped, 'HBT 853'. I locked the wine cellar and drove to the nearest town to get another lock for the gate, then headed back to New York. HBT stood for Harlem Bank and Trust, a little neighborhood bank on 125th Street. It had a few dozen customers, the biggest one being Nicolas Rocci. I'm almost sure he owned it.

I got to the bank, asked for the bank manager, and we went into his office. I told him, "I'm an associate of Nicolas Rocci. I have this key for his safe deposit box. I need you to open it for me, discreetly."

"Let me first say how sorry I am at his passing. And his wife… a terrible accident with the heater and all that. I was good friends with them for years." The bank manager was an elderly black man with a cotton ball afro. He had a warm, kind smile that made you feel at ease. If he were crooked, you couldn't tell by looking at him. "Morris, that key isn't to a safe deposit box."

"You know who I am?"

"Indeed I do," he nodded. "I told you I was friends with Nicolas and Lucille for years. You know, she had pictures of you, Nicky, and Sal at Christmas, Thanksgiving, and the Fourth. All the major holidays. Lucille called you her third little man. Both were very fond of you."

"They were family to me too. So, if this is not a safe deposit box key, what's it for?"

"Come, I'll show you," the old man rose slowly from his big leather chair, "when you are my age, it's as hard to sit down as it is to get up. And walking is no joy either."

They took a small deathtrap of an elevator down into the basement vault area. Across from the vault where all the safe deposit boxes were was a steel door. "The key opens that door.

It's heavy, you're going to have to pull pretty hard to open it. I keep forgetting to get my son to oil the hinges."

He was right about the hinges needing oil as the stubborn door creaked loud as it slowly peeled back. I pulled the light string to the one bulb hanging from the ceiling in the center of the room. There were file boxes stacked around the room against all four walls. Some stacks were three and four boxes high. There was a solid wooden dining table, one chair, a 13-inch television on it, and two video recorders, a beta and a VCR machine. And one VCR tape sitting on the table.

"You can only plug in one machine at a time," he informed me and left.

MORRIS REMEMBERS, shortly after seeing Nicky in the hospital after his fake shooting in '76, Nicky told him how he was cornering the market on the newest thing in home electronics, the video cassette recorder. A back room in the mansion was stocked floor to ceiling with both Betamax and VHS machines.

Nicky bragged, "These just fell off a truck down at the docks. The latest models out of Japan and Korea. And I know what you're thinking, what happens if Betamax turns out to be more popular than the VHS? That's why I got them both, and cameras too."

"Cameras?" I've been out of the country for the last few years, I'm not up to date on the latest American fads.

"Oh, yes. These machines can record TV programs, or from video cameras, or the cameras themselves can take a tape and make a recording that can be played back on the machine. They are going to replace the 8mm films. People love making home movies of birthdays, weddings, all that crap. And they can watch it right away." Nicky lowered his voice to just above a whisper. "And the cameras are quiet, really, really, quiet. Not like the clicking noise from 8mm, so people won't know they are being recorded. I got dad to replace the cameras in the shops on Forty Deuce with these babies. And we are converting all our triple x movies to videotape. That's a real boon, pervs don't have to go to the movies on the Deuce to get their jollies, they can whack off in their own living rooms."

"Isn't that cutting into your sex business? Aren't you losing money from the live shows and movie houses?"

"Hell, no," Nicky bragged, "it just changes the way we collect it. I can record one live sex show to two hundred tapes at once. That beats the hell out of eight dirty old men watching around the old octagon peep booth. Plus, we still have the old octagon booth, and the movie houses. You know, for the young boys who can't watch these shows at home. And the old pervs who just like to jerk off in public. And the movies still serve as a place for the girls to take a date for a quick handy or bj."

"I guess your father is right, sex is still the best business to be in," I agree.

"My dad let me hook up all our hotels too. You'd be surprised at all the people we have on tape, and 8mm. It's good to have an ace in the hole."

"I often wondered how your dad never got popped. Especially with you for a son. Nails, you are not exactly discreet," I joke.

I OPENED a bunch of the boxes in the room. Naturally, they contained videotapes and 8mm film. Some of the tapes and film boxes just had dates on them, dating back decades. The boxes on the bottom mostly had 8mm and a few converted videotapes from the Fifties and Sixties. Other tapes had names and dates, famous people, politicians, judges, police officials, actors, actresses, singers. Anybody and everybody was on tape. Nicolas was very busy.

The tape on the table was unmarked. I wondered, was this Nicolas' Watergate? Thirteen years ago, Nixon was ruined by his obsession with recording people. Had Nicolas recorded someone he shouldn't have and gotten himself and his wife killed because of it? It was quite possible for the FBI, CIA, NSA, or other black ops groups to stage a killing and make it look like Sal did it. Was this tape his Watergate?

Nicky had the county medical examiner declare his parents' death an accidental asphyxiation due to a faulty furnace in the home, then had them cremated to prevent any further investigation. For a man like his father, the death would not go unchallenged. Nicky could not let the authorities question Sal, or anyone else who was in the house at the time. The local officials were very understanding, and cooperative in his time of grief. Now I wondered what Nicolas had on them.

I had gone through a good number of the boxes, looking at the names, dates, and places. Not all the recordings were made on the Deuce, or in New York. Nicolas went after people he could use, wherever he could get to them. Finally, I sat down in front of the TV and popped in the tape on the table. It was why I was here. The video wasn't made too long ago, judging from the lack of dust on it. Although, the room was very clean, it wasn't airtight. The ventilation system brought in a bit of dust and there was a fine layer on everything in there.

Whatever Nicolas wanted to tell me, whatever he wanted me to know was on this tape. The TV showed black and snowy for the first minute, then Nicolas' office in the mansion. *Interesting, I didn't think he came to Long Island anymore. Not since Nicky started running the operations.* The room was empty, the clock in the lower right corner of the screen showed 6.12.1978 8:00:00 am. The recorder had been on a timer, it must have started recording every day at the same time. That was my first impression, but I was wrong. People started filling the room. I saw Nicky, Pauley, Fat Joe, Icepick Louie, Mr. Pierre the Undertaker, Christopher Carmine, and his newly wedded wife Carmella.

This is three months after the Jimenez' killings. Nicky's plan had worked, and I guess Chris and Carmella are being welcomed into the family. These tapes are eight hours long, so if this tape starts and stops automatically when someone enters the room, I could be watching a lot of home movies junk.

But as it turned out this was a business meeting. Chris and Carmella were introduced to Emelia, affectionately known as Grandma Coco in the cocaine business, on the phone. They were being told who to meet with in Florida and where to stay. Icepick was being sent with them as Grandma Coco was not to be trusted. She had a reputation for getting rid of people that got in her way. Nicky liked her, I more than once suggested we feed her to the alligators.

Icepick was a good choice to keep an eye on our business. He was experienced, where Chris and Charms, as Nicky called her on the tape, were not. And Icepick earned his name the old fashioned way; a number of bodies turned up with stab wounds from his weapon of choice. Quite a few people in the Mob used an icepick, as it is untraceable, but Icepick Louie would take out people eyes, before or after they were dead. It was the punishment for traitors. Icepick Louie was a respected and feared enforcer. Grandma Coco would not readily go against him, and that meant not making moves against Chris and Charms either.

The tape breaks there and the next segment is of Nicolas and Pauley. It is January of 1980. *Oh, yeah, my Venezuelan vacation.*

This ought to be interesting. I expected them to be talking about finding me, but this meeting was about getting the goods on someone in the District Attorney's office. Nicolas knew there was a mole inside one of the families, the FBI's Organized Crime Task Force was making arrests of some of the top bosses. Nicolas needed his own mole in the Bureau and in the DA's office. Someone who could tip him off and get rid of evidence when necessary.

Another few hours of family business pass by on the tape. Vinny takes a five-year hit for gambling charges and racketeering. Nicolas uses his ADA to get convictions against other families. He is strengthening Nicky's position. In June of 1984, Nicolas turns over the operations to Nicky and throws a lavish party.

At 9:30, Nicky pulls Carmella into the office. First, he compliments her on the job she is doing in Florida, then he starts groping her. She pulls away and he get furious, "what do you think this is? I'm the boss now. You do what I want when I want."

"So, your first act as the head of this family is to rape me," Carmella defies him, "how will that look to the rest of your men? They will be looking to get rid of you before the night is over."

"Nobody is going to know because you are not going to tell anyone. You got that?" Nicky has her pressed against the wall in full view of the hidden camera.

Ah Nicky, this is going to be your Watergate, not your father's.

Carmella pushes him back, "I won't have to say anything. Things like this never stay secret for too long. I see how you look at me, Rozalina sees it too. And by the way, Chris is not too fond of you calling me to meetings without him. It will only be a matter of time before you are the joke on the street." Carmella walks to the door then stops. "If you want me that bad, Chris is going to Colombia next week…"

"I know," Nicky says, "I'm the one sending him. So, you'll stick around until he's gone. This relationship can have benefits for both of us. And by the way, I see the way you look at me too, Charms."

Ok, I can see why Nicky was going to catch a bullet. But it's been five hours, and nothing here speaks about Sal.

The next section of tape clarifies his involvement. The date stamp is March 12, 1986 2:00 pm. Carmella enters the room. I expect to see Nicky following behind her. I'm surprised to see Nicolas with her. He positions a chair at an angle and sits her down at his desk. He looks directly into the camera. Directly at me. "Nicky is away on business, that's why I called you here."

Carmella is scared stiff.

I'm guessing things had been going on for a while between her and Nicky. Now Dad is about to put an end to it.

"Is everything ok? Is there something wrong with Florida, or the football tallies."

Nicolas comes straight to the point, "I wish it were that simple. I know what you did to get into this family."

"What do you mean?"

"Look, I knew from the beginning how Nicky got you to plot against your father and Lucas. I didn't like the plan, but it worked out for the better, so I gave you your bones. And your crew have been steady earners. This thing you got going with Nicky, I don't care. Well, I do, but you're going to have to work that out with him. I'm sure you have learned by now, there are hard choices to be made in this business."

"I…"

"No, no need to explain, I'm sure this is more Nicky's doing than yours. But that is not why you are here today. Back then, when you proved you could do the hard task of watching your father's friend die, you proved you could be counted on. Now, I have a hard task and you are the only one I trust to see it done."

"Ok, whatever you need," Carmella says with certainty.

"I need you to kill Sal."

"SAL? Sal who?"

"You know who," Nicolas says and looks past her at the camera again. "My son Sal. Not now, but when the time comes, and you'll know when that is… I don't want him to suffer. It has to be clean. You understand what that means."

"Yes, I know. He won't feel a thing." She says soberly, "but why?"

"NEVER YOU MIND WHY." Nicolas wipes his hand across his face and composes himself. "Because Nicky or Morris could never do the job. And I can't ask them to, I just can't make them do this. You have never met Sal, I made sure of that. To you, he's just another person, a name without a face."

"What will happen when Nicky finds out? I mean, you are asking me to commit suicide." Her demeanor was stern but somehow very sympathetic.

"Not to worry, you won't be harmed. I will make sure he knows this is a sanctioned hit, by me. No retaliation of any kind," Nicolas took a deep breath as if what he said took all his strength. The added, "As long as Sal doesn't suffer."

The tape cut off. Black and white snow filled the screen. I spent the rest of the day going through the other tapes. I was looking for the ADA, the FBI agent, and some others that Nicolas had mentioned in the tape. I wanted to know what he had on them and how I could use it. This room was a treasure trove of blackmail.

Morris returned the next day to the mansion and told Gisella she had to go home right away, saying the situation was about to get worse before getting better. Indeed, if Nicky didn't pull through, things would get very bad, the family would more than likely fall apart, meaning a power struggle for his businesses. She argued but he put her on a plane anyway. He wanted Rozalina to go with her, but she vehemently refused, saying she had to be there when Nicky woke up.

Morris told Pauley he needed him to call a family meeting, needing to speak to all the capos and lieutenants at once. Pauley objected, "They will not respond positively to you. Most of them know you, but you are still an outsider."

"Then don't tell them I'm calling the meeting. Tell them their boss wants them here."

"I'll do it," agrees Pauley, "but why?"

"I've got information from Nicolas about the family."

"I was Nicolas' second-in-command for years. I would know if he left any information behind."

"Then you know about the videos?" I asked.

He nodded.

"Well, he left one for me specifically for after Sal's death. You know the family was in trouble."

"Not the family," Pauley corrected, "Nicky and you. You two fucked up badly. Nicolas was trying to clean up your mess. But in the middle of it all, Sal killed him. You say he left you the reason why?"

"Kinda, you get everyone here. I'll do the rest."

NICKY'S CONDITION was a tightly guarded secret. Few people knew he had been shot; less than a handful of his capos knew he was in a coma. About thirty of Rocci's top men, which included some from the Della Russo and Lucas families, filled Nicolas' office. Which, as big as it was, could not hold that many people comfortably. They sat on folding chairs shoulder to shoulder five rows deep. Quietly, some asked about Nicky's whereabouts, and the strange sounds coming from upstairs.

I entered from a door behind Nicolas' desk that led to a private suite. Thug One and Thug Two, two of my biggest and best bodyguards rolled out a television on a cart.

The room came alive with questions, "what's going on here," and "where's Nicky?" A few challenged Pauley directly.

I yelled above the noise, "Nicky is upstairs, in a coma from an assassin's bullet!"

The room got quiet.

I continued, "we are here to find out who fired said bullet. You all know me, or of me. I have been a trusted and loyal associate of Nicky's and Nicolas' for years. And if you don't believe me watch this."

I pressed play on the VCR and Nicolas began speaking to Nicky, Pauley, and Vinny. "Nicky, anything should happen to me, trust these two men, and your friend Morris. He's probably more Italian than all of us combined."

They laughed.

Nicolas continued, "He's smart and you may need someone from the outside looking in, once in a while. Morris is the man I would pick."

The room exploded with shouts of, "BULLSHIT!" and "THIS IS A FAKE!"

"You remember that day, don't you, Pauley?" I ask.

He nodded.

"Ok, so now that's out of the way, let's get down to business. You guys may not know this, but anyone who ever had a meeting with Nicolas in this room, and some other choice places, is on tape. I have viewed a lot of them… not all, not yet. I am going to ask all of you some questions about what you have been doing, and I'll see if what you say now confirms what is on tape."

Again, the room breaks into a riotous and tumultuous tone. Chairs falls as a lot of the men either try to make their way to the desk or the door behind them.

I pull out an Uzi from under the desk and yell, "Everyone sit the fuck down!"

The men gather their chairs and calm is restored.

"Now, obviously, everyone here could not have been involved in Nicolas' death and the assassination attempt on my friend Nicky. But one or a few of you are, and I will find out who. Now, you can either answer my questions, or my associates here will have much tougher ones for you."

"Morris, you are insane," Pauley gets up, "as tragic as it was, Nicolas' death came at the hand of Sal, that poor crazy bastard."

"Really? because in light of what happened to him and Nicky, I'm not so sure. I know what you told me. I know you are the one who found their bodies the next day. You are going to have to persuade me."

"I've been this family's number two man before you were born…"

"Maybe you thought it was time for a change. Maybe you thought turning the family over to Nicky was a big mistake. And maybe you thought you could become number ONE!"

"That's it! I'm not listening to anymore of your ravings. Because you're Nicky's best friend and I think you mean well, I am not going to put a bullet in your head. But this meeting is over." Pauley storms out, slamming the door with a boom that shakes the whole house.

All eyes are on me. My hand is still resting on the Uzi on the desk. A few more seconds pass and then gunfire erupts outside the office.

BOOM! BOOM! BOOM… BOOM… BOOM.

"Ok. If anyone else wants to leave the party early," I chide.

"The door is there." I wait a few long agonizing minutes, painful for the others, not for me. "Chris. Christopher Carmine where are you?"

"Here." A hand goes up in the middle of the room. He is sitting next to Carmella who is holding his other hand.

"For the sake of appearances on the street, you are now running the day to day. Nicky trusted you. Nicolas trusted you. And I found nothing on the few tapes you are on to make me not trust you. Don't prove me wrong." I stand up and put the Uzi in the desk drawer. "Everyone is taking orders from Chris. Chris, you are taking orders from me. As far as the street is concerned, the orders are coming from Nicky. You all can let the word out that he's been shot. But tell your people he is tough as nails. He is fine. Oh, and one more thing, you know in the old gangster movies when they say, 'No one leaves town'? Yeah, it's like that, no one leaves the house until you are cleared by me. Got it… I'll be calling everyone in one by one. I need to be persuaded, capisce."

I went back out the door I came in. The rest sat in stunned amazement. After a few minutes there were quiet grumblings and softly offered curses to me and my lineage. But they quietly filed out to the bar, everyone taking a quick glance up at the second floor, where the noise suddenly became a familiar sound, hospital equipment. They also looked at the large amount of blood on the foyer floor and the drag marks going out the front door.

5

BLACK BLOOD

S tarting with the most recent tapes and working backwards was the quickest way to find out what Nicolas was up to. It didn't take long to find a tape from 1986 where Nicolas and Pauley are talking at the farmhouse. *Nicolas had Nixonitis bad.*

Nicolas was in the living room drinking a wine—not from his cellar—when Pauley arrived and complained about the drive up as usual.

Nicolas ignores his complaints, "pour yourself a drink and sit down, we have a problem."

"What did Nicky do now, Boss?" Pauley pours a glass of bourbon, "man, it's still cold up here. You should come back to the city. This mountain air can't be good for your health."

"My health is just fine," he answers defiantly, "and it's not what Nicky did now, it's what he did years ago that's the problem. I got a call from Mark Hampton. He said the DA is reinvestigating the Banoa murder."

"What the fuck! Why is that cocksucker, District Attorney, looking into that? Whose, the fuck, cares who whacked Banoa. What'da he thinks, he's gonna have every boss in cuffs?" Pauley's accent becomes more pronounce as he gets angry. "I tell ya, Boss, somebody oughta put a present up his tailpipe. Retire him before he does some real damage."

"No. That will only prove he was onto something. Besides, you know killing a DA will cause a Fed Task Force to look for his killers. We don't need another fucking fed task force crawling around. I have a better idea," Nicolas pours another full glass, then sits staring out the bay window and not looking at anything.

Pauley waits for a few minutes, then finishes his drink. He looks at Nicolas for another moment, "so what's the plan?"

"What plan?"

"About Banoa's murder? What do you want to do?" Pauley asks, hiding his disbelief.

"That fucking degenerate, Mark Hampton, called me today. Said the DA is reinvestigating the case."

"Yeah, you told me that," Pauley looks at Nicolas with concern, "are you drinking that poison from the wine cellar? You know that stuff is only good for target practice."

Nicolas continues like Pauley hadn't said a word. "Hampton, that fucking prick, said the DA is looking into the whole war with Banoa. The Raven shooting, the hijackings, the construction mishaps, every little detail of his life, and mine. If he keeps digging, he will find something that ties the boys to Banoa. I can't let that happen. When did Vinny get pinched?"

"In 1980, I think. I can check on it, get you the exact date. Why?"

"No. That's good," Nicolas says looking around like he has lost something.

Pauley watches his head bob and twitch, "what's wrong, boss?"

"Where's my vino?"

"It's in your hand, Boss. Are you sure you okay?" Pauley was very worried.

"Oh, what? Like you ain't getting old, you fuck," Nicolas

berates him. He smiles and says calmly, "I'm going to go and confess to Mark Hampton, that no good bastard, to killing Joe Banoa."

"WHAT? ARE YOU FUCKING INSANE?"

"NO! Hear me out. The only way that prick of a DA will stop looking for Banoa's killer is when he finds him. I got all the details from Sal, that boy don't forget nothing. I'm gonna be the inside shooter, you and Vinny are going to be the outside guys. Once I'm convicted, you can clear your name. You weren't even in the country at the time. I don't know what the fuck Vinny was doing back then, probably jerking off somewhere. Anyway, I'm sure he can prove he was busy elsewhere and couldn't be outside the Bella Rosa that night."

Pauley sat stunned for a time. He poured another drink and sipped it slowly, mulling over Nicolas' plan. Finally, he gave his opinion, "I don't know, Boss. Nick, you put your head in a noose like that and you are liable to get hung. Maybe you wait, see what the DA comes up with."

"Too late, I already arranged to give that little prick my statement. He'll get the case and I'll make sure he sticks to the script. I will remind him; we still have his little girlfriend on tape. I'm sure he doesn't want the world to know what happened to Adrianna."

Pauley didn't know what to think. Nicolas could recall details about a murder four years ago, a dozen years ago, but cannot remember he's drinking his wine. Sure, he had an alibi. He and Vinny get separate trials, they will get off, but Nicolas taking the fall for Nicky and Morris, that does not end well for Nicolas. He watches his boss wander aimlessly around the room mumbling to himself.

Nicolas comes back from another trip to Lalaland, "Pauley, not a word to Nicky. I want this thing over and done before he has a chance to fuck it up."

Wow, Nicolas was going to take the rap for Nicky and me. Wait... not for us, for Sal, he was the triggerman. But what went wrong? Did one of Banoa's guys decide to dispense a little mob justice? Did the ADA, Mark Hampton, do a flip and have Nicolas killed? Wouldn't be the first time a worm grew a spine when being blackmailed and faced with losing everything.

I find a tape marked, Adrianna 1980. This has got to be about the ADA. Adrianna Nunez is a beautiful Puerto Rican girl with black luxurious hair down to her ass. She has thick black eyebrows and natural long lashes that make her look exotic and mysterious. She cannot be more than fifteen or sixteen in this tape. Adrianna is a stripper in several of Nicolas' clubs. She goes by different names but there is no mistaking her face and deep accent. Nicolas was obviously taken by her, there were twelve tapes of her dancing, performing in the booths, having sex in hotels with johns from 1980 to 1984.

It is on a tape in '82 she is first introduced to Mark Hampton at a strip joint. He looks like a fresh and wide-eye college boy. She must have been told to show him special attention, because she was rolling around in front of him each time she took the stage. Sliding up and down the pole and shaking her pussy in his face until he could take it no more and made the stiffy walk to the door.

The first time, Mark was brought into the club by a guy I figured worked for Nicolas. After that, he was hooked. He sat stage side in the dark club and ordered a hundred-dollars' worth of drinks each night. Adrianna was great at what she did. She had several regulars who came just to see her. And they would spend an hour or two in the private rooms, costing them hundreds of dollars more. Nicolas used her as bait to trap some of the most influential men and women in New York.

Then I found a tape named, Hampton 84. I popped it in and immediately Mark was on top of her. He looked drugged. His speech was slurred, "Eyes luvs you Annie. Marry me. WEE will runaway…"

She laughed, "Youse already married. Oh, did you forget about your wife again?"

"My… wife… no, she don't need to know… I told her I am working later…"

The recording skips and then he's yelling and screaming like a madman. Adrianna is naked and huddled in a corner of the room. Mark is naked and trashing the place. He throws the lamp and hits her in the head. She falls over. He rushes to her and begins choking and beating her head on the floor. The tape skips.

They probably got him dusted. Looks like PCP or bad acid.

Some man stands in the doorway, the morning sun shines on Adrianna's dead body on the floor. Mark is naked, sitting on the bed, hands and body streaked with blood. The man speaks slow and clear, "hey, don't worry about this. You had a bad night, that's all. A little too much to drink, a little too much up the nose, these things happen."

"But what about Annie?" sobs Mark.

"Who? I don't see no Adrianna. You see an Adrianna?" The man opens the door, "look, you're an important guy with important friends, they are going to take care of this. If it wasn't you, it would have been some other guy. That's how these girls like to live. They like to party. And sometimes they party too much, too hard."

"I don't know."

"What's to know?" the man said angrily. "I called your friend from the club, Peter, he's bringing you clean clothes. Wash up, tell your wife you fell asleep at the office, buy her something nice and take her out for diner. Forget about this, it never happened."

I would bet it didn't. Adrianna had been killed at least five times on tapes already. *Nicolas, you cagey old fox, getting the johns drugged and passed out, so when they wake up and find her bloody and with faked stab wounds, they bolt.* A great scam and blackmail plot. She played the part well, but this tape was too real.

But Mark could not forget about it, Nicolas made sure of that. Also, on that tape, Peter tells Mark they need evidence against a drug dealer to disappear, to mislabel the bags for destruction. And he did. And when they came to him to get a conviction, he falsified evidence. On the rare occasions Mark's morals stood up to Peter, his handler for the Rocci family, the name Adrianna came up. He was even shown the tape, unedited, of him killing her.

Mark knew he had been drugged and he should have turned himself in immediately, but he was panic-stricken and after the body was gone it was too late. Peter told him the body was dumped out of state, a Jane Doe murder victim. Her murder would remain unsolved, the police in the town had nothing to go on. The only way to identify her was through the tape of her murder.

It did not take him long to figure out who had set him up; the favors he was asked to do mostly benefited the Rocci family. Either by helping them escape prosecution or convicting a rival. Coercion alone would not have worked for as long as it did. Peter fed Mark information such as where evidence could be found, or witnesses that would be forced into testifying. At times, he was sure the testimony was fabricated, or the evidence planted, but he used it anyway and his career benefitted.

It becomes easier to justify one's actions when there are no other choices. Peter soothed his conscience by telling him, "these people deserve the jailtime you're getting them," and, "we will get these guys put away, if not by you, then by someone else we have on the team. You are not our only ace in the hole. So why let someone else get the glory you deserve?"

Mark began looking at his fellow members of the legal system in a different way. How deep Rocci's influence ran was beyond him. It wasn't hard to trap him, and others had bigger, better careers to protect. There were judges who seemed to favor his arguments in court. So much so, that in front of some benches he brought the bare minimum to trial and still won. Rulings that made his hair stand on end were commonplace in his trials.

Sure, the courts and legal system overall was overworked and bursting at the seams, politicians pushed the war on drugs to the voters, drug dealers pushed crack on the streets to the poor, heavy hitters like Peter plied doctors, lawyer, politicians, and the social upper class with the fun drug, cocaine, and Rocci kept the entire system spinning, sending the right people to jail and keeping his businesses humming along. But he was just one cog in a giant corrupt machine, the drug business. And it was deeply embedded in American society. Its roots ran to the very bedrock of the country.

Mark Hampton belonged to Nicolas Rocci, body and soul. His only way out was through death, his own. He contemplated it, wrote a suicide note. Drank a bottle of Scotch and took a bottle of pills. He would have succeeded if he had picked any place other than a seedy lower westside hotel. One he had frequented in the past. A place where streetwalkers took him to when his life spiraled down the drain after an easy win in court. A place owned by Nicolas Rocci.

Peter was there when he awoke in the hospital. "Hey, buddy. How are you feeling?"

"What happened? Where am I?"

"You did something very stupid last night," he admonished him. "Let's start with going to a fleabag hotel alone. No one goes to those places except to get laid or to off themselves. Then there is writing this note." Peter held up the paper and began to read. "I am a disgrace to my family and my profession. I am a fraud, a liar, a cheat, and a murderer. I killed a hooker… no, a lady, whom I loved, name Adrianna."

Peter crumpled up the paper and threw it in Mark's face. "It goes on. The liquor and pills must have kicked in because after that your handwriting is atrocious. What the fuck do you think you're doing? We have plans for you. Big plans. And you go and pull something like this."

Mark turned his face in shame.

Peter took the crumpled paper from the bed. "I had to go to the Big Man myself and beg him to give you another chance. Next time, we let you die, but this little note of yours, well, it might get reworded. I don't know, maybe talk about fraud in a different way, like embezzlement. How would you like it if your wife were implicated in a bribery kickback scheme? You'd be dead, she'll be sitting in jail with a couple hundred G's sitting in an account, and an assistant district attorney vowing to bring your family to justice."

He started to cry, "Leave her out of this. I'm sorry. I won't do it again."

"Hey, get your shit together, man. This is no way for your wife to see you. She is on her way up. We… the doctor, told her you have the flu. You were found passed out on the train in Brooklyn. It's all very innocent. Happens to the best of us. They'll keep you in the hospital for a couple of days, then you go back to work."

Helen Hampton rushed to her husband's side, hugged him, and kissed his forehead. "You don't have a fever. That's a good sign."

"Probably all the good drugs they are pumping into him," Peter laughed, "still, I'd be careful, so don't get too close. And for God's sake, when he gets out of here, you two take a vacation somewhere warm. Our golden boy is working himself to death.”

Helen nodded and thanked Peter for being such a good friend.

When Mark got out of the hospital, he didn't go back to work. First, he and his wife were invited by the state senator to a holiday party. Several big names from New York's elite praised his work to his wife. They toasted his successes in helping clean up the streets. Two judges, whom he knew well, pulled him away from his wife for a private talk, taking him to an upstairs den. They left him with an older man with a pleasant smile and subdued voice. “Mark Hampton, right?”

“Yes. I would venture you are Mr. Nicolas Rocci?”

“I'm told that trying cases is starting to wear on you. I understand. This thing, facing all those degenerates, day in and day out, not knowing if what you're doing is helping anyone at all. Don't worry about it. Come Monday, you'll have a new job.”

“No. Thank you. I can do my job. I like what I do…”

“Maybe you do,” Nicolas said, “maybe you don't so much anymore. The fact is… everybody needs a little change of scenery once in a while. You will still be in the DA's office, but you'll be an investigator. Better paid, less stress. Your friend Peter won't be coming around anymore.”

Mark looked panicked, “No, I like Peter. He's an OK guy.”

“Hey, don't worry, Peter is just fine with it. Besides, you don't need him in this job. You just go to work, do your job, and everything will be fine. Now, you'd better get back to the party before somebody tries to steal your pretty little wife. And have a Merry Christmas.” *This is a much better use of this asshole. Instead of feeding us information and trying to change things that already in known, we can be in the driver's seat directing how and where the investigations will end up.*

The two judges open the door and lead Mark downstairs. They chat with him about the Knicks' latest winning streak and end when they meet up with his wife. Five minutes later, Mark is ushering his wife into a town car and away from the party. He is both relieved and frighten by the night's events.

"LUCILLE, IS NICOLAS AROUND?"

"No, Pauley, he took Sal to the doctor today. Or did you forget it's the first Tuesday of the month?"

Pauley takes her hand and leads her to the sofa. "I know, I'm here to see you. Has Nicolas been feeling ok? Has he said anything to you? You know, about not feeling—"

"You see it too," Lucille interrupts, as her eyes well up with tears. "I've tried to get him to see a doctor, but he insists he's fine. Just getting old, he says, but with my health and Sal's condition, I think it's just getting to be too much. I worry about him."

"Has he been forgetting things he said, or the things he's done?" Pauley asks.

"Yes. And it's getting more frequent. Sometimes, I'll catch him staring off into space. Or he will just not be there in the middle of a conversation." Now tears are rolling down her cheek. She continues, "I think all these… things Nicky has started is also wearing him out. I suggested he turn everything over to Nicky. He's more than ready to handle the business. Maybe, you can suggest it too."

"I will. It's a hard thing for a man to think about retiring," Pauley says compassionately. "We'd all like to play the game forever. I will also try to get him to see a doctor. It's probably nothing, or that rest and getting rid of the stress won't cure. I'll come back tomorrow, and we will talk."

The next day Pauley showed up early in the morning with a box of cannoli. "Hey, Nicolas, how are you doing?"

"I'm fine. What are you doing here?"

"I bought you cannoli from that place on Orchard Street you like," Pauley smiled and watched Nicolas' face, trying to judge his reaction.

"I didn't ask you to bring me anything," Nicolas said confidently.

Pauley smiled. It was a good sign. "No, you didn't. But can't an old friend come by and shoot the breeze for a minute?"

Lucille comes to the living room door and smiles at them, "He woke up cranky this morning, Pauley. Watch out he doesn't shoot you for being too nice. I'll take those."

Pauley hands over the box and Lucille returns to the kitchen down the hallway.

Nicolas waits another minute and then says, "OK, the truth. Did Lucy tell you to come check up on this old man?"

"The truth?"

"Yeah."

"I came to check on you myself," Pauley sat down on the same couch.

Nicolas remained standing.

"You might want to sit down; this is going to take a minute." He waits.

Nicolas sees Pauley is not going to leave without saying what is on his mind. He sits.

"Now, that is not so bad, is it? Basically, Boss, I am worried that you are overworked. And I don't mean with just these last couple of weeks. I mean for a year or more. You seem to be slipping…"

"Slipping, huh? You think I'm too old to run things anymore. Or maybe you think I lost my mind because I want to protect my sons."

"Not exactly, I was thinking maybe it is time we turn the

business over to the boys. Enjoy our life. No law says we have to go out in a blaze of glory, you know. Some of the best guys went quietly, at home in bed, surrounded by their families. And maybe you go to the doctor, make sure you can enjoy your retirement in style."

"I don't need to go to the doctor," Nicolas says bitterly at the suggestion, "because I've already seen the doctor, three of them for your information. I just haven't told Lucille, with her heart and all. And don't you tell her either, the doctors aren't exactly singing her praises either. I know I've been having trouble remembering things, so I went. They said it's Alzheimer's disease."

Pauley's mouth falls open.

"Great poker face. I guess you know what that is. I didn't but they explained it to me. One day, and apparently not too far from now, I'll be wandering around here with a cowboy's hat on and no fucking pants… Feel free to laugh now."

"So that's why you want to cop a plea for the Banoa murders," Pauley regained his composure. "If you think they won't try you, you're wrong. Alzheimer or no Alzheimer, they will still stick you in jail."

"Yeah, but if I don't do it now, I might not remember everything Sal told me about that night. If I slip up and they figure out I'm lying, they'll come after the boys."

"What do you need me to do?"

"Drop me off at the DA's office," Nicolas says, "I prepared a written statement. You can't wait around, since I'd be implicating you too. I'll give you a copy, then get word to Vinny through the lawyers, he has to know what he can say and what he can't."

Nicolas enters the District Attorney's office at 26 Federal Plaza in lower Manhattan. The dusty rose granite stone building was erected in the middle of the 19th century and housed the city and federal legal offices. He waits at the green iron elevator doors in the north corridor and admires the relief on the door of two opposing groups of people gathered on the scales of justice. Sun rays shine down the middle of the doors equally on both sides.

A small group of men and women gather around him this early Wednesday morning. He nods politely to police in uniform. Smiles at the young woman in the gray skirted business suit. Another man fumbles with his briefcase and coffee as he tries to clip on his FBI ID badge.

"Here, allow me," Nicolas offers and takes the man's coffee cup.

"Thanks, Mister," he manages to affix his badge and retrieves his cup. "Coffee shop around the corner to the right. Coffee's a hundred percent better than the swill you will get in here."

"Good to know."

The doors part right down the middle of the sun beams and the base of the scale. A dozen people file into the tiny elevator car and start calling out floor numbers. The young FBI agent is pressing buttons, "and you sir, what floor do you need?"

"Seventeen," Nicolas answers as the doors slide shut.

They ride up in silence and he steps from side to side to let others off before him. The few conversations that were going on outside of the elevator were put on hold until the people got off. The car stops at his floor and as he exited, he smiles to the only two left, the skirt suit businesswoman and the FBI agent waiting anxiously to drink his coffee. No one eats or drinks in elevators either.

He says, "Enjoy your coffee and have a good day." Then walks down the aisles of gray fabric cubicles. Phones are ringing, people pecking away at computer keyboards, and occasionally someone glances up at him, not to offer assistance, but to make sure he's not checking on what they are doing. *This floor is one large square of boredom. It's enough to drive someone crazy. How can these assholes stand it?* Finally, he finds a gray wall with the nameplate, Mark Hampton, velcroed to it. *Instantly replaceable. How fucking demeaning.* Nicolas stands in the opening, "OK. Let's get this over with."

"Yes, sir, Mister Rocci," Mark says, surprised to see him. "But not here. I must take you upstairs to the twentieth floor. That is where the interview rooms are. You'll make your statement before another assistant DA."

"I told you I was turning myself in to you!"

"You are," Mark cowered, "but I am an investigator. There will be another trial attorney there. Probably quite a few. You didn't come with your lawyer?"

"What for? I have a written confession. There will be plenty of time for lawyers."

They took the elevator up three floors. A crowd awaited them. All very politely ushering him into a glass-enclosed room. Inside, video cameras were set up in each corner, four microphones on the table, a dozen chairs on one side of the long mahogany table, and just two on the opposite side. Nicolas took one of the two and six others filled the other side of the table. A heavy-set man, but not fat, with a full head of wavy black hair and graying sideburns in a blue pinstriped suit pressed a button on the table to start the recorders. "18 March 1986. Present is Marissa Kristian, assistance district attorney, me, George Jarvis, district attorney for the Manhattan circuit court, and various other witnesses to be named at the conclusion of these proceedings. We are here to take the confession of... can you please state your name for the record..."

"Nicolas Angelo Rocci."

"To the charges of murder of one Mister Joseph Banoa, in particular, and the conspiracy of murder of several of Mister Banoa associates. Is that correct, Mr. Rocci?"

"Yes, that is correct," Nicolas said, showing he was a bit annoyed with this arrangement.

"Let the record show that Mr. Rocci is not at present represented by counsel," Jarvis stated, "do you wish to wait for your counselor to arrive, or do you wish the state to provide you with one at this time?"

"As I told Mark here, I have a statement I'd like to read. I don't want this thing to take all day." They went silent. The cameras were rolling.

Nicolas made the last video of his life. "On the night of April 5th, 1972, I met with Joseph Banoa to discuss difficulties between our two families. The conversation was of a personal nature. About an hour into our talk things got heated. Insults were thrown by both of us. He reached for his gun. I pulled my .22 first and fired three shots. One hit Joseph Banoa in the head, killing him. On hearing the shots fired inside the Bella Rosa, my private security personnel, Paul Perelli and Vincent Masserole fearing for my life opened fire on the occupants inside. Whom, by the way, were trying to kill me. I dropped the gun and fled the scene. I did not go to the Bella Rosa with the intention of causing Mr. Banoa harm and I deeply regret the events of that night, and my part in it."

"Thank you, Mr. Rocci," Jarvis said. He stood up and motioned for two uniformed officers to enter the glass cage. "Based on the statement you just gave; I hereby place you under arrest for the murder of Joseph Banoa. Officers, will you please take Mr. Rocci into custody."

Nicolas stood up and placed his hands behind his back, "I would like to call my lawyer now."

"Of course," Jarvis stopped the recorders. "Officers, remain here with Mr. Rocci. Miss Kristian, can you please get a phone and plug it in here. After you make your calls, the officers will take you into custody and bring you downstairs to booking. Thank you for your cooperation, Mr. Rocci." Jarvis was the last to leave. He stopped just outside the door and said, "you can make as many calls as you think is necessary."

Marissa, the woman from the elevator in the gray skirt business suit, watched Nicolas led into the elevator in handcuffs. She was just outside of Jarvis's office. He was with Mark Hampton. She leaned in and said, "Wow! That was surreal. Do you think he's telling the truth? Not about it being a family dispute, but that he was the one who shot and killed Joseph Banoa."

"Yeah, sure," Mark quickly replied. "Why would he lie? He could have just kept quiet, couldn't he?"

"He's lying," George Jarvis stated bluntly. "My best guess would be he's dying, so he's trying to bury the case with him. I already called to have a medical exam preformed when he gets to lock up and before his lawyers can get him out." Jarvis leaned back in his chair and stared at the ceiling for a moment. "I don't know why he decided to confess to you, Mark, but you will be lead investigator on this. Marissa, you are going to take first chair. I want to make sure we make these charges stick."

"Even if he is not guilty?" asked Marissa.

"Doesn't matter to me," Jarvis said in a callous tone, "if he wants to go to the gallows for this crime, I'll be glad to pull the lever. And Mark, find the other two men, his so-call private security team. I want them behind bars too. Rocci is trying to play the self-defense angle. He thinks that will keep him off death row."

NICOLAS ROCCI WAS BAILED out of jail before nightfall with a clean bill of health. The DA office made no mention of his arrest to the newspapers, Jarvis feeling the fewer people who knew about it, the easier it would be to find witnesses. They always seemed to disappear when someone like Nicolas Rocci was involved. Although Nicolas kept a low profile, he was well-known in society circles and underworld mobs. And when those two groups crossed paths, investigations turned sour fast.

Jarvis was also worried about the son, Nicky, who was more brash and flamboyant than his father. When he entered the picture, which Jarvis knew he would, the prosecution of the case would get crazy. He envisioned death threats to his people, and perhaps attempts. He wanted to go through as much of the evidence as possible before Nicky Nails Rocci tainted it.

Nicolas showing up without a lawyer probably meant he had not informed his son either. He didn't know how long he could keep this thing under wraps, but he'd be happy if he got through the weekend before the shit hit the fan. But that was not going to be the case.

Before the elevator's door closed and Nicolas Rocci could be fingerprinted and photographed, a call was made. "Mr. Brunello, this is Richard Webb… Yes, from New York, the DA's office… You'll never guess who just came through this office with a story to tell… Nicolas Rocci. He just confessed to Joseph Banoa's murder… Yes, sir. You're welcome."

Beniamino Brunello was very interested in what was happening in New York, but especially interested when he had to do with the Rocci family. Nicky, but more so Morris, had cost him a large fortune, so he was looking for any angle he could use to bring the family down. He knew Nicolas well enough to know that shooting someone in the face was a last resort. Him confessing to it, or any crime, was even more of a long shot. Whatever was happening in New York, he wanted a piece of it.

Brunello dialed the Las Vegas sheriff' office, "Sheriff Chennain, how is the wife and kids? Good, I'm glad to hear that. Is that package still at the Stagecoach Saloon? Good… Oh, yes, if you would be so kind and pick it up for me… No, just hold onto it, someone will be along in a couple of days for it."

MONDAY MORNING MARK HAMPTON called Nicolas from a payphone a block away from his office. He kept looking around the booth while the phone rang. He was anxious to get the call over with before he was missed at the office, "Hello, Mr. Rocci?"

"Yes, who is this?"

"It's Mark Hampton, sir. You said to call if I had any news about your case."

"Well, let's have it, boy," Nicolas barked.

"Yes, sir." Mark was terrified. He felt Nicolas Rocci could reach through the phone and choke the life out of him at any moment. "DA Jarvis went over your statement and said there were inconsistencies with the evidence."

"What kind of inconsistencies?" Nicolas began to worry. He had written down everything Sal had told him about that night. At least, he thought he had. He must've, he had Sal go over it countless times. The DA was trying to trap him.

"Mr. Rocci, did you hear what I said?"

"What? No. What did you say?"

"You told Jarvis that you shot Banoa once and dropped the gun. But the murder weapon wasn't recovered at the scene."

"Oh no?" He had to think. *Did Sal ever say he dropped the gun? That would have been the thing to do. Nicky would have told him to leave the gun behind. But Sal never said he dropped the gun after the shooting.* "It must have been mixed-up with the other guns. I am sure it was there."

"No, sir. I am sorry, they ran ballistics on every weapon found in the Bella Rosa. Not one matched the gun that killed Mr. Banoa. And that's what got Mr. Jarvis questioning your statement."

"So, what? Maybe I stuck it in my pocket. Who remembers the small details? it was over a decade ago. Everything else checks out, though, right?"

"No, not exactly. Mr. Jarvis went over everything. All the photos, the witnesses' statements, all the forensics, whatever was at the Bella." Mark became extremely nervous. "The photos showed a blood trail leading out of the club. He assumed it was the inside gunman's blood since it didn't match any of the victims. And it led away from where Mr. Banoa was shot."

"So..."

"Well, you didn't mention being wounded in the attack..."

"Goddamnit! It has been years, who remembers these little details?" A picture flashed inside his head. Nicky, Morris, and Sal in his kitchen. Morris is wrapping Sal arm. He had forgotten about the flesh wound. Nicolas grumbled, "So, what are you trying to tell me, is the deal off the table?"

"I don't know," Mark replied, "I don't think so. I think Jarvis is waiting for the forensic guy to tell him something."

"You need to make sure this investigation goes down the way we discussed. It is why you are where you are in the DA office."

"I understand," Mark is very careful about what he has to say next, afraid if he isn't of any further use to Nicolas, he will wind up dead, "but this evidence was collected years before I was even in the department. There's not much I can do. But I will try."

Nicolas slammed the phone down, then paced the living room floor. *The blood, that's going to be the thing. Sal's type is O, the same as mine. It's got to be. I can't let this thing drag on, can't wait for it to go to trial. A Deadman's confession, that's the thing. No one questions that, it's an open and shut case. A slam dunk for the State, they won't pass it up.* Nicolas listens for a moment; Lucille is upstairs getting dressed.

He goes to the kitchen and comes back with clear plastic wrap, then calls Sal to the living room. "Sal, you must promise to do exactly as I tell you, or you can't go to Heaven with your mother and me. You have to be a good boy and obey your father. Do you understand?"

Sal nods.

NICOLAS MADE Lucille a cup of tea then doubled the dosage of her heart medicine into it. A few minutes later she was sleeping peacefully. He wished he could fall asleep. He kept watching the bedroom door. Finally, it creaked open and he watched Sal slowly walk to his mother. He heard Sal sobbing softly… he had told him not to cry, but he understood.

Sal took the plastic wrap and pulled off a foot. He had run to his room bawling aloud when Lucille asked if they had seen it after dinner. She was putting away the leftovers and wanted to cover the bowls. Nicolas told her to use aluminum foil.

Now, Sal stood over his mother with a piece of the missing wrap. A look of terror and fear gripped and twisted his face, his mind spinning in turmoil. He plunged the wrap down over her face. It forced her head down into the pillow. The heart medicine kept her asleep. She didn't struggle. She did not gasp for air. She died peacefully.

Nicolas would not have it so easy. He had to be alert. Make sure Sal followed his instructions. He told himself not to struggle. *Just let it happen.* But dying is not as easy as it seems, even when you plan it.

Sal walked around to his father.

Nicolas took his wife's wrist, there was no pulse. "Good Boy. I'll see you in Heaven."

"Goodbye, Papa."

Sal gently covered his father's face with the plastic wrap and pressed hard. His father started kicking and reaching for him. Sal's arms locked like steel beams holding up his body, remembering the words. *Don't you let up. No matter what I do, you keep pressing down until I'm asleep with your mother. Then you throw the plastic wrap away. Uncle Pauley will come for you in the morning. You don't tell anyone about this, especially Nicky. If you tell Nicky, he won't let you go to Heaven with us.* Sal pressed harder. Sweat ran down his arms and tears dropped onto his father's face. His father stopped struggling and went to sleep. Sal fell down beside the bed grabbed his hair, pulled hard, and started crying. He sat on the floor with the piece of plastic in his hand crying all night.

Pauley let himself in the next morning. He called for Nicolas, then Lucille, and finally Sal. No one answered. He walked around the farmhouse and finally ended his search in Nicolas' bedroom. He saw Sal sitting on the floor besides the bed, plastic wrap in his hand, still crying.

"SAL! WHAT THE FUCK?"

"Momma and Papa is sleeping in Heaven. I'm a Good Boy."

●
6

DEATH IS VERY REWARDING

Morris interviewed all the capos and their lieutenants. He knew who was behind Sal's killing, now he wanted to know who tried to take out Nicky. Was Chris and Carmella pulling a coup? Did someone else find out about Carmella's contract and decided this was their chance to make a move? Nicky had replaced most of Angelo's men already. Some retired, got out of the game on their own. Others were caught by the police and federal agents as the war on organized crime continued across the country, heaviest in New York. By the time Nicky was shot, all the higher-ups in the family were handpicked by either him or his father.

When Nicolas died it created the opportunity for one or a group of capos to make a move against his son. That's the way it is in this business. If Nicky showed any signs of weakness he would be replaced; his weakness would be another's strength. Power changes hands quickly in the underworld, so one must keep a firm grip on the reins. People must respect you, fear you, and love you. Everyone is out for the big question, 'what's in it for me?' And the answer must always be, 'Your Life.' Because when people start thinking they can survive without you, or worst, are better off without you, that's when they start thinking of replacing you.

So far, the capos came up clean, all going about their business as usual on that day. None had outside interests that would make him suspicious. So, it came down to Chris and Carmella. Were they conspiring together? Or did Carmella get tired of being Nicky's bitch? Or did Chris find out about them and decided to get rid of his boss? All good scenarios. Each with merits and possibilities, only Nicky could sort it out. He needed to talk to Nicky.

"OK. Tell me. Why is Nicky still getting a morphine drip?" I asked.

"He had a very serious injury; the bullet nicked his spine and punctured his lung. There is a lot of pain with an injury of this nature. Swelling around the spinal cord can cause severe pain."

"Gisella has reviewed his latest scans; she said the swelling is minor now. He may feel some discomfort but that's all. His breathing would improve if he were off the drip too."

"How would she know?"

"She's a doctor, a very good one, and I sent her the scans," I informed him. "I had her double-check everything you've been doing since we got here. She thinks your treatment is going over the top. Who's ordering you to keep him on the morphine?" I took out my Berretta and started aiming at his head.

The doctor ducked and covered his head with both hands. "Nicky! Nicky didn't want me to stop the drugs. I told him he would get better faster without them, but he threatened to kill me if I stopped. And now, you are threatening to kill me if I don't."

"Tuff decision, hey Doc. Let me make this easy for you, I have a fully loaded pistol pointed at your head and I'm ready to blow it wide open if you don't stop dosing him. Nicky, on the other hand, couldn't hit the broadside of a barn right now." I looked at him with a smile.

He nodded sheepishly.

"You're not going to tell Nicky you are taking him off the narcotics. You go up there and replace his bag with plain saline solution. And I will handle Nicky Nails."

IT TOOK a week before the morphine wore off. Nicky kept pressing the button to add more drugs to his intravenous tube, the pain was gone but the high he was craving did not come. He was angry calling for the doctor to come and fix him. The doctor left the premises immediately following Morris instructions. Morris sat in the kitchen for two days listening to Nicky's withdrawals. He allowed only food and water to be taken to him. On the third day he took the tray of food.

"Morris, when the hell did you get here?"

"I came as soon as I got word," I said. "I've been around a couple of weeks, now."

"You heard about it on the streets, I supposed." He seemed ashamed.

"No, Cherry Bomb called me."

"That's Mrs. Cherry Bomb," Nicky laughs weakly. "Anyway, I'm glad you're here. I want you to go shoot that damn doctor. The drugs he's giving me ain't worth shit!"

"That's because I told him to stop giving you drugs, or I'd shoot him."

"WHAT? I take it back, I'm not glad you're here." Nicky looked around frantically. "Where's my gun? I want to shoot you."

"Yeah, I thought you might react that way. I took them. They're downstairs," I pointed to the door. "If you want to shoot somebody, even me, you will have to get out of bed."

"I can't. I'm hurt. I've been SHOT!"

"I've been told," I answered calmly, "But you are all better now. Nothing keeping you in that bed but your own weakness. You don't need drugs, or doctors, you need a bath!"

"I have a nurse for that," Nicky snapped, "or did you fire her too."

"No, Mrs. Cherry Bomb did. Get your fucking ass up, Nicky. We have work to do."

Nicky sank deeper into the bed. His voice lost strength. "You know I died on the operating table?"

"Is that what's bothering you? Welcome to the club. Hell, I died before. Twice."

"Fuck you, MoJo! Why are you always trying to outdo me? Just leave me alone." Nicky rolled over. He sighed a long heavy breath and angrily ripped the IV tubes from his arm.

"So, is that it, you just want to be some pathetic drug addict junkie now?" I seethed.

He stuck up his middle finger and blood ran down his arm. "You're no better than me. You get high all the time. So, kiss my ass."

"Yeah, I get high. But for fun, not to hide from the world. You want to get high, I'll get high with you, but first you are going to get out of that bed."

"Look, MoJo, my father is dead. My mother is dead. My brother is dead. I should be dead. Just get out of here so I can die too."

"That's it then. You are going to let them die and not avenge their death. Their lives meant nothing. Their killer goes free."

Nicky didn't respond, lying motionless in a fetal position with his back to me. I stormed out of the room and went to the kitchen.

Three of Nicky's soldiers sat at the table drinking cappuccino.

I said, "Get a fire extinguisher and put it outside of Nicky's bedroom. Do not go in there!"

"Why?" asked one of the three. After a dead cold stare from me he got up and ran from the kitchen.

I walked outside to my car and returned with a full five gallons gas container. "Whatever happens, do not come up there."

The man who ran for the fire extinguisher asked, "what are you going to do with the gasoline?"

"I'm gonna get your boss out of that bed and on his feet, even if it kills him."

"I can't let you do that," another of the three bodyguards said and jumped up.

I shot him in the thigh a few inches above the knee and along the outside. He fell to the floor, grabbing his leg screaming, "ARE YOU CRAZY?"

"A little. Don't come upstairs. And you," I pointed my gun at the guy who retrieved the fire extinguisher, "take your friend there to the hospital. He's making a mess on the kitchen floor."

I re-entered Nicky's bedroom. He was still curled up in a ball, unscrewed the cap on the gas can, and splashed a little on the foot of the bed. I waited until the smell of gasoline was noticeable in the room. I waited for Nicky to respond.

"Are you back, MoJo? What the hell is that smell?"

"Of course I'm back. What kind of friend would I be to leave you to wallow in misery? You said you wanted to die, I'm here to see that you do. Shooting you didn't do it, so I'm going to send you straight to FUCKING HELL." I flicked my gold lighter and tossed it onto the bed where the gasoline had soaked in. There was a swoosh and an instant blaze.

Nicky looked over his shoulder and kicked the covers from the bed. Then he jumped off and scrambled to the corner terrified, screaming, "ARE YOU FUCKING CRAZY?"

"Yeah. A little, I think. Dying tends to do that to a person," I picked up the fire extinguisher from outside the door and sprayed down the bed. "Why didn't you stay in bed? I thought you wanted to die."

"Not like that, you sick fuck!"

"Dead is dead. The second time I died, I was beaten to death. I thought immolation would top that. Just giving you a chance to be number one. Well, now that you are up, I thought we'd get to work on who shot you."

"And killed Sal."

"I already know who killed Sal," I told him. "Let me correct myself. I know who gave the order and to whom. But we have some digging to do to find out who and why they took a shot at you too."

"If you know who shot Sal, then you know who shot me. Had to be the same person, right?"

"Doesn't have to be," I said, "I had a look at the police reports. Sal's body was still at the scene, and you were rushed off to the hospital. But from where Sal's body was and where you fell, it suggests multiple shooters. The angles don't add up, the shooter would have to be one fast dude to make both shots in so little time. The shots look like they came from different floors and different buildings. So, multiple shooters. The real question is, were they working together?"

"I want the sonofabitch who shot my brother," Nicky demanded. The fight was back in his voice. The fire put the spark back in him, or maybe it was the fact I knew who killed his brother.

"That is going to be complicated. You get cleaned up. I have somethings to show you."

NICKY CAME down to the kitchen hours later. Dressed and angry, "Where's my gun?"

"Here you go, boss," said fire extinguisher man. "Morris had us take it from your room because he was afraid you'd harm yourself. You know, with the drugs and all."

"Oh, yeah," Nicky seethed, "Morris is a great friend."

I waved at him from the table and continued drinking my Irish coffee, with extra Irish. It was mostly whiskey with just enough coffee to make it go down smooth.

Nicky sneered at me. "So, you thought it was a good idea to let that crazy motherfucking nigger into my room with a can of gasoline?"

Fire extinguisher man spoke up quickly, "when you came out of the coma, we told you Morris was here running things. You said to follow Morris' orders. Remember, Boss?"

"Yes, I remember." Nicky exploded, "but that doesn't mean you let him murder me, now does it?"

Limpy, the bodyguard I shot in the thigh hobbled over to Nicky, "I tried to stop him, Boss. But he shot me in the leg."

"Really, good man, which leg?"

"Right here," he pointed to his upper left thigh.

Nicky fired into his right thigh at the same height. "You mean like that? Is that how he shot you?"

Limpy was back on the floor howling in pain. He was grabbing his right leg and trying to push away from Nicky with his wounded left.

"Where're you going? I expect when someone is trying to kill me, you will fire back. Where's your gun?"

Limpy fumbles inside his jacket and drops his pistol on the floor.

I laugh.

Nicky throws me a look. "Maybe it's a good thing you didn't go for your gun, MoJo would have killed you and I wouldn't have gotten the chance to myself," he takes aim at his head, "you morons, take this idiot to St. Joseph and have his other leg stitched up. He's bleeding all over my marble tiles."

The other two bodyguards quickly pick up Limpy and rush out the kitchen. They are in no hurry to get Limpy to the hospital, they just want to get out of the line of fire before Nicky caps one of them.

I hear a familiar female voice from the other room cry out, "not again. What the fuck is wrong with you guys?"

Nicky takes a seat across from me. His gun in his hand lying on the table pointing at my chest. He stares, no words, just anger pouring out of him.

I tell him, "I'm not going to apologize for setting your bed on fire. Nor shooting your guy in the leg. So, if you plan on shooting me, go ahead."

"Why? So, you can shoot me in the gut under the table?" Nicky spins the gun on the table, and it stops in a non-threatening position. He says, "Besides, you haven't told me who killed Sal yet. And as for you setting the bed on fire, the bed came from the hospital, so I don't care about that. But the sheets and things, they belong to Rozalina, she just might shoot you when she sees what you've done. And don't think I'm gonna stop her."

"I'll buy her new linens," I stand up and Nicky sees I am unarmed. "Come to the study, I have a lot to show you. And let me warn you, you are not going to like what you see."

"I don't like anything you've done so far. Where are those drugs? You promised to get high with me."

"Let me ask you something, MoJo." Nicky says in a demurred voice. "Don't laugh or get all philosophical about this. Just answer me truthfully."

"Yeah, of course, ask me anything." I already knew what the question would be.

"When you died, did you see your life flash before your eyes?"

"No. The first time there was a lot of pain and I was cold. I was in the river; I don't remember dying. But the villager and Gisella said I was dead, so I have to believe I was. The second time was a lot more painful. But no memories of running through fields of grass, or alleys of broken bottles like in the South Bronx where I grew up. Just pain, then nothing, I supposed."

"No white light. No family member coming to greet you?"

"None of that bullshit," I sneer, "I was dead then I wasn't."

"Me either," Nicky scoffs, "all that crap the priest fed us about going to Heaven or Hell. I saw none of that. I expected… I guess to see my Mom. Or maybe my Dad if I was going to Hell. But not to see nothing at all, that's what really got me down. And I was dead for like fifteen minutes they told me."

"They told you!"

"Yeah! Fucking doctors, like they were bragging or expecting a tip or something for saving my life." Nicky gets animated. "I'm dead fifteen minutes, and where the fuck is God? You'd think He'd have a minute to pop in to say a little something. Or someone in my fucking family would want to greet me."

"Why the fuck do you care? You're not dead now. The next time you die stick around a little longer, who knows, maybe they'll send out the fucking welcome wagon."

"Do you think, maybe I wasn't dead long enough? How long were you dead?" Nicky asks with a gleam in his eye. "The second time, I know it would be hard to judge the first time."

"How the fuck do I know? I wasn't counting Mississippis." Nicky was pissing me off. He still wasn't out of bed. "I can go get the gas can, we'll see if you can set the record for being dead."

"Ok, fuck it! If this is going to piss you off so bad let's drop it." But Nicky couldn't let it go, though. "Hey, after all you been through, do you still believe in God? Heaven? Hell?"

"You want the truth?"

Nicky nods.

"I don't believe in anything. I didn't believe before I got shot and died. I don't see any need for God. Not like they taught us. Not in the biblical sense. Look at all the fucked-up shit in the world. Look at all the fucked-up shit we have done. Do you think you deserved to be saved?"

"Maybe you're right. It's just hard finding out the shit you believed in all your life is a lie."

"Do you really want there to be a Heaven and a Hell? A place to go to after you're dead, with all the shit you've done here on this Earth. And do you really want to run into your dad in the afterlife? No offense, but if he's your guide, you are in for a HELL of a time."

Nicky nodded his head. "Hell, yeah! I'd want to see my dad. He was great, at least to me. He treated you pretty good too. Well, if there is or isn't a God, it's too late for some people anyhow. While I was upstairs getting dressed, I was making a list of people who have been taking advantage of my predicament.

Most of these guys are in my family, there are a few who are rivals here, New Jersey, Chicago, LA, and Florida."

"Don't you think we should find out first who wanted you dead before we go on a shooting spree?" I counsel him.

"Oh no, they are not on the list because I think they tried to have me killed. What's the saying, 'when the cat's away, the mice will play'? These guys are the biggest rats in the organization. I need them gone and I want your guys to do it. And note, there is one or two of your people on the list too. They have been scheming and skimming, I guess you have been a little busy with me to notice."

"Consider them gone. But when did you have time to come up with a list?"

"The boys have been giving me reports during my lucid moments. I guess you had them scared and they wanted me to know that they were on the up and up."

I WENT after my guys first. Nicky was right, I had let some things get past me, and I took offense to it. This was not going to be anything fancy. Nicky needed to send the message that he was still in charge, and he was not happy. They got what they deserved in an old-fashioned drive-by shooting.

I sent word I needed to speak to my men. Told them to park on a corner in the Bronx and to wait for my call on the pay phone. A car pulled up to the parked one and opened fire with a couple of .22s. Then my own personal touch, I told the hit squad to torch the cars and bodies. They poured gasoline in the vehicle —two of the four men were in pain but still alive—then they threw in a lit matchbook and everyone died.

The others were similar operations. Two gunmen walked into a bar, restaurant, or night club, find who they are after and start shooting. A minute or two apiece and then they move on to the next target on the list. The killings were in the morning papers like the weather, late last night it rained bullets in the Bronx, Queens, Newark. Within a week, more than a dozen known and suspected members of organized crime families were dead. The hit parade had the desired effect on the underworld, everyone knew Nicky Nails Rocci was alive and still in charge.

HOWEVER, the tactic is a double-edged sword. Yes, it keeps your people in line. Protection money rolls in on time. No one dares dip a hand into the pot for fear of having it cut off. Nicky personally cut off the hands of a courier whose daily drops were light a thousand dollars. Then he shot him in the face while his wife and kids looked on. We left him sitting in his barber's chair. It had a real old style feeling to it that Nicky liked.

Nicky and I went after some of his most egregious associates. One pimp was using Nicky's girls for private parties and pocketing the money. He wasn't even paying the girls, telling them they were being punished for not meeting the new quotas set by Nails. Naturally, Nicky hated the way his good name and reputation was being abused. He gathered the girls, twenty of them, and told them to cut or stab the pimp once.

They could inflict any injury they wanted but it had to be non-lethal, he didn't want the girls charged with murder. And they could not cut off his penis, Nicky reserved that honor for himself. We left his body in an alley a block from the precinct house. The police report showed he spoke one word before bleeding out, "Nails."

Although the police knew whom he meant, it wasn't enough to warrant bringing Nicky in for questioning. But the more bodies surfaced around New York, the more the DA called for Nicky Nails' arrest. And when executions started happening in other cities around the nation, the FBI put together a task force specifically aimed at the Rocci family.

But it wasn't the number of hits that drew law enforcement's attention, even if two dozen in one month was a bit excessive, it was the viciousness of the murders. Nicky had outdone the mobsters of yesteryear. Rival families who thought they could muscle in on Rocci's businesses received a care package delivered to their doors. The package exploded minutes after being brought into the premises. Instead of receiving their supply of guns or drugs, they received a going out of business notice.

Nicky was called to two sit-downs during the 'Month of Blood', as it was dubbed by the press. They warned him to settle his differences peacefully and gave him millions as compensation for his losses. Nicky took the money and agreed to end hostilities. As a Godfather was leaving the meeting, his name would be added to the list of murdered Mafia Men.

Vinny 'the Viper' Victorinni came to the meeting from Los Angeles. He was dressed in his trademark snakeskin greenish gray jacket and tan boots. Even though he was freezing in the Windy City's harsh weather he maintained his Hollywood image. The son of a mob boss, his image was all he really had. He talked a good game, but all his men were loyal to his father and happy to let him be the face of the operations. He received his cut, substantially less than his father commanded, but enough for him to call himself the boss.

The Viper, as he had all his men call him, was skinny and slippery as the name suggested. He could have been a real mobster if he had more venom than verbosity. He was added to the list of guests at Nicky's request. He had a side hustle his people didn't know about. He was running a couple of Home Growers out of Humboldt County and cutting Nicky's weed prices. The marijuana out of Humboldt was good quality and Nicky supplemented his Jamaican and Mexican products with homegrown weed. It also made good business sense, interstate smuggling was easier and cheaper, meaning a larger profit.

In the war on drugs, marijuana was considered low level crime. The police hardly bothered going after dealers and smugglers unless they were involved in cocaine or heroin trafficking too. Except for the occasional shootings between the Jamaicans in Brooklyn, 'those crazy guys' he complained to MoJo about regularly, marijuana busts never made the papers. However, it was a billion-dollar business and Nicky did not stand for anybody cutting into his business.

As Nicky had all the parking spaces taken up in front of ChiTown Pizza, a renowned restaurant where they held the meeting, the Viper foolishly let his driver park half a block away. After the meeting ended, he walked back to his car flanked by his two bodyguards. On the way, they passed a man sitting on the ground wrapped in blankets begging for change. A few steps away, the beggar threw off the blankets, revealing a sawed-off pump action shotgun, with which he pumped out four shots, leaving one to cover his escape down an alley. The blasts left Vinny the Viper and his bodyguards a bloody mess on the Chicago sidewalk. Nicky had no intentions of ending his purge, or feared being caught by the authorities, until the names on his list were all crossed off. He sat in the restaurant and finished his lunch while the others scurried off before the police arrived.

NICKY RETURNED from the dead as some men do, without any regards for the life of others. Having been in the darkness and felt the emptiness, nothing scared him anymore. Nothing could sway him from getting what he sought. Revenge was the drug that kept him satisfied. Like all drugs, the more he had, the more he needed.

The second sit-down was more formal, and I attended that one as Nicky's third. Each Godfather was accompanied by three other persons, his consigliere to give him advice, his head capo to trade in case things were left unsettled, and a bodyguard to protect him. The bodyguards were the only ones at the meeting allowed to have a single pistol. I was there, against the objections of the other family heads, as Nicky's consigliere. Although they objected to my role at the meeting, I am sure they were glad I was not the one carrying the gun.

I wasn't sure why Nicky wanted this meeting. He demanded Beniamino Brunello from Chicago be present. I was sure if anyone wanted Nicky dead it was him. Our business in South America cost him billions in oil. Federico Giganti, known as Freddie the Fixer, because he owned a string of electronic repair shops in Florida, and betting against his horses or dogs in a race was a good way to lose your money. I believed Freddie was using the races to move drugs and undercutting our business. Then there was Pasqual Duranti, Pistol Pete, he pistol-whipped a man so bad the judge gave him the same amount of time as if he had shot him. Pasqual was the oldest of the group, already in his seventies.

Rumors were spreading that Nicky had his father killed so he could have unrestrained hold of the family. It was a long-held belief that Nicky had little self-control and a violent nature. Those two qualities made him a very dangerous boss. The other Godfathers from around the world felt only Nicolas' guiding hand saved them from Nicky Nails worst predilections. Whether Nicky killed his parents, or someone else did and then tried to take him out too, they knew the underworld was about to face their dreaded nightmare scenario, Nicky Nails Rocci untethered and out for revenge.

Nicky started the conversation off, "Let us dispense with the pleasantries and get right down to business. Since I was indisposed as it was, each of you have been trying to muscle your way into my pockets."

No one confirmed or denied the statement.

"Benny, you have long been after my gambling houses. Freddie, you are trying to take my drugs distribution and electronics businesses. And Pistol, you would love to add my girls to your stables, stretching your prostitution ring from Vegas to New York as I am working it now. I am not above having everyone in this room done away with, as I think you all know. But, in all honesty, a war between us will do more harm than I am willing to suffer at this particular time. And with the Feds snapping up everyone that runs for help these days, it would not be wise to give them more people to flip."

"Then what are you suggesting, Nails?" Benny wondered. "We all go back to our corners and play nice?"

"Yeah, something like that," Nicky snarled.

As much as he wanted to kill Benny and for as long as he wanted to do it, he showed remarkable restraint. Probably because I wasn't behind the gun this time.

"And to make sure we all do play by the rules, I suggest we trade capos."

"This has been done before in difficult times," Pistol Pete seemed agreeable to the idea. "But there shall be no torture, drugging, or attempts to flip the capos, agreed? We have unfettered access to our man."

"Of course," Nicky agrees, "he is just an insurance policy. If everyone does what they are supposed to do, no one gets hurt. Right? As a matter of fact, don't take this fool here," Nicky pointed to Ronnie Patronno, the man with a bullet hole in each leg, "instead, take Christopher Carmine. During my recovery he was handling the day-to-day family affairs. Now that I'm back, he returned to the operations of my drug business. He's in Florida; I'll have him report to you immediately. I'm sure I can say, he'll be in safe hands with you."

"I don't like this idea," I whisper in Nicky's ear.

The other bosses complain that Christopher was not present and how would they know if he was actually delivered. The meeting started to break up as voices began to rise.

"If he's not then we will pay Nicky a visit together," Pistol Pete confirm then passes his man to Freddie, and Freddie sends his guy over to Benny, leaving Benny's man with Nicky. The meeting is over.

Before they leave the Park Avenue hotel suite, Freddie asks, "how long do we hold onto these guys?"

"Back in my day," offers Pete, "the deal was for a year. Long enough for tensions to ease, and not too long for our pawns to get to liking their new home."

"I'll go along with this to keep the peace," concedes Benny, "but I don't trust Nicky Nails for a moment."

"You have my number, Benny. If you feel your man is getting anything less than the royal treatment, give me a call. I don't pistol-whip anymore, don't have the stamina, but I can still pull the trigger." Pistol Pete's assurances were extended to the others as well, "Back in the old days, if one guy broke the rules, the others in the pack would exact punishment. We are all our brothers' keepers. Is that clear?" It was a question that did not require an answer and the old man left.

Nicky and I left the meeting in our car. Benny's man and Ronnie were in another. He would be taken someplace where a prisoner could be kept safe.

I told Nicky, "I wouldn't put it past Benny to have his own man killed and turn the other two against us."

"I agree. Plus, I wouldn't let Benny's rat anywhere near our operation."

"Then why in God's name would you let Chris go?"

"Don't worry," Nicky said in that silky-smooth tone that means he was hatching another plan. "I can reach out and lay hands on him anytime I want. Peter is one of my dad's oldest and most trusted friends. He helped me put this sit-down together, so we can get our hands on that fat bastard Benny's man." His face was dark and malevolent as he ruminated. "Don't think I forgot about the pain he caused you, MoJo. Because I haven't. Not for a moment… if he's behind the attack on me, we will find out. And if not, then he will pay for Venezuela. In either case, we are going to introduce Fat Boy Benny to a very excruciating death. I promise you."

7

THE TRUTH BE TOLD

After Nicky and I had our heart to heart, we poured drinks from his father's best bourbon. He had been off the morphine for a few days before I went into his room. His mind was clear and sharp again. This was his first day out of bed, but I knew he was ready for what he had to see. After our little interlude in the kitchen, I thought this would put his life in perspective. And on the other hand, I feared it could destroy him. Whatever was to come next he had to know I'd be there for him. "Here, let's look at this tape first. Maybe it will explain why your dad didn't come visit you in the afterlife." I played the tape of Nicolas hiring Carmella for the hit on Sal.

He sat stunned by his father's actions. "I'm going to kill her. Contract or not, I'm going to blow that fucking bitch's brains out."

After a couple of seconds of snow on the screen, the tape started playing again. "Nicky, this part is for you. Ask Morris to leave the room, although, he probably has already seen this part." I nod, confirming Nicolas' belief. Nicky waved his hand, signaling me to stay. "You already know why I picked Carmella. And I know it's probably screwing with your head because

123

you're fucking her. But I had to make sure the job got done and I know she wouldn't use it to make a move on you."

"Wrong there, Dad," Nicky tells his Dad on the screen.

"Nicky, I have Alzheimer's. It won't be long before I'll be too far gone to help you. What you did to Sal… although I know you wanted him to have his revenge for the way he turned out, put a noose around his neck. He's incapable of telling a lie, and when he talks, you and Morris are going to hang with him. Carmella has a few contacts I gave her; she'll know when the time is right. Morris and Carmella are your two best assets, use them wisely. I hope you gave Sal the sendoff he deserved. He did the hardest thing I ever asked any of you boys to do. Nobody but Sal could have pulled it off. And I am sure he kept his promise not to tell you." The screen turns to snowy images again.

Nicky sits in shock for a long time. I sit in silence with him. He is running through scenarios in his head. Trying to figure out where things went wrong. "He's wrong, we could have protected Sal."

"He tried. There is another tape, he took the rap for killing Banoa. Pauley and Vinny were going to back him up. The DA took his statement, arrested him, and charges were filed against him."

"How come I never heard about this? Why am I just finding out about it now?"

"Because it wasn't very long after he made the statement to the DA that Sal killed him and your mother. There's no tape of him getting into Sal's head, but he did. I'm sure Nicolas thought his confession and death would end the investigation. I guess he was wrong about that too. Now, we need to know who Carmella is getting her info from, but I think I know."

"Good, because I am going to kill her," he threw his glass through the big screen TV.

"No, you're not," I say fighting back my tears. No matter how many times I watched that tape it was always hard to take.

Knowing the torture Sal must have gone through, his father leaving him totally alone. I'm sure Nicky didn't hide his anger with him either. "Your father was right about one thing, we wouldn't… couldn't kill Sal. If someone put it together that Sal was the gunman, he was as good as dead. He would go down with us, or better said, we would go down with him. He'd be in the gas chamber and not know why. What we need to do is find out who knows what. Because you and me, we are still very much facing a death sentence. And that's why you are not going to kill Carmella."

"Ok, you just lost me around that last turn," Nicky joked.

"If Carmella really wanted to do you in, she just had to let things play out. Sal gets arrested. He tells the police everything, as we know he would, and you and I would be done. So, her following orders saved your life. And I don't think she saved your life and then shot you."

"You talked to her," Nicky asked.

"Yeah, but not about this," I admitted. "I think she knows about the tape. I questioned all your capos and lieutenants. Some, I showed tapes to when there was something to be gained from it. But I wanted to wait for you to be better before we confront her with it. She can tell us what she knows about the investigation. She won't lie. I think you know why?"

Nicky's mind slipped away from the study. Away from Morris and Sal and everything that had happened. He couldn't help himself. He was back at The Garden. Springsteen, The Boss, was doing a week of shows. As powerful as Nicky was, Carmella had insisted on meeting him someplace where they would not be seen. And if by chance they were, it could be explained as a coincidence.

Nicky laughed, "And you think we won't run into any goombahs at a Springsteen concert? They think he's Italiano."

"You can send Chris out of town, but he can still have someone watching me. In a place like The Garden, I can easily get lost."

After the lights went down, Carmella left her front row seat and slipped out to the VIP lounge. She ordered a drink and waited for the last of the latecomers to make it into the arena. Bruce was doing *Dancing in the Dark*. She goes up a stairwell and finds Nicky waiting for her there.

He pounces on her. She tries to slow him down, but he's too eager. His hands are under her blouse one minute, down the back of her skirt the next. He smiles, "No underwear. I like your style."

"Not style," Carmella presses against him, "practicality. How am I going to get them back on if someone comes up these stairs?"

"Smart," he agrees, "but you could have gone out the door to the hotel across the street. I told you I have a room for us."

"Yeah, and when the show is over and I'm not back in my seat, what do I tell Chris?" Carmella starts kissing his neck and undoing his belt. "No one is going to come this way for a while, so shut up and fuck me."

Nicky does as commanded. Letting his pants drop to the ground he lifts her up by her butt and sits her on the handrail.

She shrieks, "Oh, that's cold!"

"Here's something to heat you up."

The stairwell makes a perfect place for their interlude. Carmella spreads her legs wide and rests her left foot on the higher step. Nicky humps her with savage force. He has been waiting years for this. Their first time was over too quickly, she was a virgin and much too tight. She did as she was told and didn't enjoy it at all. Now, she was open, wet, and willing. She slipped off the railing and down on him. She invited his hands and mouth to explore her body. They were in the stairwell until *I'm on Fire* ended with a blazing finish of their own.

She returned to the VIP lounge bathroom to clean up before the second set, Nicky went upstairs into the darkness. She couldn't help looking back during the rest of the show, feeling his eyes on her. She was sure his weren't the only ones. Nevertheless, she went to every show that week and met him. On the third night she gave in and left after the first set to go to the hotel across the street.

"Why are you doing this?" Carmella finally got up the nerve to ask.

"Because it's fun," Nicky responded without hesitation.

"Is that all I am to you, a toy?" She was annoyed by his flippant answer.

"What? You expected me to fall to my knees and profess my undying love for you?"

"You've been after me for years. And all you think of it is… it's fun."

"Ok, let me ask you this," Nicky countered, "why are you here? Why now?"

"Because you are the Godfather," she said sheepishly. "You can have anything you want. Get anything done…"

"Hold it right there!" Nicky interrupted. "Don't try and pull you're afraid for Chris bullshit. Over the last eight years, I have never threatened or done anything to you or him. You are here because I am the Boss. You want to feel that power. Admit it!"

"No, it's not like that, but lately, you have been sending him on dangerous missions. First, it was to track down your friend. Now that he is back, I don't know what Chris is doing in Colombia. I love him, he's good and kind."

"Not exactly the qualities that makes for a good Mafioso," Nicky laughs. "He is in Colombia replacing Morris. Being good and kind doesn't make him a good choice for an enforcer, but he is a good manager. No one will touch him because they don't want Morris to come back and manage things. And while he's on these business trips, I get to play with you."

"Well, I'm not a toy. And don't think I will come running any time you call. I was a little curious to see what you are really like, but I'm married and so are you. I hope you had your fun because I won't be coming back here again."

If only I could believe she meant those words. I should have told her how much I loved her. She had just the right combination of brains and looks that could cook a man from the inside out. That first night was to get her loyalty, but these times were for her heart. Something she never could give completely to me. I could kill Chris, easily, and not by my own hand, but then I'd lose her forever. No, Chris has to live, and she will keep coming back to me. She needs me as much as I need her.

"Hey, where are you?" I snapped my fingers. "I've been talking for the last five minutes and nothing. It took me a while to figure out that last move with the other bosses, but you wanted to send Christopher away for good. Or at least a good long time. Give your girlfriend a call, it's time we have a Come to Jesus moment."

"I'll have her here in the morning," Nicky was weary.

"You didn't ask me why I objected to trading Christopher."

"I don't know. I guess you think they'll force him to talk, like the way I'm going to force Danny Boy to give up the goods on his boss Benny."

"No, that's not why," I said, "I was keeping my eye on him,

tracking whom he made contact with. Who's on his side? What's his end game? It can't be to replace you, he's not high enough on the food chain. If he had anything to do with the hit on you, someone put him up to it. And probably didn't have to push him very hard, just let him know you're doing his wife."

"Did you find anything?"

"Nothing much, yet. There were two lieutenants and a capo I was interested in, but they're dead now. Thanks to you and your overzealous need for a clean house."

"Who were they," Nicky demanded.

"Why? Are we going to shoot them again?" I asked. "Don't worry, I have plan B in the works."

Nicky was nodding off; the effects of the morphine hadn't completely left his body. He got up and stumbled to the door. He hadn't spent much time in the den before, now, he was there all-day watching tapes. "I'm going to bed now. If that's ok with you?"

"Give my love to the beautiful Mrs. Cherry Bomb."

"These nights, I can't even give her my love," Nicky sighs.

"It's the morphine. Leave it alone and it will leave you alone," I encouraged him. I couldn't be sure, but I had a feeling Nicky was still using.

CARMELLA ARRIVED EARLY in the morning. A private jet from Miami and then a helicopter out to the island. She was the head of Miami Golden Real Estates, a conglomerate of real estate investment companies that was driving the building boom. Miami Golden Real Estates, and all its subsidiaries were shell companies for laundering drug money.

She cooked the books from building cost to how many units were leased. The hotels were the easiest, at least on floors worth of rooms that were rented and empty. Not always the same rooms or hotels, it was one humongous shell game. She also had commercial properties that were built, furnished, leased, and completely vacant. Some address, usually outside of the major cities were recorded as constructed, demolished, and rebuilt. But the land had never been touched. Not so much as a shovel had ever sank into the ground.

Carmella was the queen of taking mob money, dirty dollars, and banking it as legitimate lease payments. Billions of dollars flowed through hundreds of fake companies and accounts to be returned to Rocci Construction Company.

She walked into the den in a blue pencil skirt, white see-through blouse, no bra, and a blue blazer that covered her when she wanted. "Oh, Morris… I didn't know you were still here."

"Obviously."

"I heard Nicky was on his feet and back in charge."

"I am," Nicky entered the room and grabbed her ass as he passed by. "Nice to see you. Go ahead and plant your fine ass in that chair over there." He pointed to a beige leather chair by the window affectionately called the hot seat. Partially, because when the sun shone on it, it was very uncomfortable. And more importantly, because it was an overstuffed leather seat, and was easy to wash the blood off.

"Where did you send Chris this time?"

"Colombia." Nicky didn't have to lie. He could have said Chris was in Las Vegas, but he felt himself incapable of the truth. "What did you have to do for my father? What kind of arrangement did you two have?"

"I don' understand. I didn't…"

"Let me refresh your memory," Nicky fumes and presses play on the video recorder. The new giant screen plays Nicolas ordering Carmella to murder Sal.

"Ah… Yes… Well, as you can see, I was given a contract—"

"YEAH, OK, we know all that." I interjected as Carmella squirmed in the chair. "Nicolas spoke of informants, who are they?"

"FUCK THAT! We will get to that in a minute," Nicky was standing behind her with his hands on her shoulders. *I should snap your little soft neck right now.* "How did you pick the time?"

She felt his hands on her shoulders very close to her neck. *Nicolas, you promised no harm would come to me.* "I have two men in the FBI and one in the Department of Justice. I just had to mention one name, Adrianna Nunez, and they were very cooperative. That tape was made in '84. After Mr. Johnson here, returned to New York to do some late-night remodeling. That alerted the Feds and NYPD that you two were still in the game, and just as dangerous as in the seventies during the Banoa war. And when Nicolas turned himself in as the shooter, he didn't know the gun was miles away at Morris' home."

"Because he got a fact wrong, you decided Sal needed to die?"

"No, Nicky, of course not. But his confession would turn a spotlight on your family. They wanted to take your father down, if for nothing more than a symbolic gesture, putting the top man in the New York Mafia behind bars would send shockwaves through the criminal world. But they realized he was sacrificing himself to protect someone else. He unwittingly pointed the finger at you. But then I heard something that meant I had to act quickly."

"What was that?" I asked. I was watching Nicky. His hands and arms were tense. One wrong word and Carmella would be dead before she could finish her sentence.

"Do you know a Nathan Napolitano?" she asked innocently.

Nicky's arms went limp, his hands dropped to his side. He staggered away from her like he had taken another bullet to the chest. I took him by the arm and guided him to the chair behind the desk. I sat him down and his head dropped onto his folded arms on the desk.

Carmella looked bewildered and turned to me for an explanation.

"We know who he is," I said without any further clarification. "What do you know about him?"

"Nothing. My contacts in the FBI said he surfaced in a Las Vegas prostitution raid and the whole case against Nicolas took a one-eighty degrees turn. I contacted the man from the DOJ whose name Nicolas had given me, but he clammed up too. All he told me was that Nathan Napolitano went deep into the WPS, you know, witness protection service."

"We know what the WPS is," Nicky fired off, "it's how we get to our most wanted stoolpigeons. The government promises them protection, it's like putting a bullseye on their back and a neon arrow over their head. We follow their agents, and it leads us right to our prey. That's what we'll do with that fucking little fag. And this time, no mercy."

"I don't know about that, Nicky. The DOJ man said this Nathan fella is off the map. They got him in a black site or something. No contact with anyone outside the small group of agents who are always with him. From what my contact said, they don't contact anyone either. What does he know anyway?"

"Everything," I tell her. "Here's the million-dollar question for you. Think carefully and answer truthfully because it will determine if you walk out of here or not."

"Christopher probably is behind Nicky's shooting," Carmella offered.

The tension in the room skyrocketed. Nicky's rage turned him red.

Carmella's demeanor stiffened, and her words were as sharp as a razor. "What did you expect was going to happen when you're fucking another man's wife? You being the Boss only deepens the pain and strengthen his resolve for revenge. I can't say for certain that he pulled the trigger, so my guess is he hired someone from the outside to do the job."

I saw Nicky was about to pounce. Maybe it was lucky she was still in the hot seat and he at the desk. "You didn't think to warn him?"

"OH, I WARNED HIM." She screeched.

Maybe it was a good thing they were a room apart.

"I told him often and continuously that Chris was good and kind to me. To others he could be quite cruel and ruthless. I don't think he would have survived in South America on your reputation alone, Morris. Anyway, I don't have any proof that he's behind your shooting, Nicky. He never said or threatened you in my presence, but the way he looked at me, the way he said your name. I warned you, you were playing with fire. And what did you say?"

"I like it hot." Nicky smiled.

"What would you do, Morris, if someone, even Nicky, was fucking your wife? Or women? Or whatever you got going on over there in Greece."

"I wouldn't leave him alive," I confessed. "You don't know who he hired?"

"No. I hired the Syrian and his girlfriend. They are the best, and they didn't know the target was your brother, Nicky. But as your father wished, it was a clean shot. Don't go after them, we need their services. Like I said, if it's Chris, and YES, he is the logical choice, he had to go outside the family. Way outside the family. Please, tell me, where did you send him this time."

Nicky smiled a very sadistic grin, "he's a prisoner of war. He'll be ok, but if I find out he's behind my shooting and working against this family…"

8

ON THE HOOK

The Las Vegas Sheriff together with LVPD raids The Stagecoach Saloon on the outskirts of the city. It's an unlicensed brothel offering women and men prostitutes and the predawn raid captures twenty-two sex workers. They are handcuffed to a long chain and led into the police station for finger printing and mugshots. After a check for outstanding warrants which takes an hour or two, the workers are released with a court date. In Las Vegas it's a routine occurrence. Many sex shops are unlicensed, or, their workers are, and the police sweep the businesses often.

By 8 am the police are down in the hole, the basement of the precinct where the cells are. They call each person by name and issue them a bench warrant to appear in court. Fifteen females and six men are released. One person, in a red floral Chinese dress is left in the cell. The blonde grabs the bars of the cell door, "what about me?"

"Let me guess," the officer looks down at his list, "you're Nathan Napolitano."

"Yes." Nathan's voice jumps, sensing something is wrong. This is the first time he's been arrested. He had been careful

134

working mainly the revues that did not have direct mob influences. He was mostly a dancer working the shows, and occasionally worked the sex clubs for extra cash. He has become very good at spotting undercovers trolling the clubs and slipped out before any trouble started. He could spot newcomers to Vegas, and those who wanted what they were afraid to do back in their hometowns.

"Hmmpf. Says here you gave your name as Nancy Tano. I guess from the way you're dress you thought we wouldn't find out who you really are," the police officer says sharply.

"I'm not trying to hide anything," Nathan says sincerely, "I've just identified as Nancy for so long it's who I am now. I'm sorry, I'm not in any trouble, am I?"

"I don't know," responds the cop, "you tell me. Fingerprints don't lie, and yours says keep me here, there's someone who wants to talk to you… Nancy."

"Talk to me! What for? I have never been in trouble. I've never been arrested," Nathan panicked.

"Again," he said with a sour tone, "I don't know. But I bet you're in trouble now. Go sit down on the bench and wait." Then he added with a chuckle, "Like a good little girl."

Nathan could not sit down. He paced back and forth in the cell for hours. Other prisoners were brought in and put in the other holding cells, each time he questioned when he was getting out. None of the officers knew or cared. One told him every time he came down, he was taking him back up with him, then left laughing.

He was in the cell all day and all night alone. Even when the other cell became overcrowded with drunks, prostitutes, and bloodied combatants, Nathan remained the sole prisoner in his cell. One man in a cell across from him had put up a losing battle with the cops. He lost badly from the looks of his face and clothing.

He called out to Nathan, "Hey, Queenie. What they gotcha in for?"

"I don't know. They won't tell me."

"They gave you a private suite. Whatdiya do? Bite some john's dick off when he found out ya not a bitch? Com'on, you can tell me."

Nathan stopped answering and turned away.

"Hey, it's ok with me. I'll keep you company, darling. You can suck me off, I don't care if you're a dude."

BENNY BRUNELLO CALLED the FBI office in Las Vegas.

"FBI field agent, Daniel Webb, how can I help you?"

"Danny boy, it's how can I help you."

"Excuse me, sir?"

"Danny, are you familiar with the Joseph Banoa murder case from '72?"

"Yes, I heard of it. Do you have pertinent evidence concerning the case? I can connect you to our Organized Crime Division," the agent responds in a professional manner. He knows the murder took place in New York and considers this a crackpot call. He has received more than his share of calls from people reporting all sorts of things, from alien abductions to where Jimmy Hoffer is buried. "Let me get your name and number before I transfer you to an agent in that division."

"Danny, this could be the biggest break in your career, and you want to give it away. If I wanted to talk to OCD, I would have called them," Benny assures him. "You work the Vice Unit. Right now, there is a guy who has lot of information about the Banoa case. He was picked up on a prostitution beef in your town, but if you don't act quickly, he'll disappear again. And with him, the identities of Banoa's killers."

"Ok. Who is this person?"

"His name is Nathan Napolitano," Benny informs the agent. "He doesn't have a record, so he won't be held very long. But if you run his prints against evidence from the Banoa murder... well, I think you will be very surprised."

"Ok, I'll call up OCD and have them pull the records. And what is your name?"

Instead of an answer, Daniel Webb heard a click and a dial tone. He logged the call then called Central Booking, "This is FBI field agent Daniel Webb, do you have a Nathan Napolitano in holding? He would have been brought in today on prostitution charges."

"Let me check," was the response before he was put on hold. A few minutes later the man's voice returned, "no Nathan, but there was a woman prossie arrested by the name of Nancy Tano. We didn't get a hit on her prints. That is unusual for her line of work. What do you want to do?"

"Send me the prints and keep him... her, there until I get back to you."

Late in the evening, Daniel Webb, and Ellen Dyer from OCD, are at Central Bookings. Nathan has been in the holding cell for almost two days. When the police come for him, he's happy, thinking he's being release. His heart jumps into his mouth when he is led into an interrogation room and the two FBI agents are waiting for him.

Daniel looks him over; Nathan's makeup has sweated off and

his dress is disheveled. His bleached blonde hair is shoulder length, unkept, and he looks like someone who has spent the night in lockup. *Maybe in the right light and better circumstance he could pass for a woman.* Daniel starts, "Nathan Napolitano, I'm agent Webb and this is agent Dyer from Organized Crime Division. We have a few questions for you."

"Should I get a lawyer?" Nathan asks softly. He feels the lights getting brighter and the room getting smaller. The police officer sits him down and clicks his wrists in the handcuffs welded to the steel table.

"Do you need a lawyer, Nathan?" asks Ellen Dryer. Then she says in a warm and friendly voice, "Do you prefer to be addressed as Nathan or Nancy?"

"I went by Nancy for years trying to avoid ending up here. I guess it doesn't really matter now."

"Do you have a lawyer? Do you want us to wait until you can get one?" Daniel asked.

"No."

"Is that no, you don't have a lawyer? Or no, you don't want to wait for one?" Ellen asks. She is dressed in a blue dress down to her knee and flat shoes. She is the same height as Nathan but better built, more muscular and better curves.

"Both."

"Ok, then I guess we will continue," Ellen slides a photo across the stainless-steel table. "Do you know this man?"

"Yes, that's Joseph Banoa. I was his driver." Nathan fights to remain calm. He's conscious of the bead of sweat running down his face, unable to raise his hands, he dips his head to wipe it away on his forearm.

"Do you know what happened to him?" she asks in the same warm and friendly voice.

"He died. Ten years ago, or something."

"He was murdered," she slides another picture across the table. This one is a morgue shot. Nathan looks down at the table but not at the picture. She slides another picture at him, "do you recognize what this is?"

"It's a gun." More sweat starts down from his forehead. He lets it run its course. His fingers dance on the stainless-steel table, unconsciously tapping them so fast and hard red flakes of nail polish fly off. His eyes can't fix on one spot either, he looks from the photo to the woman to the man, afraid to spend much time looking at any of them.

"Oh, not just any gun. That was the gun that killed Joseph Banoa. Would you like to tell us how your fingerprints are all over the murder weapon?"

"Because I killed him," Nathan sheepishly admits. His eyes and hand freeze in place. He stares at his hands, unable to lift his head. The full weight of his situation now clear in his mind. He is never leaving a cell again.

"You! You killed Joseph Banoa?" she asks in disbelief. "Give us a minute."

The two FBI agents left the interrogation room.

Nathan stares at himself in the mirrored wall across the room. Horrible images come flooding back… He's dizzy and about to throw up. It has been more than a decade since the torture he endured, but it just as well could have been yesterday. The shame, the pain, it's all right there staring back at him.

Ellen watches through the one-way mirror. "That guy is no killer. He couldn't have killed Joseph Banoa, who was one of the toughest Mob Bosses in New York. Hell, I doubt if he could take my eighty-year-old grandmother. Something is wrong here."

"I'll say," Daniel agrees. The dress notwithstanding, Nathan is a puny runt, with the look of a person in perpetual fear. Daniel had come across murderers in his time that did not fit the bill; old men, young innocent girls, but they all had a certain look. Something in their eyes or reflected personality suggested there was more lurking beneath the surface. Not this guy, everything was in plain sight. There was much more going on here, and this guy was somehow in the middle of it all, "this whole thing stinks. From the call I got yesterday, to this… this creature sitting in that room. It smells like a setup."

The two agents re-enter the interrogation room. "So, you're telling us that you took part in the most brutal mob hit in history. The Joseph Banoa killing was worse than the St. Valentine's Day Massacre, and you're saying you were the triggerman? Sorry, I'm not buying it," Daniel says.

"Why not?" Nathan is nearly in tears.

"In this job, you have to be a good judge of character," Ellen answers. "You don't have the character of a man who can shoot a guy in the face. Who are you protecting? What have they got on you?"

"Nothing. No one. I did it and I'm just tired of running and hiding. Lock me up," Nathan starts crying.

The two agents leave him alone again.

"I've never seen a cold-blooded killer break down and cry like a baby before. Even those trying to put on an act haven't looked like this guy. Whatever he's involved in, he's too deep to see his way out. I say we help him see exactly where he's standing… how close to oblivion he is. He wants to take the fall for Banoa's killers, ok. I wonder what he'll say when we hit him with the other two murders?" Ellen tells Daniel then steps back into the room. "Ok, Mr. Napolitano, you are under arrest for the murder of Joseph Banoa, and Detectives Fitzpatrick and Mancotti. I think you are going to need that lawyer now."

"No, wait. Not Fitzpatrick and Mancotti, I didn't say anything about them. I didn't kill them," Nathan starts looking around wildly. If he weren't handcuffed to the table, he'd be climbing the walls.

"Oh, but you did." Ellen raises her hand and a voice from the speaker acknowledges her. Then she commands, "play that tape I left in there."

The loudspeaker poured out, "I followed Morris Johnson

back to his house. Where his house used to be, he went into the shed behind the garage with the gun in a paper bag. When he came out, he didn't have the paper bag. If you want the man who killed Joseph Banoa, go get the gun from his toolshed."

"You remember making that call, don't you, Nathan?" asked Daniel. "We've been running a voice comparison, so we know it's you. Why would you call those two detectives and tell them where the murder weapon was? The weapon that has your fingerprints all over it?"

"Yes, that's me. I made the call but that is all I did. I didn't kill them."

Ellen jumps to her feet; she was nose-to-nose with him. "Oh, no! That toolshed was a trap. It fucking blew up when they went in to find the gun. You sent those detectives to their death. You might as well have put the last two slugs in their heads. We did retrieve the gun. It wasn't destroyed as you had planned."

Daniel stands behind Nathan, his hands pressing on Nathan's shoulders. "I say you'll probably get off with a few years for killing a douchebag like Joe Banoa, but killing two of New York's Finest... Oh, you will fry for that. No lethal injection and a goodnight's sleep for you. They are going to strap you in that hard-wood chair and give your head three hot jolts. Three, because the first zap doesn't usually kill you, just gets you all warmed up inside. Then the second shot comes, I hear people try to jump out of the seat so bad that they break their arms and legs. And finally, when you get hit a third time, your brains smoke from your ears and eyes blow out of theirs sockets. Not a pleasant way to die at all."

"Do you still want to cop to this murder rap?" Ellen asks softly. "Or are you ready to tell us what the fuck you're involved in?"

"I can't," Nathan drops his head on the steel table as if he wishes his skull would crack. "Nicky Nails and Bulletproof Morris Johnson would do worse than kill me."

"You haven't been keeping up with the times, Nathan, Morris Johnson died years ago. We can protect you from Nicky Nails Rocci, you'll go into the witness protection program. They obviously set you up to take the fall for them. Aren't you tired of wondering when he will come to finish the job?" Daniel sat on the edge of the table and unlocked the handcuffs. Lifting Nathan's head by his shoulder, he sat him gently back in the chair. "You've been living a nightmare, but you don't have to, not anymore. Tell us what you know, and I promise, I'll make Nicky Nails Rocci pay for every minute."

Nathan started talking, and once he started, couldn't stop. He began with the shooting at the Raven; how he didn't want to go with Joey Banoa and his gang. He stood and watched as Joey killed Maria, Morris' girlfriend, for insulting him. The others shot the rest of Rocci's gang. He was there, but never fired a shot. But that did not matter to Nicky or Morris because weeks later, they found him and sent him to a house of horrors. He described every sexual act forced upon him.

Each rape left a mark on his soul. Every depraved act he performed for a scrap of bread pulled him deeper into a well of despair. He was ashamed of the stories he told, every act he performed, the people killed in his name, and at the same time, was relieved to tell someone. The years living as a transvestite prostitute to punish himself for not standing up to Joey Banoa, Nicky Nails, and Bulletproof Morris Johnson.

His confession went well into the night. Daniel and Ellen were horrified by what they heard. In their collective thirty-seven years in the bureau, Daniel having spent eighteen years in vice, they had never heard a more twisted and sickening tale. All they could do was reassure Nathan that Nicky would get the death penalty for his crimes.

Nathan was sure Nicky would somehow make him pay. He understood if he was ever caught or questioned, he was to take full responsibility for Banoa's murder. Nathan gave them information on his boss, the man he was forced to work for. And when the time came, he stranded Joseph Banoa at the Bella Rosa, knowing they were waiting there to kill him. However, he did not know the detectives were also killed. He had left town right after making the phone call, as instructed.

He kept telling the agents that a person like Morris could not die. He could feel him deep inside his heart. Morris' love for Maria had consumed him, and his hatred for those who took her away kept him alive. He would not die until he had his revenge, complete and total, which meant Nathan had yet to pay for his part in her death. After all he'd been through, it would not be enough to satisfy Morris.

Ellen Dyer called the New York District Attorney's office and put a stop to Nicolas Rocci's prosecution. The FBI was officially taking over the investigation. Any deal they had with Rocci would be null and void. She gave the DA no explanation either. Two days later, Nicolas and his wife were found dead in their bed from carbon monoxide poisoning due to a faulty space heater. They were cremated the next day. Then came a lengthy court battle between the New York District Attorney's office and the FBI over whose case would go forward and whose would be buried.

I DON'T WANT to say it but there is no way around it. This is an 'I told you so moment'. Nicky isn't going to take it well, although he knew it was coming.

We dismissed Carmella and she left in a hurry. She was staying at the hotel where Nicky kept a suite for her under the name Lisa Westerly. Nicky was sure no one knew she was there, especially not her husband Christopher. I poured him the last of the bourbon.

"Go ahead, just say it."

"I told you we should have killed that little fagot, the day he made the call to Batman and Robin. Loose ends always come back to trip you up," I told him. I saw the look on his face when Carmella mentioned Nathan's name. I'm sure he could read mine.

"Yeah, we all know murders only compound, and never go away," he argued. "We should have killed Joe Banana and the cops and given them Nancy. That was the plan. If we killed him then they'd be looking for his killer. That little sausage bender knew what would happen if he talked. He's gonna pay."

"Ok, but your father, mother, and brother are still dead. If you had trusted me, the cops would have had the gun and the shooter that killed Banoa, the person who setup two crooked cops, and one suicidal homo who tied it all together. They wouldn't have looked too hard after that. And he would have gotten what he deserved, a short flight off a Bronx roof with a very bloody landing."

We sat in the study for the rest of the afternoon. I showed Nicky more tapes, ones I thought would be helpful in light of what we knew now. We formulated plans and bounced ideas off of each other between tapes, like "that guy is now the police commissioner, I bet he'll know if there are any special details being assigned," or "this guy is the bureau chief for the FBI, if we can get a list of their safehouses from him, we can find Nathan quick." Then we both said, "BINGO! We got us a federal judge."

Nicky got tired of the Nathan affair, his focus returning to Chris and Carmella, "so, what do you think I ought to do about them?"

"You have to kill Chris," I said coldly. "Her, I don't know. You love her, so it's gonna be hard either way. I mean, once you kill him, you can't be sure she won't put a knife in your back. She looks like she still loves her husband, even if she's fucking you on the regular."

"Yeah, that's a hard one to figure out," Nicky lamented, "she's not just a great lay, she really works the business too. And you know how it goes with childhood sweethearts. She has outgrown him but at the same time can't let him go. I definitely have to kill him. But first, I'm going to have Pistol Pete beat the information we need out of him."

"And that's why I was mad you sent him away. There's an easier way of getting the information and finding out if Carmella is in on the plan. But Elie and Stephanie are another story, they are my best assassination team. I'd hate to lose them."

"But if they took a shot at me…"

"Without a doubt they're gone. Elie doing your brother, that's a given. He works alone or as a team, never with anyone else. But Stephanie couldn't make the shot on you. She works best up close, using her looks and then taking a person down with small arms, knives, poisons, that sort of thing."

Nicky rattled the ice in his glass for a minute. "What if Elie trained her, or better yet, set the shot up for her. All she had to do was wait for me to walk into the crosshairs."

"That is a possibility. Could also be why you're alive today. If Elie targeted you, he would not have missed. I'll have a talk with them, ask a few questions. You know what I mean." The sun had shifted, and the hot seat was very comfortable. It was like sitting on a cloud. You could easily doze off there if you did not think about the number of people who sat there and never got up. "What about that guy, Deano, Benny's man?"

"Oh, his beatings have already begun," Nicky laughed. "He knows, if Benny calls to check on him, to say he's having the time of his life. Or else we cut him into little pieces and feed him to the fish."

"Have you gotten anything useful out of him yet?" I got up,

walked over to the liquor cabinet, poured a twenty-year-old whiskey, and returned to the comfort of the hot seat, "if you want, I will pay him a visit. I told you, we needed to take out Benny two years ago."

"I agree with you," Nicky leaned back in his chair and put his feet up on the desk, "but we have to do it right. Or we risk starting a war with the rest of the families. We have our rules and Benny has his friends."

"Sometimes, the best way to deal with a problem is head on," I smile and take a sip, "and by that, I mean dropping his head on the concrete from say… a twenty-story building."

"How about this, when the time comes, I'll let you give that fat guido bastard a flying lesson. Lord knows I don't need back problems." Nicky laughs and finishes his drink. "Hey, how come you didn't show up for my parents' service?"

"You got the flowers, right? And Elizabeth and Yana were there. I tried to get Maria to come along but she's still… resistant to coming back to New York. You know why."

"Yeah, but that's not the same thing."

"Well, if you noticed, past those flowers there was another funeral going on," I told him. "A black family was burying their ten-year-old son who died from cancer. I arranged their funeral, so I could watch yours from a safe distance. Away from all the cameras."

"You killed a ten-year-old?"

"Noooo, you fucking degenerate. What's the matter with you? I paid for the funeral, so they could hold it on the same day. I have been meaning to ask you, why the caskets and burial service? Didn't you have your mother and father cremated? Why the expense and drama of a full funeral?"

"For Sal," Nicky dropped his head. "I never told him they were cremated. The medical examiner knew instantly they were smothered. Especially Dad, so I had to do away with the evidence of that right away. I didn't know if he understood what he had done, or what the effect of them being cremated would have done to him. Hell! I should have put a bullet in his head and here I am worrying about his fucking feelings."

"Well, it seems your father took care of that for you," I could feel his pain, it filled the room. I now understood why he wanted to die. "He took care of it so you wouldn't have to, maybe when you finally do die, he will be waiting for you… upstairs."

I TAKE a quick trip out to the west coast. I'm at a very posh hotel called The Four Winds. It sits on a bluff overlooking the Pacific Ocean. It's a short walk down the boardwalk and there's a flight of steps to the beach. There is a narrow path of sand between smooth gray boulders at the bottom. The hotel brochure tells of the expense and foresight of the builders to truck in the boulders from Oregon to stop the erosion of the beach and bluff or else one day the hotel might topple into the sea. Long before the rest of California does.

"The sunset is spectacular isn't it, Elie?"

"Mr. Johnson, what brings you to my little establishment?"

"I must have one of your specialties," I smile up at him, "can you make me a Pirate's Bloody Hook?"

"I'm not sure I know what that is?" The smile fades from his face.

"Come to my room, twenty-one twelve, and I'll show you how to make it."

"I don't get off 'til midnight," the worry lines deepen as his eyes narrow.

"That's ok," I say, still wearing a carefree smile. I start

walking toward the hotel lobby and say, "Stephanie will keep me company until you arrive."

Elie knocks on my door five minutes after I get there. He's perspiring and breathing hard. "Where is she? Is she ok?"

"Come in." I shut the door.

Elie sees the open balcony door, the curtains blowing out, and waving goodbye. He rushes to the rail and almost falls over as he looks down on the rocks below. "Where's Stephanie? I know why you are here." He returns to the room scanning frantically for a sign she was here. "It was a sanctioned job. Carmella ordered it, said it came straight from Nicolas himself," he confesses, "I didn't know the target was Sal. I didn't know it was Nicky's brother. How would I have known? I thought it was an old vendetta he wanted purged after his death. I swear."

"Well, that didn't take long," I laugh, sitting down on the oversized couch. "Have a seat. Do you want that drink?"

He sits across from me on the other large sofa. His eyes are looking through me. Fear is gone and the calculations of a killer's mind are at work. "Where is Stephanie?"

"Stephanie," I call out, "come in here and bring that tray of Pirate's Bloody Hooks with you, please."

She comes from the kitchen with the tray and sets it down on the glass table between us. She takes a seat next to Elie and holds his hand.

"Why is everybody so glum?" I take a glass from the tray and take a sip. "Ah, perfect. I thought you wouldn't be here so quickly, so I taught Stephanie the recipe for the drinks. You call it a recipe not a formula when you are talking about drinks, right?"

"Yes, that's right," Elie answers.

"Well, you are the bartender, so I'll yield to your expertise. Go ahead and take a sip. Tell me what you think." I pull out a white pistol as they pick up their glasses. I see their eyes widen at the sight of my gun. "I had Stephanie make the drinks, so you know they are ok. I'm having a drink with you, so you know we are all still friends here. And we will stay friends as long as you two answer my questions honestly and without hesitation. Now, I know you're thinking about this gun. When I was a kid in the South Bronx, we couldn't get our hands on a real gun. That was the good ol' days, now, a six-year-old can buy a gun, if he buys it from me.

"Back then, we either made our own guns, you know, zip gun, but then we needed bullets. Again, not easy to get as a kid. So, I'd carry water pistols filled with battery acid. Battery acid is not as deadly as a bullet, but extremely painful if you shoot someone in the eyes. I guess you figured out by now that at this range I'm a dead shot."

"Morris, Elie already told you it was Carmella who hired us," her voice was strong and unapologetic. "We didn't know who he was. You know how these things operate. We are only given a face and a place."

"Of course I do," I say and sip on my drink while keeping the gun pointing at her. "In this gun is fluoroantimonic acid, or a superacid, which is a billion times stronger than sulfuric acid and probably a billion times more painful. It will burn the flesh off the bone in seconds and then dissolve the bones. Now, I'm going to ask Elie the questions and if he gives an answer I don't like, Stephanie will be the first to know. One bad answer and you will have a permanent role as the Phantom of the Opera. If you live. Elie were you alone in the high rise?"

"No, Stephanie was with me. She was acting as my spotter. And I was training her to be a sniper."

"Ok. Did either of you shoot Nicky?"

"No!"

"No need to take offense." I put my glass down. I am watching their muscle tension, eye movement, nostril flair, any sign that they are lying or about to strikeout at me. "Did you see another shooter?"

"No. But I did see Nicky go down. I thought we had been set up. But then I thought who else knew we would be there that day. No one."

"Why?"

"We were in that apartment staking out the site for weeks," Elie seemed to relax. "We knew Nicky was building a crypt for his family and were given information that he showed up there with the target before. Like I said, I did not know it was his brother, I thought it was just another capo in the family. When he went down, I knew we would be blamed for both shooting."

"So, why didn't you run? Why come back here like nothing happened?"

"If we run, we are guilty," interjected Stephanie.

"Yeah, but not running does not mean you are innocent," I wink at her and she shuts up.

"You would show up wherever we went," Elie continued her thought, "sooner or later you would track us down. It would be better if we did not make it hard for you to find us. I actually thought you would have been here weeks ago."

"Well, I only found out about your involvement recently. Carmella wasn't exactly bragging about your success. Where did the second shot come from?"

"I'm not sure. We fired from inside a bedroom window. We had no peripheral view. But I believe the shot came from above our position. We were on the fifth floor; Sal was pushed forward and then down." Elie got a very professional tone to his voice. "I fired a fyv-FYV-six NATO round enough to kill with a single hit but not to destroy the target completely. Camella was clear the target was not to suffer. I thought it was odd. Nicky was knocked down, doubled over like he got punched in the gut. Plus, the bullet exited the middle of his chest."

"You saw all that?"

"Not the exit wound info, that I got from the medical records," Stephanie volunteered.

"Mr. Morris, if I may," Elie asks, "when I said I expected you much sooner, I thought Carmella would have told you about the hit she ordered. When you didn't show, I began to think that maybe she hired the second shooter. But if she did, she didn't tell him about us because our shot threw his off. It's the only reason why Nick is alive today. Back in Syria, we knew there would be multiple snipers, we always reacquired our targets before firing. But now that you are here, asking these questions, I'm beginning to think she didn't know about the second shooter either."

"Really? One last question then, for all the marbles, were you working with anyone else? Someone who may have learned of where Nicky would have been and when."

They shake their heads vehemently, almost spilling their drinks.

Elie says, "We never discuss a job with anyone. After I saw Nicky go down, we changed our exit plan. Broke the gun down into two different bags as usual, but we both went down the same stairwell and out the same exit. Those buildings, as you probably know, have multiple exits facing all sides. We got in our car and circled the buildings once looking for a second shooter. I didn't see anyone that would have fit the bill and then we got the hell out of there."

I put the pistol on the couch next to me and picked up my drink. I finish it in a satisfying gulp. "I don't know who made fluoroantimonic acid, or why, but you guys should look into getting some. It's great for getting rid of bodies. However, you will need to keep it in Teflon," I pat my white pistol on the couch, "that stuff will eat through everything else."

Elie and Stephanie finally drink theirs. Elie's face is a little strained.

"Stephanie, why don't you go make another round of Pirate's Bloody Hooks."

9

HANGING IS TOO GOOD FOR HIM

Morris is reading the morning paper. He is flipping through the pages and stops on a centerfold spread.

Nicky enters the kitchen and says, "You're in the wrong magazine if you're looking for nudies."

"No, I'm not looking for those pictures. These are pictures and timeline for this guy, Ted Bundy's victims. They fried that nut job in Florida last night."

"Look who's calling the kettle black," Nicky jokes.

"Oh, come on," I protest, "what I do is for business. This whacko was a rapist, serial killing creep. You know he fucked his victims for days after they were dead. You can't compare what he did to what we do. He did it to get some kind of morbid pleasure."

"Relax," Nicky said with a smile, "I'm sure you stopped fucking that girl in Venezuela after an hour or two. Anyway, what are you doing here? It's cold as hell outside."

"Who're you telling? We got to go into the city. There has been some development on the Chris Carmine front."

THE ROADS off Long Island were treacherous, and Rocky is driving like it's a spring day not the end of January.

The car fishtails on the Long Island Expressway, causing Nicky to yell at him, "IF YOU FUCKING CRASH THIS CAR, I WILL KILL YOU."

"And after he does, I'll bring you back and kill you again," I add.

"Really, you can do that?" Rocky turns back to look at me. "Because I heard you knew some kind of voodoo. That's why everybody is afraid of you. They call you Bulletproof, right?"

"Bulletproof, yes. Mangled and crushed to death in a car, NO. Where the hell did you get this yahoo from?"

"Hey, keep your eyes on the road and slow the fuck down," Nicky reaches forward and slaps him on the back of his head. "He's actually a great get-away driver. He just doesn't know the difference between a drive and a police chase."

"Yeah, I've been driving getaway cars since I was twelve. I was tall for my age."

Closer to the city the roads cleared up and driving was as normal as any other day. The morning traffic on a Wednesday is a bit lighter, most deliveries are done for the week, only garbage trucks and ambulances are cruising the streets of Manhattan this early. We head down the west side towards the Deuce. Rocky pulls the car into a parking spot on fortieth and ninth avenue.

"So, I wait for you here, Boss?" Rocky enquires, not sure of our plans.

"Yeah, we'll be in the club around the corner," Nicky informs him.

"Why don't I just drop you off around the corner? It's freezing out there."

"Because I don't want anybody to know I'm here, capisce?"

"Yeah, yeah. I got you now."

"He must be one hellava getaway driver," I tell Nicky as I step out into the cold city wind.

We enter the strip club known only by the address above the door. The black window makes it perpetually night inside. Red neon lights in the figure of a shapely girl dances across the glass in a series of three provocative poses. Repeating itself every seven seconds. Inside the door there is a short narrow hallway at a right angle designed to keep the light out and customers under control. The hallway is six-feet long and three-feet wide, and one must enter the club in single file formation. There is a plexiglass window to pay the twenty-dollar entrance fee at the end, a fortified black steel door at a sharp left turn, and a formattable two-eighty-pound doorman in front of it to wand you down.

They don't expect any trouble at these places. Most of that occurs inside the club where half a dozen other bouncers inconspicuously stand in the darkened corners. The hallway is a mantrap to keep the police out for as long as possible. Inside the club the girls may be performing more than dances on stage or in the private booths for the right price.

The red-light bulb in the hallway makes identification of patrons difficult, again by design. Nicky slides a twenty under the narrow cutout in the plastic window and turns to be wanded. The doorman goes up and down his front and then his back with the metal detector then buzzes him in. I follow the procedure and meet him on the other side of the door talking to a topless waitress. Music assaults the ears, making conversation less than an inch from mouth to ear impossible. I take his arm and lead him down the right side of the stage.

The chairs along the stage have five guys staring up at the three pole dancers slithering before them. *Regulars, sanitations workers just getting off, in more ways than one.* We pass behind them in total darkness. Another foot to our right is a raised platform and four tables around a small stage and pole. There are six of these areas in the club, three on each side of the main stage. Behind those, along the walls are small, curtained booth, a bright pink neon sign proclaims on one wall, "PRIVATE DANCES" and, "LAPDANCES" across on the other.

White and blue spotlights shine down from the blackened ceiling onto the various stages. We come to the last little square stage in the back. A man is watching a very pretty black dancer twirl around her pole. She leans forwards and squeezes her breast together in front of him to receive her fare. Then quickly slips into her bra and panties as we reach the table.

Nicky squints and looks hard at the graying man in the dark, "Pauley? No fucking way. They told me Morris killed you."

"Really, and yet here you are with him."

"He said he had a good reason. I was going to take it up with him again at a better time," Nicky consoles him.

"As you can see," I intercede, "I did not have him killed. We needed people to think that I did or wanted to."

"Wanted to?" questioned Nicky. "I understand you didn't want anyone to challenge your authority while I was down, but what do you mean by wanting him dead? He's either dead or not."

"Let me explain," Pauley said.

A girl came by, looking for a dance and her tip and I took hold of her arm. A bouncer near the bar and one across the club stepped from the shadows. I whispered into her ear to bring three straight vodkas and tell the other girls not to disturb us. The bouncers disappeared back into the darkness as the girl left the table.

"We faked the shootout in the mansion, and I went to Chicago. We wanted it to look like Morris had usurped power here in New York and I was now on the outs from the family. His plan was for me to get in close to Benny Brunello. Let's face it, Brunello hates you two guys with a passion. I knew if he wasn't behind your shooting, he sure takes advantage of it."

"So, is he behind it?" Nicky asks just as our drinks arrive.

"I would say so," Pauley says but admits he's not one hundred percent sure. "He had been talking to Christopher Carmine since the shooting and seems way too familiar with him. I think he has been working him for quite some time now. He put me in touch with his guy here in New York, whose only job is to keep tabs on you."

Nicky shoots down his drink. He's getting angry. "How's he able to do that?"

"I would say he got someone on the inside," Pauley surmises.

"Carmine, that sonofabitch!"

"Maybe," Pauley confirms half-heartedly, "but I think this guy's been on the job longer than that. I think he may have been the one to flip Christopher."

I have been watching the girls on the main stage and following the conversation with my ears. I turn to Pauley, "then who's this guy's contact?"

"I think it's someone who came over from Lucas' organization," Pauley tells us. "Nicky, I think we have a bigger problem than what you think. Peter Lucas never got over Angela's death and he blames you. If Christopher told Benny that you had his daughter killed, well, the two of them together coming after you… You see what I'm getting at."

"Yeah." Nicky sat back in his chair.

"Yes," I agreed and finished my drink.

Pauley finishes his drink and puts up a hand for a girl to take the stage besides us. It would make people suspicious to see the three men sitting there and no entertainment. We had picked the place because we didn't want to be identified. A blonde, white chick with large fake boobs stepped carefully onto the stage. Even in the dim light, I could tell she had been in the business a long time. Stoney face and lined, makeup could only do so much. Her body, fake boobs and a taunt ass, made up for her age. She moved well to the music and flipped and spun around the pole with ease. Upside down, right side up, one leg hooked around it, her clean shaved and puffy pink lips commanded our attention. When she was done, I threw a twenty on the stage. Pauley tucked one between her breasts. And Nicky rolled his lengthwise and slid it in her wet wide-open hole.

"Buy a lady a drink," she said as a younger waitress with a boob job placed a champagne flute on the stage. I threw another twenty and the waitress filled the flute with champagne. Without a word, the dancer slid down on the glass until it disappeared. Then she did a back flip back to a split and slowly raised up off the empty glass. "AH, that was refreshing," she smiled, grabbed another couple of twenties from the stage, and was gone with her dress over her shoulder.

Pauley smiled, "I will be going back to Chicago to dig deeper and stay close to Benny."

They brought over another tray of drinks and a lanky blonde girl, younger than the last, started slipping out of her undies under the white spotlight. She bent, dipped, spread, and rolled to our delight. We tossed her a couple of fish, and two other Latino girls came after her. The lunch crowd, if five more men consti-tuted a crowd, filled in the tables around the club. Then we left.

"HOW WAS NEW YORK? Do you miss that garbage dump?" Benny asked as Pauley climbed in the back of his limousine.

"Hey, nobody talks about my city or my Knicks, got that?"

Pauley laughs, "you didn't have to come pick me up. Don't tell me you missed me that much."

They cleared the airport traffic and headed out of town. "Not at all. But since your ex-boss has been up and around, he has been messing with my businesses. First, he killed so many of his own people my connections in New York are afraid to do business with me. Then that whole exchange of hostages deal I was forced into has made me restructure my organization from top to bottom. I know Nicky and his Darkie is going to beat his secrets out of him. I got to get ahead of them."

"That still don't explain why you personally came to get me from the airport," Pauley said.

"I couldn't wait to hear what happened when you met with some of your crew," Benny said with glee. "Were they shocked to see you alive? Were they ready to follow you into battle against Nails and the Niggers?"

Pauley came to Chicago and hided out in one of Benny's hotel. It wasn't long before he was recognized by Benny's men and paid a visit. Benny had heard Pauley was killed in a shootout in the Long Island mansion by Morris' gang, so he was very interested to hear how Pauley had managed to escape. Pauley told him it was easy; he was the first one to draw and fire. He killed three of Morris' men and dragged them to his car. He drove off Long Island and had been driving ever since. He told Benny, Morris must know he is alive but for appearances and to keep a hold on the family, Morris let's people believe he's dead. Pauley told him he was not looking for help, just needed to lie low while he came up with a plan. But Benny was eager to help.

"No, it was nothing like that," Pauley admitted, "I met with a couple of capos who go back with me a long way. They are ok with how things are now that Nicky is back running the business. Most of the people that got whacked were low level soldiers who they thought had it coming. Morris is still around, he's running security, my old job. Christopher Carmine going to Vegas left everybody skittish to make a move."

Benny was not pleased by Pauley's report.

But Pauley was not trying to make him happy, he needed Benny to show his hand. Benny was having trouble keeping his businesses out of trouble. The law was moving in on his gambling dens. The blacks were taking over his crack houses. His loan sharking business was the only thing that was doing well. A good report about New York might make him a little reckless.

Benny did not let Pauley in on any business decisions, saying it was to keep the secret that he was still alive. Pauley doubted it, it was all about trust. But if Benny wanted to bring down the Rocci family, he was going to have to open up.

"I didn't think you get much out of your meetings with your old pals." Benny said. "Nicky has all but severed ties with anyone from our generation. Did you meet with my man in New York?"

"Yes," Pauley had met him before going to the strip club. Made sure he would not follow him there. "He had practically nothing to report. Nicky almost never leaves the mansion. If I had to guess, I'd say he's paranoid."

"Good. Good. That can work in our favor." Benny was pleased. He was quiet for a long time, like the conversation was over. Then he announced, "I'm going to put you in contact with someone from Peter Lucas' family. He's been working with Nicky for a couple of years, but he's really on my payroll."

"What does that make him, a triple agent?" Both men laugh.

"He had a crush on Angela, wanted Nicky's head when she died. He was heartbroken when Peter didn't go after Nicky. All very sad," Benny feigned regret. "I think if you feed him some damning information about Nicky and Carmella, you know what I mean, it will get the ball rolling again with Lucas. I opened

Chris' eyes about his wife, but he dropped the ball. And I'm afraid he's out of the game now."

"You know, Nicky and Carmella hooking up now doesn't mean they were involved in a plot against Angela. In fact, I know they weren't."

Benny's face and mood turned sour. He was still careful what he said to Pauley and gave his bodyguard a look in the front seat. Pauley sat behind the driver putting him in direct line of fire from the passenger in the front. Picking him up at the airport meant he didn't have time to get strapped up. Pauley was a big man, with decades of experience killing with his bare hands. But digressions worked better than bravado. He did not want to provoke him too much.

"I know you think Nicky is back on top, but Chris told me personally that Morris Johnson has taken over the family. He kept Nicky doped up, so he could get rid of anyone who stood in his way, like you. Now, Nicky may be up and about, but I'll bet it's Morris Johnson who's calling the shots. I think it's time a man like yourself took the reins. What do you think?"

The ride from the airport can only go one of two ways. Either he agrees and accepts whatever deal Benny has in mind, or this ride ends at a shallow grave in the woods. He has been in the game a long time and knows you always have a man meet you at the airport with hardware. The upswing in plane hijackings during the seventies also meant security was getting tighter at airports.

He picked up a .38 snub-nosed revolver from the paper towel dispenser in the men's bathroom and strapped the ankle holster to his left leg. Most pat downs did not go all the way to the ankle, some people were just too lazy. Others found it somewhat difficult to get that far down, while others felt that if a guy went for an ankle gun he'd be killed before he could get off a shot. But the fall backwards, draw, and shoot from the ground maneuver had saved his life on several occasions. He practiced it regularly and always carried a S&W .38 on his left leg. He had a Beretta .25 on his right as a backup; less powerful but had more shots.

He did not need them for Benny, he was old and overweight, a hard word and he'd keel over from a heart attack. But the muscle in the front seat was a different story. He had been caressing his iron the whole time; waiting and wanting to get the order to pull it out and put it to use. Sitting in the back seat he would be hard pressed to get to either gun fast enough. "Maybe you're right. Nicky is too reckless to run the family business. And as long as he's got that blackie by his side, he'll never be my Godfather."

Benny smiled, took hold of Pauley's arm, and gave him a reassuring shake. He looked up to the rearview mirror and nodded. The passenger in the front seat relaxed. Benny opened the bar in the console between them and took out a wine bottle and a pistol. "Here you go," He handed over the gun in a clip-on holster. "I bet you feel naked without one of these. And I'll bet you thought this was going to be one of those rides."

"What ride?"

"You know… I'm sure you have taken others on them. The ones that end at an unmarked grave in the woods." They all laughed.

Snow started falling on the windshield. "I don't think I'll ever get used to this. Snowing without a cloud in the sky."

"It's called lake effect snow, from the wind blowing the water off Lake Michigan," explains the passenger.

"I know where the snow comes from," Pauley says, "I just don't think I can get used to it. I'll be glad to get back to New York. Chicago is too weird for me."

The two men sit back and sip wine as the car speeds along towards Benny house in the affluent suburbs of Chicago. His mansion is two hours from the crime-ridden streets of the city on the North Shore in Lake County. The rest of the ride is a mini question and answer period between Benny and Pauley. Benny wants to know how many capos can be flipped when the time comes and how many soldiers they command. He also wants to know how many men Morris commands.

Pauley says truthfully, "Nobody knows for sure. Maybe Nicky may have some idea, but with Morris, things are always moving. Too bad he's not Italian."

"Really. You know how those jungle bunnies are," Benny says with a slight grin, "they multiply like... well, like rabbits." The car erupts in laughter.

THIS WAS the first time Pauley had been to the house in Lake Bluff. Brunello had one of the three mansions on Sunrise Avenue, the biggest one. It was nestled back from the road in the park neighborhood. The long winding driveway maintained his privacy and the bay doors of the sunroom gave an exceptional view of the beach along the lake. It was the type of place a man of his stature should call home. Beniamino Brunello considered himself an old-time gangster, right up there with the likes of Capone, Dean O'Banion, and "Big Jim" Colosimo.

He left Pauley in the sunroom to take a call. An informant inside the FBI had sent him a package and was anxious to hear his reaction. Benny opened the envelope and read the transcript of Nathan Napolitano's confession. He was overjoyed, especially by the last few paragraphs where Nathan described reporting on Joe Banoa's daily whereabouts, and then stranding him at the Bella Rosa the night he was murdered. And lastly being given the murder weapon by Morris and sending the cops to their deaths. All under orders from Nicky Nails Rocci.

Benny laughed so loud on the phone to his informant Pauley

heard him two rooms away through closed doors and the windswept waves on the lake. Also clearly hearing him say, "Nicky put nails in his own coffin this time. That little fuck always thinks he's so clever, I'd like to see him get strapped in the chair myself."

Then there was some cursing before he heard, "Ok. It doesn't matter but try to find out where he is being held. I'll work things on this end to make sure he gets a fair trial before he hangs."

PISTOL PETE ENTERS a small room on the top floor of a rundown hotel miles outside of Las Vegas. Chris hops off the bed and backs up to the wall. He is weaken and barely able to stand from the lack of food and liquids. Peter closes the door, "Relax, I'm not here to hurt you. I'm too old for that. I'm just here to talk."

He takes a seat in the chair by the door and gazes out the window at the sand blowing through the ghost town. There are about a dozen buildings along the main street, and a few dots the other street that intersects it. The landscape beyond is sagebrush and empty desert.

"Tell me," his voice is that of a kindly grandfather, "do you know why you're here in this little corner of Hell?"

"I am a hostage," Chris answers, "a guarantee that you and the other bosses don't try to take over the Rocci's business."

"That was the cover story, alright. Here's the real deal," Peter tells him. He's a thin but muscular man for his age, the veins in his arms pronounced. "Let me tell you why I'm called Pistol Pete. Back in my day, I would much rather beat a person in the face and head with my German Luger than shoot him. I would start with a good crack across the bridge of the nose. It's hard for a man to fight back when he's drowning in his own blood. Then a smack by the schmuck's eye." Peter jabs a finger into Chris' face at his cheekbone. "That lets him know this is going to be a painful talk. A pistol whipping really does terrible damage to a person's face and leaves very little evidence the police can use. And if the person refuses to talk, I'd either beat his brains out through the top of his skull, or as a last resort, use the business end of my luger. Well, that's my story, let's hear yours. Nicky thinks you tried to kill him. He believes Benny the Ballbreaker, that's what we used to call him, either put you up to it or was helping you get it done."

"NO. NO. Tell him that's not true. Tell him to speak to Morris…"

"Listen, cowboy, it doesn't matter to me if you did or didn't. I don't know Morris, but from what I hear, he's not as stupid as you might think. He let you believe he trusted you to see if you would take another bite of the apple. He's a patient man, Nicky is not, he is more of a get-it-done-now guy. Nicky thinks you did and wants me to get the truth out of you. Like I said, I'm too old to beat it out of you. But I can bring in a couple of guys if that is the way you want to do this. I trained them well, like any artist passing on his talents. Or I could just leave you here in Satan's Retreat for a few more days. The hundred-and-twenty-degree days and twenty-degree nights makes this little shithole a real pleasant place to die."

"That son of a bitch was sleeping with my WIFE!"

"Ah, there it is. Doesn't it feel good to get that off your chest?" Peter stands up and opens the door, "Let's go downstairs. I got a couple of cold beers in the car; you can tell me all about it."

"So, you are not going to kill me?"

"Not unless Nicky tells me to," he smiles and lets Chris go down the stairs ahead of him.

Chris feels a little bolder. "You came out here alone. How do you know I wouldn't kill you and run?"

As they get outside Pistol Pete tells him, "Look around. You can go a hundred miles in any direction and still be in the same place. And if you drive five miles in the wrong direction my man will put a bullet in your head. This is not my first rodeo, cowboy." He reaches in the back seat of his red convertible Cadillac and grabs two beers out of the cooler. He uses the back of the massive diamond ring on his pinky to flip the caps off. He hands Chris his beer and starts back to the hotel, "grab the cooler and let's get out of the sun. It's not doing either of us any good." He uses his Stetson to dust off a table and chair in the ramshackle lounge. He sits down. "Ok. So, Nicky Nails, your boss, was sticking it to your wife. That used to be called the right of kings, but I guess I'm old fashion. Not that anybody liked it when we had monarchs. So, you tried to have him killed or did you take the shot yourself?"

"No, I didn't take the shot." Chris downed his beer. He pointed to another in the cooler. "May I?"

"Knock yourself out. This is your party."

He drank half of it, then said, "When Mr. Brunello's man told me Nicky was sending me out of town, so he could sleep with Carmella, my wife, yeah, I wanted to kill him. As I thought about it, I told Brunello's man to shoot him in the back. Like he was doing to me."

Chris' last word came out with such venom that Peter took a hard swallow of beer. He coughs a little and chokes it down. "Ok, I'll leave that part out. I'll just tell him you found out about him and… Carmella, was it? I'll tell him it was his old friend Benny the Ballbreaker that got inside your head. Between your jealousy, and his pushing you to do something stupid, you lost control. What about the rest of the business with the family? Were you trying to help Benny take control? Don't you lie to me, cowboy? I have look many a liar in the eye and I don't like what it makes me have to do."

"No, nothing like that. He just supplied the hitman. I guess he thought I'd kill Nicky and that would make him happy. Then Morris put me in charge of the family… I didn't know why."

Pistol Pete got up and started walking towards the door. He left the cooler on the table.

Chris followed him out to the car.

"I'll send my guy in with some food and a blanket for the nights. Don't think about killing him and driving off, he's not as nice as I am. And you still wouldn't get more than five miles down the road before you'd be out of gas and stranded in the desert. By the way, this road only goes another five miles in that direction, then it turns into nothing but desert. I'll provide you a daily supply of food and water… beer. No reason why we can't be civil. No more. No less."

Pistol Pete drives out of the desert. *That poor stupid idiot. No matter how I spin this, Nicky is going to hand him his balls. Well, maybe she's worth it.*

10

BENNY'S GRAND PLAN

Benny has a room made up for Pauley, two floors below on the north end of the mansion and watches him closely since his return from New York. With extra guards on duty if Pauley came back with orders from Nicky, he'll put an end to their friendship quickly. Two locked doors separate the north end of the mansion from the south. *What a stroke of luck that Morris tried to bump off Pauley. He played right into my hand. Now, I can go back to plan A, and forget about Chris and plan B.*

Plan A came to him a few years ago when he sent a man to collect a debt in Los Vegas. A Serbian named Miloje, owed him a large amount of money on a heroin shipment that went missing. While the Serbian was teetering on the railing of a balcony twenty floors up, he was trying frantically to make a deal. "Tell your boss I got information that's worth his weight in gold."

"The boss told me to come back with one point two million in cash, or your head in a basket. That last part was figurative," sneered the nondescript man in the black suit. He was holding a gun on the Serb and forcing him to take drinks of vodka. "You don't have the money, so when they mop you up on the sidewalk, the blood alcohol level is going to tell the police you are just another drunk idiot in Sin City. Which you are for trying to cheat Mr. Benny."

"I'm not the idiot, you are! I hope he finds out that you blew his chances of taking down the Rocci family!"

"You know I can't shoot you," the clean-shaved, short black haired, Italian said politely, "but I can push you off the railing. You and that bottle is all I really need to call the job done."

"Come on, call the Boss, Dukes. Just let him hear what I have to say. And if he tells me to jump, then I will."

"I told you never call me that!" Aldo 'Dukes' Romano was a heavy weight fighter, a good puncher but a slow-moving target in the ring. At two-eighty he left the fight game when a man from Benny's camp paid him to take a fall. When he got up off the canvas it was the last time, he would ever touch it again. Afterwards, he worked his talents in alleys against opponents half his size for twice the money. The hitman picks up the phone by the bed. He dials a number and says, "Put me through to the boss." He waits as the call is transferred to another number. "… no, it's not over yet. This weasel doesn't have your package. But he is giving me some cock-and-bull story about New York. He thinks it might be worth you hearing him out… Yeah, he thinks it's worth his life." Aldo listens intently to the instructions on the other end. Then he motions the Serb to come take the phone.

"Thank you, thank you, thank you," he says to Aldo as he hops off the railing and rushes to the phone.

"Make it quick and make it good," the gruff voice orders over the phone.

"Ok, I was giving this he-she a magic carpet ride… no, nothing like that! I gave him some product and the place to use it. He was in one of my joints. While he is riding the wild horses…"

"Your code words are a fucking joke," Benny yells into the phone, "just tell me what you know about Rocci."

"Yes, sir. This guy gets high and starts talking about him

setting up Joe Banoa's murder. He goes on and on about Nicky Nails and some guy MoJo put him up to it. He is crying about how he's sure his fingerprints are all over the murder weapon. He thinks every mobster is looking for him."

"Is that all you got?"

"His real name is Nathan Napolitano, but he dances as Nancy," Miloje says with a smile on his face and winks at Aldo. "He must have been telling the truth because after that day, when he realized what he said, he swore off the hard stuff. He hasn't been using in a month."

"So, you're telling me, you had this information for a month and I'm just hearing about it now? Holding it to save your sorry ass!"

"No. No sir. I was going to tell you before. But the whole mix up with the shipment…" Miloje wishes he hadn't said that. "I mean. When you are standing on a ledge your life flashes before your eyes. I remembered it and thought it would be a shame if I died without giving you this very important message. Knowing how much you hate Nicky Nails."

"You're right, this is really great stuff. Put Aldo on the phone."

"Here you go, Dukes," Miloje hands Aldo the phone with a big smile on his face.

"Yeah, okay, Boss. Right away." Aldo drops the phone and grabs Miloje by the neck and his boxer shorts. He drags him to the balcony, tosses him up and over the railing, then throws the half bottle of vodka after him. He adjusts his black leather gloves, hangs up the phone, and leaves the hotel by the back stairs. He passes a gathering crowd in the parking lot around the splattered body of Miloje, close to the building as if he fell from the upper floors.

ALDO 'DUKES' Romano locates Nathan and is told to keep track of his whereabouts. Benny wanted to know what the police knew about the 'Bella Rosa Massacre', as it was labeled in the papers. He wanted to know if they made the connection between that shooting and the shooting a couple of years earlier at the Raven Social Club. It had also made headlines, but neither told the true story. Although the papers hinted at a Mafia connection in each incident, the owners of each place, at least on paper, had no connection to any mob family.

His connection in the New York District Attorney's Office, a low-level clerk by the name of Robert Richards, said they were listed as unsolved armed robbery attempts resulting in multiple homicides. Bobby, as everybody knew him, was a squat, balding man with thick glasses from years of routing around in files. He had access to all the police records, court files, including FBI reports. He was an invaluable source of information to Benny Brunello and was paid well for it. He informed Benny that the two cases ran out of two different precincts. The Bella Rosa robbery made little sense with only one gunman inside and two shotgun-toting bandits outside. Plus, the cash register was not opened. Because of whom was killed, it looked like a mob hit to the police. The Raven shooting made less sense, a neighborhood poolhall with little cash in it. Maybe a local hood would try and stick the place up, but three or four gunmen for less than thirty dollars in cash did not add up. But in that case, the victims were neighborhood kids and a couple of old men, nobody of importance in the Mafia. The Banoa-Rocci War was played down by the police, and not even mentioned in the newspapers, but it got the attention of the FBI's Organized Crime Unit.

Benny decided he would reach out to another contact he had in the NYDA office and spark his interest in the Bella Rosa case. "George Jarvis, this is your old friend Benny. How is your day going?" He listened to the small talk for a minute, then said, "Have I got a story for you. I hope you're sitting down because this is going to floor you." He gave him enough information to tie Nicky—his friends being the ones murdered at the Raven—to Banoa, especially after Joey's hunting accident and sudden death, to the Bella Rosa hit. He held onto Napolitano's name as the source. He planned to release it when Nicky Nails was in the hot seat. He was no stranger to making a witness disappear and neither was Nicky.

Everything was going well until Nicolas Rocci showed up to confess to Banoa's murder. Naturally, Jarvis would take the bait to jail the senior Rocci over junior. You always go for the big fish in these cases. Benny had not foreseen the father stepping in to rescue his son and ruin his revenge. Benny decided to give Nathan Napolitano to the Feds. Then it was on to plan B, the direct approach.

For Benny, the direct approach was to kill Nicky Nails Rocci and Bulletproof Morris MoJo Johnson. However, he could not get involved directly. The New York families would not like it if Chicago was operating on their turf, not without permission. Benny knew he would have to get the hit sanctioned and he knew just who to turn to for that, Peter Lucas.

He thought something was going on between the Della Russo family and the Roccis. He called Peter Lucas, "Hello, Peter, this is your old friend, Benny B. How are you doing?"

"I'm getting by," he answered disinterested. *This guy comes crawling out of the woodwork like a roach when the lights go out. What's he after now?* "What a pleasure to hear your voice. How are you?"

"Like yourself, trying to make an honest living in this world. You know how it goes, my son is starting college in the fall, the girls are getting big. All the things that would make a father proud." Benny let's his last words eat into Peter Lucas' heart before continuing, "Aunt Maria, you know, the one who married the Irish, will celebrate their eightieth anniversary next weekend. I hear it's going to be a gala affair."

"That is wonderful. It's good to see a family showing respect like that. Give them my best." Peter hung up the phone and called one of his capos into his office. "Benny B wants to have a meeting this weekend at the Shamrock Inn. Find out who we can trust in Florida and get some eyes on the place. I'm not sure what he's up to and I don't want to be surprised by a prick like him."

PETER LUCAS MET Benny and his capo in the hotel bar. Lucas had two men in the place already and entered with two more. Benny was sipping a fruity drink in a tee-shirt and knee-length shorts. Deck shoes completed his outfit. His capo was a bit more covered with a loose-fitting polo shirt that easily concealed a gun behind his back and long pants to cover the ankle holster.

Benny waited for Lucas to get within earshot and stood to greet him. "Why all the heavy equipment? This is a friendly get-together."

"Cut the crap, Benny. You Chicago boys don't like us New Yorkers and I don't care much for you either," Lucas wasted no time in getting the meeting started, "you didn't bring me down here to work on my tan. What do you want? What could not have been discussed over the phone?"

"It's not what I want to tell you," Benny sat back down, the fake smile gone from his face, "this is something you have to see for yourself. I'm sure you know who that young man in the light blue polo and gray slacks is over there." Benny turned his head and looked across the hotel lobby.

Peter turned to look in the direction Benny indicated. He sat next to Benny and spoke in a conspiratorial tone, "Yeah, I know who he is, Christopher Carmine. He took over the Rocci's cocaine business a few years ago, Brunello. What's the big deal? What's it to you?"

"I've been interested in the Rocci's coke business for a while. A little friendly competition, you know. When you had your troubles with Della Russo, I was quite happy to see Rocci lose his hold on the business down south." Benny took a sip. "Hey, let me order you one of these. Dukes, go get a couple of whatever these are called from the bar."

"Just say what's on your mind, Benny."

"It's no problem," Benny waves his hand and Aldo headed for the bar. "When all that unfortunate… well, back then I was kind of surprised to hear young Christopher went to Colombia to find Morris Johnson. I mean, what's it to him? I was quite pleased he was out of my way."

"Are you sure he was looking for Morris? How do you know?" Peter Lucas started to take a harder look at Christopher who sat in a palm straw chair reading the paper. The racing report from the looks of it. Peter also sensed he was waiting on someone.

"My people told me Morris disappeared in the jungle. A tragic accident," Benny laughed. "It wasn't too long after that Christopher showed up questioning everyone. I thought they would have killed him quick, but it seems like he had the backing and authority of Nicky Nails Rocci. So, I ask myself, and now I'm asking you, why would Nicky be backing someone he just surrendered his business to?"

"I'm sorry we don't share the intimate workings of our business with you in Chicago," Lucas says with an oozing venomous slur to his words, "but to ease any concerns you might hold, Dom ordered Christopher, and a couple of his other soldiers, to be embedded with the Roccis to watch over the transition of the

Colombian business. I'm sure he went looking for Morris to let him know he was the new boss."

"Oh, yeah, I'm sure that is all there is to it. And I'm guessing that Carmella Della Russo's marriage to Christopher Carmine two years later was just a happy coincidence." As if on cue, Carmella stepped off the elevator and Christopher greets her with a kiss. "It's no wonder Nicky took you to the cleaners. I'm amazed he left you alive. But I guess you are no threat to him."

Lucas' eyes narrowed and his men slowly moved their hands towards their weapons. He smiled and everyone relaxed. Benny was alone as far as he could tell, but he wanted to hear more, despite the insults he was casting in his direction. "As I said, it was Dominick's idea, to which Nicky objected to, and Nicolas who finally forced his son to accept. Those two men are honorable and respected, I don't believe they would involve themselves in this sort of deception. And as for the marriage, I understand those two knew each other a long time. Why wouldn't there be something between them? You come down here to stir up trouble for us in New York, I have to question, what are you getting out of it?"

"Actually," Benny sensed the tension surrounding him and pulled back a little. He also hadn't expected Lucas to be so heavily guarded. And although he had a couple of guys at the ready, they were stationed outside. "I know Nicolas and Dominick are stand-up guys, still part of the old way of doing business. But Nicky Nails is a crocodile of a human being; always smiling and strikes without warning. I wouldn't put it past him to orchestrate such a plan. And I'm willing to say that Little Miss Innocent was in on it too."

"Follow them," Lucas ordered one of the two men standing behind him.

"No need to," Benny interceded, "they are going down the block for breakfast. They will be back in an hour."

"GO!"

The man hurries to the hotel door and casually walks out into the tourist traffic.

"I'm telling you; they will be back in an hour. They live here."

Aldo returns with a tray of pink ice-cold drinks. He puts them on a coffee table in front of Benny Brunello and steps back behind his boss.

"These things are really good," Benny picks one up but doesn't drink. "That was then, this is what is going on now. Why you are here today? Christopher is going to Colombia in a day or two, it's his regular trip to oversee the business. When he goes, she will head to New York, to hop on Nicky Nails' dick. You will see, they are a regular item around Central Park." Benny drinks down the icy liquor.

"Benny Brunello!" Peter Lucas is livid. "You call me down here for some soap opera bullshit! What do I care who Nicky Nails is nailing?"

"Damn man, are you blind?" Benny is pissed, "the whole coke business was a setup from the start. Della Russo bought it from Nicky. And you know what the price was, don't you?"

"I am going to kill Dominick," Lucas said so low Benny barely heard a word. Then he said much louder, "then, I'm going to kill that bitch and her husband, and finally, I am going to burn fucking Nicky and his father alive."

"Good idea," Benny laughed sickly, "but here's the thing. Christopher, lover boy over there, doesn't know a thing. Nicky gave him the job of running the Miami Cane Company, and he does, not knowing why, or what he's giving up for the job. If you want to get to Nails, he's the way. We flip him and none of them will see it coming."

BACK IN NEW YORK by the middle of the week, Lucas calls Benny to confirm that Carmella has arrived in New York as he predicted and tells him that his men will start following her. If she meets with Nicky, the hit is sanctioned. Benny agrees to provide the triggerman to give Lucas deniability. Although Lucas wants to take credit for the hit, he agrees so that the information is not leaked in New York. Benny also has a man close to Christopher to flip him. They agree Nicky Nails will not live out the year.

With Nicky out of the way, Benny can go after Morris Johnson next. Those two had cost him billions in oil down in Venezuela. He would get his revenge and perhaps take over Morris' government arms contract. It will be difficult getting information on Morris' operation. He did not run it like a mob family. His business is spread around, different people run parts of the organization and have no knowledge or contact with others. They only know their job and it all funnels sooner or later back to Morris. At some levels they don't even know Morris exists.

From what Benny learned, Morris lives in the shadows, but at the center of a massive spiderweb of legitimate and illegal businesses. He can't even find where Morris calls home. After rescuing his daughter, Morris dropped off the face of the earth again. Benny has no idea how to get to Morris, but he is determined to find him and kill him. Once Nicky is out of the picture, he is sure Morris will surface. If for no other reasons than his friend's funeral and to avenge his death.

CHRISTOPHER CARMINE RETURNED to the Shamrock Inn two weeks later. He's waiting for his wife in his usual chair, going over the racing forms, and thinking about what he should have for breakfast when a man of medium height and heavy built drops a three by five-inch white card in his lap as he passes by.

"Excuse me, sir," Chris holds the card up to the guy, "you dropped this."

"No, it's for you." He is standing slightly behind Chris.

Chris turns the card over… his face contorts in shock then anger. He starts to get out of the chair shouting, "what the fuck is this?"

The man forces Chris back down into the plush chair with one hand on his shoulder. "It's what it looks like. If you have other questions you'd like answered, the room number is on the back." The man slides his hand from Chris' shoulder and partially exposes the butt of a gun in his waistband. He continues out of the hotel lobby.

Christopher stares at the picture of his wife, naked on a bed, in a room he doesn't recognize. *This has to be a fake. No way this is Carmella.* He turns the picture over and looks at the room number, *six o six, top floor. This has to be a trap.* He pats his pistol in its shoulder holster and goes to the elevator.

The doors open and Carmella steps out.

He says quickly and shoves the photograph into his jacket pocket. "Wait here, I left something in the apartment. I'll be back in a minute."

"Ok. Don't take too long, I am famished."

He presses the sixth-floor button, then as the doors close, he presses the third-floor button. *Just in case Carmella is watching, I don't want her to know I know about the sixth floor.* When he gets out of the elevator on the top floor, he draws his gun and cocks the trigger back. He quickly heads down the narrow hallway to the rooms at the left end of the hotel. He puts his ear to the door of room six-o-six and listens. Then he uses the barrel of the gun to knock and steps to the side.

When the door opens, he pushes the gun against the man's forehead and backs him down the short hallway, which opens to a large living room suite much like his apartment three floors below. There are four men sitting comfortably around the room. One on a barstool to his left, another on a sofa in front of him and slightly to the left, then two more to his right about three feet apart in nicely upholstered chairs.

"What the hell is this?" Christopher demands.

The man who answered the door slowly backs away from Christopher.

The one sitting on the sofa clears his throat, "AHHEM, this is not a situation that calls for violence. My name is Beniamino Brunello, I don't know if you know who I am, but I was hoping we could have a little talk…"

"Yeah, let's talk about this picture of my wife," Chris rails and turns the gun towards Benny.

The man to his left and one on the right immediately draw their weapons and train them on Christopher.

Benny waves both hands in a downward motion. "Hey, hey, hey, there is no need for all of that. Christopher is clearly upset by what he saw. I would be too. But Chris, I'm not the bad guy here. Can I call you Chris?" He continues without waiting for an answer in a smooth soothing voice. "That picture was a little crass, but I wanted you to know what I am about to tell you is the absolute truth. If you want to hear the story behind the picture put the gun away and have a seat."

Chris knows even if he kills the Chicago Don, he'd never getting out of the room alive. He holsters his weapon but stays standing at the entrance to the hallway. His eyes are fixed on Benny.

"Ok, stand if you like," Benny breaks the few moments of silence between them. "As I was saying, I am not the enemy here. In fact, I want to be your friend, we both have the same enemy…"

"Who?"

"What?"

"Who is this enemy?"

"Wait, you really don't know, do you? She's kept you in the dark the whole time, hasn't she?"

Chris' face reddens, "You'd better stop talking about my wife. I don't care if you are the Don of the Chicago Mafia." Chris' eyes scan the room briefly as if he's measuring his shots. "I suggest you stop bullshitting me and get to the point."

"The point is, Nicky Nails has been… nailing your wife, Carmella." Benny fights back a smile. "I never knew why he liked to be called Nails, now I get it. I'm guessing you don't know anything about Angela Lucas. Her murder, I mean."

"I know she was with Nicky when some hitmen tried to take him out. Lucas claimed it had something to do with Carmella and the Della Russo family, but it didn't."

Benny watches Christopher for a few moments. "I guess you actually believe that. Here is the real truth, and there is no way I can prove it, except showing you more pictures I don't think you really want to see. Nicky and the Della Russos killed Angela Lucas. I believe it was your wife who was in on the plot, not her father, and not you. That is a good thing, my boy, because Peter Lucas wants Nicky's head on a pole. And he will gladly put yours and your pretty little wife's on one too, if he thought you had anything to do with his daughter's death."

Chris shuffled his feet trying to keep his balance.

"Are you sure you don't want to sit down? Look, you are in the clear. I can tell him it was Nicky and Dom Della Russo who came up with the plan. I can tell him Nicky is forcing Carmella to have sex with him to protect her father. He'll buy it. Hell, it might even be true."

"Of course, it is the truth." Chris is desperately trying to hold onto his self-respect and his wife's honor. "She loves me! We are happy together. But there has been something hanging over her lately. He must be blackmailing her. I'll kill that sonofabitch!"

"There you go." Benny finally lets out a laugh, "now you're talking. But we have to plan this out right, and while we are doing that, you can't let anyone know you are onto them. Especially Carmella. If Nicky finds out you know, he will kill Carmella and you. I'm sure of it." Benny thinks for a minute. "Tell me, just out of curiosity, how much money are you pulling in from Colombia?"

"About a billion a year," he states.

"And it's all going to Della Russo, your father-in-law?"

"Yeah, I guess so," Chris answers absentmindedly, "Carmella handles the money. I make sure the product keeps flowing. Oh crap! Carmella is waiting for me to go to breakfast."

"Well, don't keep her waiting any longer. My man here," Benny points to the guy sitting at the bar, "is going to stay here in Florida, so he'll be your contact. I will be in touch. And remember, not a word to anyone. Nicky is a murderous bastard; he wouldn't hesitate to put a bullet in your head. Or your pretty little wife's."

Chris was glad to find Carmella waiting patiently in the lobby for him. She asked if he found what he was looking for. Christopher crumpled the photograph in his pocket and said he must have left it in Colombia. They left arm in arm for their usual place for breakfast.

BENNY CURSED HIS BAD LUCK, or Nicky's uncanny good luck. Every plan he came up with turned sour. First, Nicolas stepped in to take the rap for his son. Then, his sudden death would probably convince the NYDA he was telling the truth. With his confession on tape, they were prepared to close the case. So, he put his star witness out there, a lot sooner than he hoped. He gave Napolitano to the Feds, hoping they took over the case, and were better able to keep him safe until he testified against Nicky.

His other plan to outright kill Nicky blew up when his hitman, an ace sniper, missed the kill shot. He thought it might have been Lucas who got tired of waiting and ordered his man to shoot Sal. It was a good move to get Nicky frozen over his brother's body for a second shot at him. Not how he would have played it, but not a bad strategy.

Unfortunately, both shots being taken at virtually the same time caused his man to miss by an inch. Lucky for Nicky who survived the shooting. However, in what he thought he could only call serendipity, it brought Morris running to the rescue, as he figured it would, and he in turn, tried to kill Pauley Bochi.

Perhaps, Morris thinking his friend wasn't going to make it, spurred him to make a power grab. Wouldn't be the first time a friend became an enemy when the opportunity presented itself; not in this business. Benny counted this as a win because now, he had the number two man in the Rocci family sleeping in his house.

Although Nicky seemed to have more lives than an alley cat, he didn't know the trouble he was in. Pauley had the connections and with a little backing from Benny could take control of the Rocci family. With Nicky and Carmella's treachery exposed and Morris' attempted coup, those two were only a heartbeat away from a very bad ending.

Pauley wouldn't want to kill his old boss' son, but he would have no problem ordering his death. Benny had no problem; he would willingly put a bullet in Morris' head if he had the chance. He worked a plan to serve up Morris' head for target practice. In doing so, it would prove Morris Johnson was still very much alive. Though, he was sure the government knew that all along. He was protected because he moved arms and ammunitions around the world to people they would rather not be connected to. The Government was accustomed to looking the other way when a few deaths occurred if the greater good was being served for them. But in the long run, they were just as willing to let Morris hang to protect themselves.

If all that failed, Nicky and Morris, would find themselves facing a judge and jury for the Banoa's Murders. No matter what the outcome, Beniamino Brunello felt he was finally going to get his long-awaited revenge. And if all went right, he would finally get hold of a New York family and expand his reach in the underworld.

11

NO GOOD DEEDS

Deano Belladini, also known as One Eye Deano, because during a game of chicken with his younger brother was shot in the eye. He has one very blue right eye and one very white left eye. Mostly, you can't tell, because One Eye Deano always wears designer shades. He dresses in Italian silk suits and handstitched leather loafers. One Eye Deano, at age thirty-seven, is the top capo of the Brunello family. A made man at eighteen, he has buried more bodies than any undertaker in Chicago. He is a hardened criminal, but as Beniamino Brunello knows, over time even the strongest steel cracks.

The day One Eye Deano was handed over to Nicky Nails, Benny considered him a casualty of war. He went through great lengths to change which capos ran what businesses. He altered delivery schedules, money drop locations, stash houses for cash, drugs, guns, people. Benny reorganized from top to bottom to thwart what he saw as an imminent attack from Nicky Nails Rocci.

Nicky, however, was after only one piece of information that Deano Belladini might be holding. He wanted to know how deep into his organization Benny had penetrated. Deano was held in a meat locker on the west side of Manhattan. Gone were his fancy clothes and shoes. He hung from a pair of meat hooks inserted into his armpits. His jailer, Lenny, left him with his boxers and sunglass, because that white left eye freaked him out, and he was a gentleman and Deano did not need to have his private parts hanging out to get done what he needed to do.

Lenny started on him the first day. He and four other meat packers beat him out of his fine clothes, kicking, punching, and clubbing with rubber riot batons. After One Eye regained consciousness, Lenny and the boys stuck the meat hooks in him and hung him in the special freezer in the basement of the warehouse. Special because it was hidden behind a brick wall accessible through a narrow alley between the two warehouses. And special because it was set not to freeze, the interior temperature held at a constant thirty-eight degrees.

One Eye's shivering caused him to sink deeper on the meat hooks until he could feel their sharp points against his shoulder bones. He passed out and awoke to intense pain. Breathing was a task that took concentration and deliberate effort. He was kept mostly in total darkness, not knowing if he was dreaming or awake. And exposed to blinding lights which he began to crave for the heat it gave through the agony. His tormentor blasted ear-splitting sirens in the metal container, adding to his delirium. They sprayed him with hot and cold water shocking his body and mind. He heard voices, questioning him about Brunello, Nicky Nails, and Christopher Carmine.

The beatings came irregularly, mostly the rubber batons between his legs. He howled and screamed before passing out. He was awakened by clubbing to his ribs and buttocks. They grabbed his legs and beat the soles of his feet to the point of broken bones. His ordeal continued for five days. He told them everything he knew about Brunello and who contacted Christopher. What information they gave him about Nicky and his wife. And before it was over, who the hitman was from Chicago. Just to be on the safe side, Nicky had One Eye Deano record some statements they could use to prove he was still alive. They even beat his coded 'all is well' phrase out of him, "I'm looking forward to time at the beach house," if asked, "do you miss Chicago?"

One Eye Deano Belladini was taken from the meat freezer and sent to Lazarus Lamar, the Undertaker. Morris had used his funeral services for years to dispose of bodies quietly. Lazarus would take the body and bury it in a grave an hour or two before another legitimate burial was to take place. Or add the person into the crematorium with other bodies. As long as there was another legal funeral taking place there was always room for one more. Deano was gagged, put in a coffin with a ninety-four-year-old great-grandmother, and burned alive. He would spend eternity on the mantel of the O'Connolly family home in New Jersey.

CARMELLA WAS CALLED to Long Island once more. Nicky met with her alone this time. She saw the look in his eyes and knew she would be put to the test.

"What have you decided? Am I a Deadman?"

"Not hardly," Nicky poured her a drink of wine, "here, tell me what you think? It's from my family vineyard."

Carmella sips it and makes a face. "I'd never guess poison was your choice of weapon. This is God awful."

"There it is," Nicky claps his hands once, "that is what I need. The truth no matter how painful it might be!"

"You didn't call me here for a wine tasting. And you already know the truth. Please, just come out with it. Tell me what you want me to do."

Nicky hands her an envelope. He takes the wine glass from her hand and throws it against the wall. "You wanted to be a boss. You wanted to run a crew. You got all those things, but you never paid the price. You never got blood on your hands, did you?"

"What are you talking about?" She fired back, "you had me kill Angela Lucas to get my crew. And how many others in my own family, for me to become a capo?"

"You had them killed, you didn't kill them," Nicky whispered. "There's a difference, a big difference. If you had killed one person, you would have known the price my father paid for killing my brother. Why did you pick the graveyard?"

"It wasn't because of you; it was the only place he was accessible. It had to be a clean kill; your father was very specific about that." Carmella went on the offensive. She wasn't sure if Nicky still wanted her dead. "I'm not a killer, I'm a business-woman. I ran my father's business, and now I'm running yours. You are doing good with me looking after the financial ends. Things don't have to change. We won't see each other anymore, we can't, I think you know that. But business-wise we can get back to what was working."

"I let you into this family, but I didn't make you take a blood oath," Nicky looked at her coldly, emotionless, "that was a mistake, my mistake. You wanted to be one of the boys, and I... I didn't see you that way. Now, I do. In the envelope is a list of people you must kill. They are a threat to this family. Your oath is loyalty to this family. Protection of the family. Your life for the family. Open it."

Carmella reads the list and folds it back up. "What is this?"

"What does it look like? It's a hit list of all your friends," Nicky sneers.

"This is some kind of twisted... I'm not doing it. I told you

I'm not a killer," she complains, "and I don't know anyone on this list. Sorry, you are barking up the wrong tree. You can kill me if you want. But I'm not doing it."

Nicky is at her throat in an instant. He has her pinned against the wall; she struggles for air. "I'm not going to kill you and you are going to do this. Kill the first four people on the list. This is the life you wanted. This is what it means to be a mobster, a mafioso. I am sending Morris with you; you are going to need his help, especially with number three. Morris will train you, turn you into a killer, that is his specialty."

"The word is you were told to kill your friend Morris to get your bones. You didn't do it. So why should I do this?"

"Because Morris and I had already planned on killing Angelo Lucerella. What were your plans?" Nicky points to the door.

Carmella sheepishly walks toward it while rubbing her neck. As her hand touches the doorknob he says,

"Morris will contact you, don't disappoint me."

TEN MINUTES after Carmella had gone, I enter the office from the back room. I was studying the tapes of Nicky's and her exchange. "I don't believe she knows any of the names on the list. Not their actual names, their street names, or the phony ones meant to trip her up. I didn't get any reactions from her."

"You think she is innocent! I'll bet you she's not." Nicky fumes and pours himself a drink. He dumps a mountain of coke on the desk and inhales deeply. "What makes you think she's innocent!"

"I did not say she is," I sit across from him and sweep a line of cocaine towards me with my fingers. I take a healthy snort and lick my fingers. The freeze is instant. "I said, she doesn't know any of the names on the list. It could be she met them under a different name, or she never met them at all. Could be she was not in on the planning of the hit. And lastly, she could be innocent."

Nicky slams his fist on the desk and cocaine goes flying.

"You really need to control yourself. You damn near broke her neck."

After spending days watching Nicolas' tapes, I realized how invaluable videos could be. People revealed things that go right past us in the blink of an eye, but when you get to rewind, play those moments again, slow them down, they reveal truth that otherwise would be lost. I finally understood why instant replay became such a big thing for the NFL. I put four cameras in the office so not to miss a single moment, and to view them from every angle. "As they say in the NFL, tapes don't lie, there wasn't a twitch, a blink, no telltale sign she was lying. She didn't know any of those names, Nicky. And if she was lying, I wouldn't suggest you play poker with her."

"So, we just let her walk?"

"I didn't say that either. We stick to your plan, see if she slips up when she comes face to face, or more likely, if they know her. I'm just not so sure about your end move. If she's not part of it..."

"The end stays the same."

I didn't need a video tape to see that Nicky was dead set on his plan, all of it. I checked my watch; the machines were set to erase the tapes in fifteen minutes. A security feature I added thanks to Nixon. "If you want to watch the tape..."

"No, I've seen all I need to see. Just get this thing done."

TUESDAY, February 14th, 1989, 05:30. St. Valentine's Day, the sun has not yet risen, a long line of vehicles approaches the Long Island mansion with their lights off. The lead automobile is an armored black assault truck with ten-inch steel rolled bars covering the front. It picks up speed a quarter mile from the front gate leaving the two dozen cars lagging. It's tires squeal as it makes the sharp right turn and rams into the black wrought iron gate. The explosive sound knocked the sleeping guards in the gate house to the floor. One gate is thrown across the driveway and is dragged underneath the tank as it plows through the hedge towards the mansion. The other side of the gate takes out the brick column support and folds in half, slicing the roof off the guardhouse.

Red and white, blue and white, amber lights start flashing as the stream of cars now race toward the house. The last three cars stop and form a barricade across the driveway at the gate. A dozen agents in black ski masks and black army fatigues pour out of the cars and quickly apprehend the three guards.

The tank frees itself from the gate as it rolls down a hill going straight towards the main entrance. The cars split into three columns and start to surround the property. Twenty black outfitted commandoes spring from the tank's rear and side doors. Four of them are carrying a massive battering ram. They run up the front steps and without stopping swing it forward into the door. There is a thunderous retort as the huge wooden door rejects the men and their weapon. Some other commandoes in black with white FBI on their chest and back take positions behind their cars, Uzis trained on the windows and doors.

The four agents at the front door reposition themselves and strike the door again. Then again, and again, the door reverberates and but does not yield. One of the agents in front of the house stands up and circles his hand above his head. Four agents on either side of the house fire teargas canisters at the first-floor windows. They too bounce off and start smoking on the grass around the mansion. A white cloud drifts through the white security floodlights around the top house as the agents don their gasmasks.

The porch light comes on. It is a soft yellow moon-like globe. The four agents with their battering ram back down the six steps. Nicky Nails Rocci opens the door and looks for damage. The agents freeze with guns pointed at the figure in a white terrycloth bathrobe and black and red checkerboard slippers.

Nicky looks over the scene for a moment and puts his arm to his face to block the vapors wafting through the air. "Are you guys coming in or what?" he asks and walks back inside.

The agent who ordered the teargas attack holsters his weapon and walks towards the door. Six of his men follow still holding their guns in the ready position. The dozens of other agents remain outside watching for anybody who may try to escape. No one does.

"I hope you guys brought your checkbook," Nicky says as the agents reach the main foyer. "Somebody is going to pay for my gate."

The head agent pulls out a thick fold of papers from inside his bulletproof vest. He holds them up to Nicky who stares at him. "I'm Jason Parsons, FBI, Mr. Nicolas Rocci, you are under arrest for the murders of Joseph Banoa, Detective Sean Fitzpatrick, and Detective Angelo Mancotti."

Rosalina comes down the stairs in a full-length floral silk robe and furry bunny slippers, "you must be mistaken. My husband hasn't left the house in weeks."

"Unfortunately for your husband, these men have been dead for years," says Agent Parsons with a self-satisfying smile.

A sixty-year-old man enters the foyer from a back bedroom and holds out his hand for the papers.

Parsons shoots him a suspicious look.

Nicky smiles, "he's my lawyer."

"Your attorney lives with you?" questions Parsons.

"Of course not," Nicky quips, "he's here for the party later."

"Party?"

"Today is St. Valentine's Day," Nicky laughs, "we always celebrate the St. Valentine's Day Massacre. Don't You?"

"This warrant is for your arrest; you have to go with them. But I'll have you out in time for bobbing for bullets," Durant jests.

"I'm going with you," Rosalina demands.

"It doesn't work like that Cherry Bomb," Nicky tells her and holds out his hands for handcuffs.

Agent Parsons looks at her kindly. "She can come along if she likes, we will wait here while you three go get dressed."

"Three?" asks Durant. "I'm going back to bed. It will be a few hours before court begins. Nicky, I'll see you in the Federal building. This warrant is executed out of District One Federal Court. Mrs. Rocci, I strongly suggest you wait and ride with me."

"Yes, Honey, listen to old Robbie. I don't want you sitting around some cold office building all day. I'll be fine. With all these feds around, what could happen." Nicky kisses her forehead and sends her upstairs. "Agent Parsons, have a seat. It may take me a while to find the right outfit. I want to look good for my first mugshot. You do know you could have called; I would have saved you the trip out here. And the state's money for my gate."

"I'm not worried about that," Parson confesses, "the law enforcement is indemnified against damage claims when executing arrest warrants."

"Is that so? That does not seem fair." Nicky goes back upstairs and back to bed. It's midmorning when he comes down again, dressed in a blue suit and tie. All the cars are gone, except for Agent Parson's.

He has his driver and another agent with him. "You must have a lot of suits if it took you five hours to pick out that one."

"Did you have breakfast? I hope the boys gave you something to eat while you waited."

"We had coffee and cannoli. Thanks."

"Ah, that's what I smell. Vincent must be here. I thought it was still the teargas. He a great pastry chef but makes the worst coffee. I'll just grab a few for the road."

"If you don't mind, we would like to get back to the city. The sooner we can get you into booking the sooner you can get back to your *party?*"

"What's the hurry?" Nicky asks. "Those guys have been dead nearly two decades, they ain't going anywhere. I'll eat in your car or you can ride in mine, if you are fussy about that sort of thing."

"You can eat in the car. I'll just have to put the cuffs on you when we get to the Federal Building."

CARMELLA WALKS into the bar wearing a short black leather jacket and a tight black leather skirt as I instructed. The other girls in the bar look her over with distain. One woman, a very large black woman, who looks like she has two rows of breasts under her halter blocks her path.

"Step aside, bitch, or I'm gonna give you another opening you can charge for."

She looks at Carmella hand in her jacket pocket and laughs,

"you ain't packing nothing but a snack, little sister. He's waiting for you around the back by the pool tables."

Carmella slides into the booth across for me, "I guess you think this is funny and want to humiliate me as well."

"Not at all," I tell her. "Lucas' man, The Jackrabbit, likes only one type of girl. The trashy punk rock type. You're not wearing the stockings, I told you black stockings with holes in them."

"Don't get bent, I got them in my pocket. I didn't want to wear them in the street. You heard about Nicky?"

"Yeah, he was arrested and released under his own cognizance," I state, then add, "and half a million-dollar bond. I loved it when he paid it in cash."

Carmella's eyes widened. "You were there? In the court-room? Aren't you wanted? I mean, like on the FBI most-wanted list or something?"

"Yes. That one and a couple of others," I chuckle, "some terrorist no-fly list, but they don't have a picture of me. Well, I don't think they do. Anyway, I wouldn't have missed that for anything. But that's neither here nor there, you have a job to do, and if you pay attention and follow my instructions, Mr. Jackrabbit won't kill you."

I detail the plan for her as she slips on the thigh high stock-ings. She repeats it back to me three times before we leave the bar and head downtown to the Village. It's Saturday night, and the Village is hot with punk rockers. We are going to troll the bars until he notices us. Instead of stalking him, we let him stalk us.

"How did he get the name Jackrabbit?" Carmella wanted to know.

"He's lanky and hopped up on speed most of the time," I tell her. "He speaks with a horrible Cockney accent but has never been anywhere near England. He's from New Jersey, adopted the whole British shit when punk rock took off. But if you call him out on it, he'll stab you to death. Remember, he's a speed freak, very unpredictable."

I spot him at Max's and immediately go to work. I throw my arm around Carmella's shoulder and kiss her ear. We sit at a table off to the side of the stage, just inside the spotlight. Carmella straddles me and starts kissing my neck. I slide my hand up her back and bury my face between her breasts. She pulls my hands down, away from her bra snap.

The band takes a break and I invite them to the table for beers and a snort. They are a local three-man band, with little talent. Carmella starts rubbing the singer's chest then goes for a full tongue battle. When she finishes, I pull her back onto one of my legs and shove my tongue down her throat. I reach inside her leather jacket under her blouse and grab a handful of breast. She lets me get a good feel before pulling my hand away.

She stands over me, running her hands through my short afro and the drummer runs his hand up the back of her leg and under her skirt. She holds his hand on her ass for a moment before turning away and landing on my lap again. I yell over the din, "you guys should meet up with us over at Michael's. I've got to meet a guy there in a few. Going to hit him with a speedball tonight. You wanna get blasted, baby?"

"What's your name again?" she asks.

"Me? I'm the Wizard. I make the magic happen."

That got his attention. I see him leave the club after us. Jackrabbit can't resist a loose woman and fast drugs. Michael's is a bar two blocks away. As we walk down the street, I keep trying to put my hands up Carmella skirt. She playfully pulls it away from her ass. I spin her around and pin her against a car. Jackrabbit is a few feet behind us. I pull out a little plastic bag of smaller white glassine envelopes. "Hey, if you want some of this you better be nice to me."

"Ok, baby, but not here in the street. Wait until we get to the bar," she coos as Jackrabbit passes, "I'll treat you real good."

"I know your game; you get high then try to sneak out on a guy. I want a little feel now. See if you are worth it," I coerce her.

Jackrabbit stops. "Hey, this bloody bugger trying to give you the business?"

"Mind your own fucking business, cracker," I half turn to face him, "this ain't jolly ol' England. You'll get your ass kicked here."

Jackrabbit puts up his hands in surrender. "I don't want a roil with you, Mate." Then he takes a swing.

I lean forward for him to make contact. I drop the plastic bag and stumble back.

He grabs Carmella's hand, "come on, doll."

"Wait!" She pulls away and retrieves the bag of drug. "Now, let's go."

She runs down the block and turns the corner. She pulls him into the first alley they come to, "wait, I can't run anymore. I don't think he's coming after us. Not after the way you clocked him. My knight in shining armor."

"Yeah, that's me, like fucking Sir Lancelot."

"No, you are King Arthur, and I'm your Guinevere," she leans against the alley wall and waves the baggie before him. "Now, you'll get the damsel and the treasure." Carmella opens her jacket and invites him in.

Jackrabbit grabs the bag and starts kissing her neck while one hand frantically struggles with his belt. Finally, his pants drop around his ankles. He starts pulling on her skirt but refuses to let go of the dope. He is scratching her waist trying to get his hand inside the waistband.

She pulls a stiletto from her jacket pocket and holds it for a moment above his back. She plunges the blade between his neck and shoulder, as she was told. She pulls it up quickly. Jackrabbit is still trying to get her skirt off. She stabs him again and a third time.

His left shoulder is full of blood, his denim jacket drenched red. Jackrabbit stumbled back, tripping on his pants at his feet. He lands hard against the alley wall. Bewilderment and shock freeze his face. He says nothing, just stares at her as life drains from his body.

She stands there with the knife in her hand, looking as shocked as he does.

"Are you going to wait for the police to pass by or would you like to get out of here?" I ask standing outside the alley. She does not answer or move. "HEY! It's done. Let's go."

I take the knife from her with a washcloth I had in my pocket and drop it in the plastic bag with the fake drugs. I give her another washcloth to wipe her hands off and tell her to leave it in the alley. We walk quickly to the corner, get in my car, and drive away.

After we hit the highway she starts to come back to life. "Why did you take the knife? I thought it was customary to leave the weapon at the scene."

"It is, for guns. This is Nicky's favorite knife; he wants it back."

"So he can use it against me if I turn on him. That's the way it works, isn't it?"

"You're the Italiano, not me." I take her hand. "I'm just the lookout. I'm here to make sure you get the job done and not get killed. He was very specific about you not getting killed. Anyway, the first one is over. The next one will be easier."

"Why doesn't he just let you do it?" She was still distraught.

"I don't know," I say honestly, but I was lying, "he didn't tell me. But you did fine, you're a natural born killer." I laugh, she does not. *Well, she passed the second test. Not that Jackrabbit made much of a proving ground for her innocence, on a good day he may not have recognized his own mother. And he was probably so jacked up on speed Carmella could have been his mother and it would not have turned out differently.* "I will plan something simple for the next guy. He's one of Benny's men, so it will have to be much quicker."

"Quicker! How much quicker can it be?"

"A lot," I tell her. "We find a place where he's alone and blow his brains out. It doesn't get much quicker than that." I look over at her. She looks sick. *For someone who has been around the mob all her life, she doesn't look like she belongs in it.* "Maybe we'll blow him up. Much cleaner, no blood on your hands. That's not what Nicky wants, but it will be ok. I'll square it with him."

I drive her back to her hotel in Manhattan and wait until she's asleep. That was not part of the job, but she needed company. We didn't talk about killing anymore that night. She was concerned for Nicky and the trial. She loves him and the thought of him facing the death penalty terrified her. I assured her Nicky had nothing to worry about. And neither did she.

Unfortunately, Giovanni Gugillani was never alone. He was Benny's hitman who shot Nicky. Fearing reprisal, he surrounded himself with six hitmen who worked with him. The only time he was alone was when he was on a job, and then it was impossible to find him. I had my guys stalk him for weeks, to find a vantage point where Carmella could make the hit. Even when you know you are being hunted, a person tends not to notice the mundane, the ordinary, like the cab driver, the postman, or the meter reader. Gugillani and his team passed by a hundred people a week who were more interested in him than he was in them. In the meantime, I sent Carmella back to Florida, she had a business to run.

Gugillani was a hard target, because not only did he surround himself with a squad of killers, but he also had very few interests. He did not drink, so he didn't go to bars. He was married with two young children which meant he spent his time at home. His friends called him Father Guido, after the *Saturday Night Live* character because he had so few vices. I did find one thing he like to do regularly, he played cards with his crew. They played penny ante poker, never going higher than fifty or a hundred bucks, but they held the game at the same Italian social club in Brooklyn on Friday nights. Even though he worked for Benny Brunello, he lived in New York, which was not unusual for a high-priced hitman. They were probably the only ones in the Mafia who did not live where their bosses lived.

Gugillani and his boys met around six in the evening and played until ten. His friends would drink beer and wine, while Giovanni drank ice water. The club was not a mob hangout either, it was a storefront run by a group of World War II veterans, neighborhood guys, a block from his house.

The storefront in Bensonhurst was a great place for the hit. The large crisscrossing streets along Stillwell Avenue made for a perfect getaway route. The block of the social club was a row of two-story homes and stores. At ten o'clock on a winter's night the streets would be deserted.

I went to Miami to prep Carmella. We drove out to the Everglades.

Again, she was extremely nervous.

"Relax," I told her, "I'm not here to kill you. But for this next job you need a little training."

"I thought you wanted to do something quick," she reminded me. "You said just shoot him in the head."

"It's not likely he will ever be alone," I inform her. "he spends all his time with a bunch of killers. Two of them live in his house, so we are going to have to take a hard approach."

"What do you mean a hard approach?"

I stop the car on a dirt road a few miles from the paved highway. We are surrounded by trees and swamp. I get out and walk around to the trunk and she follows. I pull a blanket off a pair of MP5 Submachine guns.

She stares at the black pistol-like gun with its retractable buttstock and banana clip. "I can't shoot that thing."

"Of course not," I agree, "but by the time we leave here you will be able to, without fear." I point to the gun and she gently takes it out of the trunk. I stand behind her, wrap my arms around her, guiding her hands to the proper placement on the fore-end and the pistol grip. The gun was set to single fire. I point her in a safe direction, "go ahead squeeze the trigger."

A shot is fired, and the cartridge ejects. "That wasn't bad. I thought it would fire a lot more bullets though. Isn't this a machine gun?"

"A submachine gun, yes. Here." I flip a lever by the trigger. And she fires three bullets up a tree trunk.

"Oh! That is different." Then she pulls the trigger again and another volley of three tears up the tree.

"You want to lean forward and keep the muzzle pointing slightly down." I take the other gun from the trunk and take a stand beside her. Three bursts of three shots hits the same tree ten yards away. Most of the bullets hit the same area, leaving a noticeable scar. She mimics my stance and squeezes off another group, then another, hitting a tree to the left, leaving her own mark. "Much better," I commend and flip the selector switch on her gun. "Now, let's go full auto."

Carmella squeezes the trigger and bullets rattle from the gun in bursts of flames. They rip into the trees. Wood chips fly as her shots hit one tree then another. She gets control of the gun and centers in on the original tree victim before her clip is empty.

I teach her how to change clip and other functions of the MP5.

"Will I need to do all of this back in Brooklyn?"

"No. It will still be over very quickly."

Rocky is the driver. He pulls up to the club at 9:30. The street is deserted. There is a howling wind outside. I adjust the strap on Carmella's MP5, so it hangs down her side. She has a long puffer coat which hides her weapon. Mine is under a full-length black leather. Before we exit, I give her one last minute instruction, "careful, don't shoot yourself in the foot. Remember on the way out, give me the gun and you take the front seat."

"Why do you have a ski mask, and I don't?"

"Because this black face will get shot at before we can get in the door good," I joke, "and two people with ski masks will also get us shot. But my back will be to the targets, so you'll have plenty of time to get the drop on them."

We step out the back of the car and quickly go for the door. I pull down my ski mask. An old man is leaving as we reach the club. I push him back inside with the barrel of my MP5 pressed against his stomach. Carmella steps in and turns to the right. Five men are sitting at a card table a couple of feet from the door. Two of them look up at her and she freezes. Her gun is still hidden from view. The other men turn to look her over. They don't seem to notice me, or the MP5 I have. They are too busy admiring the pretty young woman with jet black bangs and eye shadow to match. But I know that will not last long. I wait for a few seconds of silence to fill the room then yell, "DO IT!"

The muzzle breaks the confines of her black bubble snaps and starts firing. Wood chips leap from the floor in a line towards the table. A bullet hits the back leg of one chair and its occupant falls in front of the next one. He screams in pain. Then he is hit in the middle of his back and falls quietly the rest of the way to the floor. She hits one of the men that looked at her in the chest as the gun continued to climb out of her coat. The suppressor made the roar of fury in the club unnoticeable to the outside world. Only the flashing lights of the blasts would have drawn attention to the carnage taking place inside, that is if there was anyone on the street outside.

I'm angled between her and three old men on the other side of the club. They are retreating to a corner. I yell over the muffled pops from the gun fire, "SWEEP THEM!"

Carmella grips the submachine gun tighter and swings her torso left and right, never relieving the pressure on her trigger. The card players are knocked to the floor. Blood sprays on Carmella's face and hands. She sweeps them twice more as they lie in front of her amongst broken wooden chairs, bloody playing cards, and an upside-down folding card table with one leg snapped off. She takes care to hit their heads on her final sweep as I told her. No chance of anyone surviving the night. The gun stops on its own having depleted its supply of bullets.

"Have a good night, gentlemen," I say to the old men huddled in the corner, "if I were you, I'd be gone before the police get here. And I wouldn't come back. There will be some people coming here who will ask a lot of questions. And they are not going to like the answers you will give them."

As I pull Carmella by the arm, she unhooks the shoulder strap from her gun and goes for the front seat. I jump in the back as Rocky floors the gas. He makes a wide circle in the intersection and heads down Bay Parkway. "Ok. Give me your coat."

The bubble coat caught all the bloody splatter. I stuff her bloody coat in a plastic garbage bag. I take the guns apart and put them in a backpack. She puts on a long wool coat waiting for her on the front seat. We ditch the car on a quiet side street and take the D train back to the city.

JACKRABBIT'S DEATH could have been attributed to his lifestyle as Peter Lucas points out, "that degenerate drug-addicted freak probably got himself killed taking it up the ass in that alley. But Gugillani and his crew were supposed to be top professionals, straight-up guys. Their murder has to be the work of Nicky Nails!"

Benny Brunello holds the phone away from his ear. "They were straight-up guys. He dropped the ball. But I'm not so sure it was his fault. Gugillani was supposed to kill Rocci, and if he had, we wouldn't be in this mess. But I think someone jumped the gun on this thing."

"Gugillani was not hired to cripple Nicky but kill him. He was your man. When I pay for a killing, I expect a dead man to show up on my doorstep." Lucas lets Benny know he doesn't have much trust for this arrangement either.

"He screwed it up," Benny agrees, but not convinced Lucas isn't the one who took matters into his own hands for the missed opportunity to reap his own revenge, "Nicky Rocci is up and walking around, isn't he? He has my man and there's no telling what information he's getting out of him. Lucky for you I put another plan in motion."

"I hope it doesn't include his man Pauley Bochi. I know he's been hanging around your guys. He's loyal to the Rocci family like an old hound dog. I'm sure Nicky sent him to finish you off."

"That's where you're wrong," Benny brags, "Nicky was still in a coma when Bochi came to Chicago. It was Morris that drove him away. He tried to have him killed. Now, he feeds me information and I'm ready to make a move on his family. I'll put Pauley in charge, and he'll work for me."

"Do you really think he's going to let you kill Nicky? Wake up, man! You are dreaming. They are playing you…"

"No, he's not. I convinced him that Nicky will go to jail for the Banoa murder," Benny says with confidence, "he thinks Nicky will be alright. But get this, Nicky Nails is going to death row. I put that in motion and by the time anyone knows what is happening it will be too late."

Benny doesn't offer any more details and ends the phone call. He calls one of his capos to find Pauley and bring him to the North Shore mansion. He also tells him to find out what went down in Brooklyn, "find out who the shooter was. I want to know if it one of Lucas' soldiers. Keep it quiet! I don't want anything coming back to us. No matter what you find."

PAULEY CANNOT BE FOUND by Brunello's gang. He's in the Chicago FBI office making a deal. They are aware who Paul Bochi works for and are skeptical of why he has decided to turn himself in.

Pauley explains, "I'm out of options, the Roccis want me dead. Brunello is going to kill me over his man, Gugi."

"What do you know about Gugillani?" asks the agent.

"I'm the one who fingered him as the shooter before I left New York. Now that he's dead, Brunello is going to come after me too. But if you give me immunity and WP status, I have something for you that you are gonna love."

"Tell us what you have, and we'll see if it's worth it." The agent is a seasoned professional. He has seen many mobsters trying to escape their brand of justice in recent years. Paul Bochi is a "made man" and a top crime boss in New York. He knows the Mafia is coming apart due to the wars and this is his chance to make a big score.

"What if I told you, Representative Jim Webber didn't commit suicide? What if I told you, Brunello had him murdered and I can prove it? What's that worth?"

"It has to be iron-clad," the agent insists. "No I-know-a-guy-who-knows-a-guy crap. You got me? I need physical, hard, evidence that puts Brunello behind the trigger. You got that, and you got a deal."

"Write up the deal," Pauley commands, "and I give you the guy who pulled the trigger and a recording of Brunello giving the order."

"You, you're the triggerman, but why?"

"The deal?"

"You got it," the agent snaps his fingers and two of his assistants take off running.

"Webber was there when Brunello killed one of the girls. It was a snuff party, you know, where you kill someone for the fun of it. The whole thing went down in Webber's place, and they left him holding the bag. It looked like a setup, if you asked me, but I don't know why Brunello would have done it. It probably was something in the works before I got here. He was afraid the fat little pig would squeal to save his life. Anyhow, he wanted me to prove I work for him now. My initiation into the family."

THE FBI SHOWED up at Beniamino Brunello's barbecue restaurant in downtown Chicago after the lunch rush was over. Benny was in his booth outside the kitchen, counting the take. With a restaurant full of agents and news crew recording his arrest, Benny "The Brute" Brunello hammed it up. He professed his innocence and railed against stereotyping and bias. He put on a real show for the evening news.

Benny was in lock-up waiting for night court to set a bond. He was in a cell alone at the end of the hall. With the number of judges on his payroll, he had no fear of remaining in jail for more than a few hours. He knew Webber, of course, he had put him in Congress. The fact that he killed one of his girls seemed like a setup, but Webber did the right thing. He shot himself before he had to testify. This murder charge was nothing more than an over-zealous agent acting on bad information.

"Is it dinner time already?" asked the police officer at the gate to the holding cells.

"It is for your star guest," replied the redheaded police office.

The graying officer at the gate came out of his office and looked over the food cart. Then he looked over the pretty young female. "I haven't seen you around before, just transferred in?"

"Last week," she smiled. "I thought I'd get a beat or something, but I'm a waitress all over again."

"Hey, don't worry, your time will come. If any of the animals say or do anything let me know. I'll go down there and set them straight."

She pushes the cart down the hall to the cheers, jeers, and lewd remarks of the other inmates in the cells. She smiles back at the gate officer and he returns to his office. He sits back and returns to the sports section of the paper. He yells out, "SHUT THE FUCK UP YOU, FUCKING MONKEYS! I'LL COME DOWN THERE AND BEAT EVERYONE OF YOUSE SENSELESS."

The female officer stops in front of Benny's cell and he looks at her disinterestedly. She glances back up the hall and stand on the other side of the cart blocking the view of the cop. She starts to lift her skirt.

"Ok. Just what I like, dinner and a show," Benny smiles and hops off the bench. "You know, I pay these cops enough, you think they'd let me work up a little appetite. What's your name, Honey?"

"Carmella. Nicky Nails sends his regards." She pulls out a 9mm pistol from under her skirt, the four-inch suppressor glistening from being in her vagina.

Benny's mouth drops open, too stunned to yell for help.

Carmella shoots him once in the mouth and he falls back onto the bench. She shoots him twice more in the chest, pulls the silencer off the gun and reinserts it into her body. It's hot from use and she winces as it slides in; Morris neglected to inform her about that. She tosses the gun into the cell. Benny is sitting on the bench, legs spread apart, and blood running down his chest from where his heart used to beat. She leaves the tray of food in the slot in the bar and pushes the cart back up the hall.

The gate buzzes, she walks out. The graying police officer grabs her arm, "anyone I need to take care of down there?"

"No. But I don't think Mr. Big is hungry anymore."

12

PARADISE AWAITS

The trial of Nicolas Rocci Jr. would have been big news if not for the conviction of another mob boss known as the Teflon Don, or John Gotti. He was sentenced to life in prison the same day Nicky's trial began. New Yorkers quickly became bored with hearing the same old story. Nicky was just another mobster in a long string of hoods being marched before a judge. The prosecutors seeking the death penalty for the murder of the two detectives, and their use of a new scientific process, DNA fingerprinting to get a conviction did not merit front page coverage.

Jeffery Gibbons, the head prosecutor, tried to have the case moved from New York City on the grounds Nicky had too much influence there to get a fair and impartial jury. The judge, Frederick Meyers, denied the motion stating in part, "if Gotti can get convicted here, I don't see why Mr. Rocci can't follow suit. It is the prosecution's case, not the venue, that determines the outcome, Mr. Gibbons."

Jeffery Gibbons was not concerned with picking a jury, he was worried about his star witness. Nathan Napolitano was terrified of having to take the stand. Facing his tormentor was going to take the fortitude of Hercules and he knew Nathan did not have that kind of strength. Returning him to the scene of so much pain and degradation in his life at the hands of the man who caused it would break him. He thought that somewhere away from New York City, his witness would feel less pressure. He pressed the judge further, "the unusual circumstances of the witnesses in this case would make it difficult to elicit a testimony in this atmosphere. The court stellar reputation for justice notwithstanding."

"I appreciate your respect for the court's integrity, but if your witnesses are testifying truthfully, they have nothing to fear within these halls of justice. We will proceed with this trial here, in my court."

Nathan's story was damning, but it wasn't the nail in the coffin the prosecution wished for. Nicky had kidnapped Nathan and subjected him to atrocities, true enough, however, it was Morris who ultimately put the murder weapon in his hand and instructed him to lead the detectives to it. Another problem concerned the district attorney; Nathan was not present at the Bella Rosa when his boss was killed. It could have been anyone who actually did the deed. Gibbons was going for a conspiracy to murder charge, a relatively new statute that removed the burden of proof that Nicky pulled the trigger, and racketeering charges, so he could use the Racketeer Influenced and Corrupt Organizations (RICO) Act, also enacted in 1970 to get his conviction. Under these laws, being part of a plot to murder Banoa made him guilty of the murder itself and exposed him to the full penalties of the law.

His opening statement had Nicolas' confession lay out how the crime was committed, presenting it as a coverup for his son. A father's desperate attempt to save his son from the death sentence he deserved. The seven men and five women heard graphic details about the war between the Banoa and Rocci families; much of the details coming from Nathan's account in Las Vegas.

Robert Durant, Nicky's lawyer, got almost all of it thrown out as unconfirmed hearsay by the judge.

Gibbons angered the court while in his four-hour opening statement he remarked, "so powerful is the Rocci family that even judges are beholden to them for one reason or another."

"Counselors, in my chambers. NOW!" ordered Meyers as he stormed from his courtroom. He waited by the door until the defense attorney, Durant, followed by Gibbons disappeared behind the bench. He slammed the door with a purposeful boom and began his tirade. "Mr. Gibbons, you will apologize to the court for your remark, and I will consider not having you thrown in jail for contempt and disbarred."

"I am trying to present a case, your Honor, against a career criminal who has stopped at nothing to get his way. I have never been before a bench that upheld a challenge to an opening statement." Gibbons was not apologetic.

"Perhaps you shouldn't have had an opening statement so full of conjecture and trying to pass it as evidence. This is your only warning." Meyers was a hard-looking man with a head full of white hair and the stone face characteristic of a judge and appeared as one of the statues in his courtroom, more than a human being. His years on the bench had earned him the reputation of a man empowered with absolute authority and the willingness to use it. He had sent lawyers to jail for contempt and had more than a few disbarred for their conduct in his courtroom.

Gibbons had been a prosecutor for fifteen years, a husky six-two ex-lineman in his colligate days, who still looked like he could sack a quarterback. He returned to the courtroom, squared his shoulders to the jury, and purposely turned his back to Meyers, "I apologize to the court and the jury if I made any statements that could be construed as impugning the honor and reputation of this court." He finished his opening statement with, "inside this courtroom, Nicky Nails Rocci, has no power. The only power here is truth and justice. That power is in your hands, the jury. The evidence will be laid out before you, you will know in your minds and hearts what is true and do the right thing."

On day three, Gibbons had a parade of detectives give accounts of the crime scene at the Bella Rosa. Most of the testimony was factual and unchallenged, the number of shots fired from the spent casings recovered, the angle and the position of the killers, witnesses who called the police when they heard the gun battle taking place, one brave witness who saw two unidentified persons outside the bar firing.

"Detective, what time did the first call come in?"

Detective Nunez, the lead at the time, now retired, responded, "4:32 a.m."

"And what time did the first police officers arrive on scene?" asked Durant in his cross-examination of the witness.

"At 5:48."

"You remember the exact time?"

"I went over the notes of the case before the trial started," responded Nunez with the animosity one would expect towards the defense council.

"Of course, you did, as you should have before giving expert testimony. An hour and eighteen minutes later," remarked Durant looking at the jury, "why the lengthy delay?"

"In about five minutes, we got calls from all over the neighborhood. We went to the places where we had names and addresses. It wasn't until daylight that a call came in about the shooting at the Bella Rosa. The caller said they saw dead bodies inside."

"You didn't investigate, who it was?" Durant walked over to the jury box and looked them over critically. "Mr. Pasqualli's eyewitness account of two men firing shotguns through the window of the Bella Rosa."

"He didn't make that statement until three days later," Det. Nunez disclosed sourly.

"Ah, so not as it happened, or in the hours that followed to the officers on the scene, as the prosecution would have us believe. But days later," Durant said still not making eye contact with the detective but focusing his attention on the jury. "How convenient."

WHEN IT CAME to his father's confession, Nicky wanted to stop Durant from cross-examining George Jarvis, the district attorney who took the statement. "Look, whatever he said does not matter now. It only proves I was not involved. Besides, when the time comes, I guarantee you will blow this case out of the water."

"Your plan may backfire," warned Durant, "the prosecutor is trying to paint you as a vicious killer and the controlling force behind these murders. I'm trying to prove his evidence is tainted and you are the one who is being viciously attacked here. We must discredit every bit of evidence they present."

Durant walked to the witness box and stopped just out of Jarvis' reach. "You originally charged Mr. Rocci Sr. with the murder of Joseph Banoa, and now you are telling the court his confession was a lie?"

"No, sir, not a lie. It was not his own. He got the details of the killing from his son and was going to take the fall for him. To protect him from jail." Jarvis was forceful and defiant.

"How do you know he got the story from his son?" Durant asked innocently.

"Because he knew details that were not known to the public. The number of shots fired by Banoa's killer, how many hit

Joseph Banoa, where the killer was standing, all those things could only be known by the killer."

"Ah, I see," agreed Durant. "And why do you now believe he was not the killer?"

"The main reason," Jarvis said confidently, "because he claimed to have dropped the gun at the scene and left. That gun was not found at the Bella Rosa. We know the gun was used as bait to kill the two detectives working in that precinct."

There was a gasp from the jury box. Durant quickly walked to their side, faced the district attorney again, and said, "Do you know how many people were at that crime scene in just the few early morning hours, before the crime scene photographer showed up?"

"No."

"I do," he looked at the jurors, "more than the number of people sitting here, three times more. A total of thirty-eight detectives and uniformed officers responded to the scene before the CSI team arrived. Every one of them, plus the dozen or so crime scene investigators, would have knowledge of the details of Banoa's killing. Not to mention the obvious fact that there was an hour and eighteen-minute gap between the time Joseph Banoa was brutally gunned down and the first police officer arrived. Anyone could have removed the murder weapon with the intent of framing my client." He nodded to the jurors, moved back to his table, and pulled a paper from his briefcase. "And since Joseph Banoa's murder, countless reports have been filed with the details of his death. I have one such report here, I got it from a reporter."

The jurors again gasped at the information, causing the judge to rap his gavel once. "I'd like to see that report."

"Of course, your honor, I was about to enter it in as evidence for the defense."

"He also didn't know the shooter was wounded in the attack," Jarvis blurts out. "Is that in your report?"

The judge pounds his gavel multiple times.

"No. No. Your Honor, let him continue," Durant says handing the report to the judge.

"There were a few drops of blood leading away from where the shooter must have been standing, out of the window where the two other men had fired. Nicolas Rocci Sr. never mentioned being wounded in any way. I'm sure that's something you wouldn't forget, or leave out, if he was the actual shooter."

"Oh, that is in here. Page two, your Honor," Durant said turning back to the jury box. "Did the blood type match his? You had a full medical evaluation done; you must have matched his blood type."

"We did. And yes, it is the same type, O negative," he admitted, "but that's a common type."

"But not a direct DNA match, I take it."

"No. And that was my next reason for dismissing Rocci Senior as the shooter."

"Then, by your reasoning, it must have matched Nicolas Junior's here?"

"No. Not an exact match…"

"So, it could have been anybody's blood. Even someone who survived the shooting with only a superficial wound and left with the murder weapon. Say… one of Banoa's men. In fact, your evidence does not prove the Roccis had anything to do with Banoa's murder. Did your test also reveal Nicolas Rocci Sr. had shown the onset of dementia? No further questions."

Durant sits next to Nicky and whispers in his ear, "That's why you challenge every questionable piece of evidence. Look at them, the jurors are wondering, and the prosecution is failing. And in this era of Mafia frenzy, you are looking like a victim of circumstance."

"Yeah, but you made my father look like an old fool," whispered Nicky. The look in his eyes displayed how mad he was at Durant.

"It is better that he looks like an old fool than you like a cold-blooded killer. Wouldn't you agree? And that is my job, you know."

THE NEXT WITNESS for the prosecution was the ballistic expert who verified the gun that killed Joseph Banoa and later was used as bait in the deathtrap for the two detectives were one in the same. Alex Byrne was a large Irish man with a rough patchy beard and mixed gray reddish hair. He began his testimony, "I have been on the police force for thirty-four years. I was the head of the forensic investigative unit at the time of the Banoa murder and aided in the investigation of Detectives Fitzpatrick and Mancotti. Both very fine men and good friends. I did the test on the .22 revolver recovered at the site of the detectives' death and the results were one hundred percent a match. We compared a test round fired from the weapon with one found undamaged in the wall at the scene. An Absolute match."

"Thank you, Det. Byrne, no further question," concluded Gibbons with a confident look to the jurists.

Durant made his way to the witness stand. He looked over the prosecution's photo and handed one to Det. Byrne. "Is this the weapon?"

"Yes."

"Can you tell the court any else about what your test revealed?"

"What do you mean? What would you like me to tell them? The ballistic were a match, there were three shots fired at the Bella Rosa and three spent shells in the gun."

An audible gasp came from the jury box and Durant turned

to them, "How about the grip of the gun? What can you tell the court about that?"

"There was some charring, and one side was shattered from the explosion that killed the two detectives."

Another louder gasp. Durant ignored the jury, "So, this gun was in an explosion but still functioned properly?"

"Yes, the explosive device must have been underneath or at least a distance away from the weapon. We found it in the yard near where the toolshed had stood. Near the body of the Det. Fitzpatrick."

"What else can you tell us about the weapon?" asked Durant before the jury could react to Byrne statement. "Did you find fingerprints on the weapon?"

"Yes."

"Where? Please tell the court."

"There was a set of prints on the grip, the side that was not destroyed by the blast. And partial prints on the bullets and spent shell castings."

"So, prints on the exterior of the .22 revolver and the bullets in the revolver. Where the prints from the same person?"

"We did not know at the time," Byrne said hesitantly.

"But you know now, don't you?"

"Yes. They are from one person." Byrne flatly admitted.

"So, the person who loaded the gun, handled the gun, and fired the gun killing Joseph Banoa is the same person." Durant said confidently.

"Objection, your Honor," Gibbons flew from his seat with hand in the air, "calling for a conclusion from the witness based on conjecture not evidentiary facts."

"Sustained."

"Ok. Here a question based on evidence," Durant looked at the jury again. "Does the fingerprint on the weapon match my client, Nicolas Rocci Jr."

"No." Byrne voice was not much more than a whisper, but still audible in the dead silence of the courtroom.

"So, the defendant did not handle the gun, did not load the gun, but you do know who did." Durant turned back to the detective in the witness stand and in a booming voice asked, "Who's fingerprint did you find on the murder weapon?"

"Nathan Napolitano."

DAY THREE ENDED BADLY for the prosecution, Gibbons was sure of it, and day four started off worst in the judge's chamber. "Your Honor, I motion to have my next witness, Nathan Napolitano's testimony be given via a video link from an undisclosed location."

"I object, your Honor," Durant immediately interjected.

"On what grounds?" demanded Gibbons, "you and your client will have access to cross examine…"

"Ah, I object on the grounds that such proceedings will unduly influence the jury, your Honor."

"Your Honor, my witness is terrified of facing this man," pleaded Gibbons, "you read his statement. You know the horrors his client put him through."

"ALLEGEDLY," argued Durant. "Allegedly, your honor. And since my client is not being charged with these crimes against Nathan Napolitano, and furthermore, the entirety of these murder charges rest on his testimony against Mr. Rocci, he deserves the right to face his accuser."

"Your Honor, the witness dreads his life is in mortal danger. He has been in witness protection for months, held under the tightest of security. We kept his identity secret until the beginning of the trial as the only way of safely bringing him to testify. He had not been alone for a minute since bravely coming forward with his story, to force him to step out into an open courtroom…"

"Your Honor, where else can he be safer than in your courtroom?"

Judge Meyers smiled at the toadyism from Durant, "motion denied."

"I CAN'T BELIEVE THIS," Gibbons rails and kicks the chair he was just in across the room.

"Careful counselor, you've been warned once," the judge told him.

"At least clear the courtroom!"

"I object, your Honor. Again, that will unduly prejudice the jury."

"I agree," said Judge Meyers, "you better go prepare your witness to take the stand, counselor."

Gibbons stormed out of the judge's chambers through the back door. He went down a hallway then an elevator which took him to the basement. When the doors opened, two FBI agents in tactical gear took aim with their assault rifles, then returned to their 'at ease' stance when they recognized him. They opened the steel door and two more agents snapped into fighting mode. Gibbons passed them and entered the room where Nathan Napolitano was being held. He was with his two constant companions FBI agents, Daniel Webb, and Ellen Dyer.

"We have to get you ready to go upstairs," Gibbons informed Nathan.

Nathan who had sprung to his feet behind Daniel and Ellen, sunk back down into the sofa. "I can't go up there. I won't. You said I could testify from here on a television camera."

"That is sometimes the case," Gibbons regretted telling him that. "But the judge denied the motion. He wants you in the courtroom. Look, you have nothing to worry about, we will all be there with you. You'll be in a courtroom; Nicky won't be able to touch you."

"Nathan, now's your chance to watch him squirm," coaxed Daniel.

"I'll sit behind him. If he so much as twitches I'll put a bullet in the back of his head," promises Ellen Dyer.

"Take a few minutes to compose yourself then let's go put the nails in Nicky Nails' coffin," encourages Gibbons. "We will be right outside that door when you are ready."

NATHAN PACES the small yellow cinderblock room, his mind racing. A low buzzing catches his attention, and he turns to look at the flashing amber light on the black phone on the wall. He's transfixed by its rhythmic pulses and feels drawn toward it. He reaches out fearfully, like sticking his hand into a beehive. He holds the handset to his head. His mouth slowly opens but he can only push out a simple, "hello."

"Nancy. Nancy. Nancy. I let you live on one simple condition, you know that, and yet, here you are, trying to FUCK ME."

"I was gonna… I was going to take the rap for killing Banoa. I was. But I didn't know you killed those cops too. I didn't know. I didn't…"

"Of course, you knew. Why else would I have you tell them where to find the gun? Nancy, they were in on the killing too. They were there when my Maria died, JUST LIKE YOU! They paid the price for their involvement and now it's time for you to ante up."

Nathan knew the voice on the other end, he'd been telling everyone all along that Bulletproof Morris MoJo Johnson wasn't dead. And he was not forgiven. He would kill him before this was over. "I guess when I take the stand you will kill me."

"No. Why would I do that? We have an agreement, and I expect you to hold to your end of the bargain," I say politely.

"But I already told them everything," Nathan's voice quivers.

"That doesn't mean anything until you say it under oath in court for all to hear," I inform him. "Now, I guess you realize the FBI can't protect you. They won't protect you. To the FBI, the police, to the law, you are just another lowlife cop killer. Once you testify, they won't give a damn about what happens to you. Do you know why we sent you to the Red Spike all those years ago? It's because you are a pussy, someone to be used and tossed aside. Because you've been a bad girl, and I can't trust you to do the right thing, I had to take out an insurance policy on you."

"An insurance policy? What do you mean? You can trust me!"

"Oh, but I don't. I never did. You are a weak little bitch. You do whatever someone tells you to do, so I'm going to tell you what to say on that witness stand. And you will say it, do you know why?"

"Because you'll send me back to Heart Attack and Off The Chain if I don't," Nathan's knees buckle, and he leans against the wall for support. His breathing starts racing.

"Hey, don't you pass out on me, you little fag. I'm not sending you back there." I hear him sobbing over the phone, but his relief is short-lived as I tell him what I have planned. "Your sister won a two-week trip for two to the old country, Italy. Paid for by me, of course, but she doesn't know that. What a loving sister you have, instead of taking off with a boyfriend or some fuck buddy, she invited your Mom to go with her. They will get off the plane in about an hour. You still with me?" I had to ask because there was dead silence on the other end.

"Yes, I hear you," Nathan's voice is low and distant.

"Good, because depending on what you say in the next few

minutes will determine if they have the vacation of their lives, or a lifetime as a sex slave in some third world shithole. And don't think your mom is too old for that kind of work, because trust me, she is not. And every time some toothless dirty diseased scumbag is fucking them—they will know and so will you—they have you to thank for it. NOW, LISTEN UP. You will say exactly what I tell you on the stand or both are in for a life that will make yours look like Cinderella at the ball."

NATHAN WAS LED out of the cinderblock room; two assault rifle-toting FBI agents in front of him and two behind, Gibbons, Dyer, and Webb ahead of them. Nathan had to testify in open court, but he could still make an impression on the jury with his entrance. Armed guards led them in and once inside, locked the courtroom doors, all of them. They pulled the window shades down, probably the first time they have been lowered. Gibbons had put a military-grade flak jacket over Nathan's blue suit; its bulk and weight making it hard to walk, stand, or sit comfortably, but it displayed to the jury the extreme danger he risked testifying today.

The judge was not pleased with the spectacle in his courtroom but was powerless to stop it. He had the bailiff swear Nathan in and then he sat down. Although on the elevator ride to the courtroom, Gibbons told Nathan to look at him only, Nathan couldn't stop staring at Nicky.

Nicky was looking at the window, imagining different scenes in the decades-old water stains on the tannish shades, seemingly disinterested in what Nathan was about to say.

Gibbons walked over to the witness stand, poured Nathan a

drink of water and said very calmly, "Ok. Start from the beginning and tell the court how you know the defendant."

"I know Nicky Rocci. I tried to pin the murder of my boss Joseph Banoa on him and his friend Morris Johnson, who is now deceased."

The courtroom was stunned. Everyone sat in shocked silence, until one of the woman jurors said, "Oh My!"

Gibbons looked at Nathan with wide eyes and asked in a low guttural tone, "what did you just say?"

Nathan dropped his head, "It's true. I shot Joseph Banoa and tried to frame Nicky Nails for the murder. I'm sorry, Nicky. I told them the truth, but they wouldn't believe me. They made me come here today."

Gibbons exploded. "Your Honor, I told you this would happen! Someone has gotten to my witness. Nathan, do you know what perjury is? Do you know you are admitting to murder charges? Why in the HELL would YOU SIT THERE AND LIE?"

Ellen Dyer and Daniel Webb shook their heads in disbelief, there was nothing more they could do.

Nathan looked around the courtroom, tears rolling down his face and saw Mrs. Banoa looking at him with fire in her eyes in the front row. Three rows behind her was his father, whom he hadn't seen since he had left New York. Queasiness dropped in his stomach and he bent over to vomit. A couple of dry heaves but nothing came out.

Gibbons said, "I have no questions for this man. You can take him away."

Robert Durant quickly jumped to his feet, "I have a few questions, if it pleases the court?"

"I don't know why you would," commented the judge, "but go ahead."

"This has been a strange case. I want to make sure all the facts are out in the open. Exactly, how did you kill your boss?"

"I shot him once between the eyes," Nathan said calmly.

Mrs. Banoa mumbled a curse beneath her breath at him.

"And in your own words," Durant looked towards the jury, "why did you shoot Joseph Banoa, your boss?"

Nathan took a deep breath and looked down at his feet to avoid the eyes burning into his soul, especially his father's. "Because I was in love with his son, Joey, and he loved me. His father would never accept we were homosexuals."

Mrs. Banoa let out an involuntary scream and passed out. Her two companions immediately started trying to revive her. Mr. Napolitano stood up and walked to the back of the courtroom, where a guard quickly opened and shut it behind him.

Nathan continued to speak, "Joey and I were lovers since high school, and we planned to run away together. Then his father sent him to Florida... I think he knew something was up, but he didn't know about me. I wanted to free Joey from the prison his father had put him in. I got two of my friends... other homosexuals like us, Jose and Miguel, and I waited until the bar was almost empty. Then I went in through the back door like I wanted to tell Joseph about his car. And then we killed those men."

Mrs. Banoa came to as Nathan was finishing his story and starts yelling curses at him in Italian.

Nicky sat laughing.

Gibbons knows he's lying but figures why bother trying to prove it, the trial had been a scam from the beginning.

Durant asks one more question, "why did you call the detectives to tell them where to find the gun?"

"They had caught Joey and me making out in a car one night. I figured if they put two and two together... they would know it was me who killed Joseph. That's when I decided to blame everything on Morris and Nicky. I'm so sorry Nicky, forgive me. Tell Morris to forgive me. I am sorry for all of it."

The judge dropped all charges against Nicky and ordered Nathan taken into custody. He was led away crying.

Later, Nicky stood outside the courthouse mocking the prosecution, FBI, and the justice system as a whole for his arrest. During his career, he tried and succeeded in staying out of the limelight. He had been brought up in the old ways of the Mafia, not to bring attention to himself and remain in the shadows. Unlike John Gotti, who was often on television, Nicky hoped this would be his last appearance. His last words to the television camera were, "I am pleased to have restored the good name of Rocci. Not just for myself and my family, but for good hard-working Italians everywhere who are persecuted just for being of Italian heritage."

13

ONE WAY OUT

Nathan sat alone in his cell. His nice blue suit replaced by a white one-piece jumpsuit. Thick white socks served as shoes. No pockets, no markings to identify him expect the black bold letters on his back, **OC**, Organize Crime. From this day forward all other prisoners would avoid him. Because of his crimes, killing a boss and two police officer, he would be in solitary confinement for his own protection. Twenty-three hours locked in a cell until he was tried and convicted, his testimony made that a certainty, and then marked for execution. The prosecution would seek the death penalty for making a sham of their case.

Nathan sent a request to speak to Ellen Dyer and Daniel Webb. He wanted to explain to them what had happened. If they knew about the phone call, knew Morris was still stalking his family, then they would know he had to go to jail. He sat alone, staring at the bare walls, listening for the sound of the bolt on the door to move.

It did once and a faceless man slid a tray of food through the slot. "Hey, take your food!"

Nathan swept the baloney sandwich and open container of

milk to the floor. "DID DYER AND WEBB GET MY MESSAGE?"

The faceless man did not answer.

Silence filled the cell as the portal in the iron door slid closed and the bolt secured it. Nathan returned to the cot bolted to the wall, then glanced at the stainless-steel commode, also bolted to the bare white wall. This would be his world from now, until the gas chamber. This morning he had glimpsed freedom, and now, empty existence. Surviving until Nicky Nails and Morris Johnson demanded more blood from him. Alive only to bring pain and shame to his family. They didn't know he was alive until this morning, when his father heard him profess his love for a man he hated. It was Joey Banoa who ordered him into the car that took him to the Raven and made him a part of a murder that haunted him.

Joey had already paid his price. Dyer and Webb told him Joey was reportedly killed in a hunting accident shortly after the Bella Rosa massacre. But he knew who had hunted him; his death was no accident, a closed coffin funeral meant he died a violent death. Nathan was glad, Joey got what he deserved. The two cops, they too were involved, and paid their price. All his friends were dead, those who took part in Maria's murder and those who were unluckily around them when payment was demanded and collected. All were willing participants, all paid their dues, all were free. He did much less but continued to pay the most. He too deserved to be free of this debt.

THE PHONE on the wall in the waiting room where he had been before his testimony and where they took him right after started ringing and flashing as soon as the door shut. He knew who was waiting to speak to him. He had done as he was told, he was ready to hear his family was safe. "Hello."

"Nancy… Nancy… Nancy, why do you continue to disappoint me?"

"No. I did what you wanted. I said exactly what you told me to say."

"And as soon as you left the witness stand, you are trying to make a deal with the FBI! Nails hasn't even finished his victory lap and you are going to recant your testimony?"

"No! Morr…"

"Yes! Yes, you are. Why else would you ask to speak with them? Tell them you were coerced; I see I can't trust you. I don't trust you. Say goodbye to Mom and Sissy."

The phone goes silent for a second and then the voices of Nathan's mother and sister are pleading in his ear. They are screaming to be set free. Calling out to anyone who can hear them.

Nathan sobs, "Mom. Mom can you hear me? It's Nathan. It will be alright."

"They can't hear you, Nathan. But I can."

"Let them go. Please! I'm begging you. Let them go…"

"I don't know. Today, you are pleading for their lives. Tomorrow they go into protective custody and you are singing like a fucking canary. Isn't that the game you're playing?"

"No. Let them go and you will never hear another word out of my mouth. I promise you. Never again!"

"You have to prove it to me. Make it quick, they don't have much time."

Nathan hung up the phone and was transferred to another holding cell. He looked around at the emptiness. There was nothing and no way out of this life. He thought about running headlong into the wall, but he heard stories of prisoners who did not die from that, only suffered permanent brain damage. There was no way to hang himself in the cell either, time was running out. Morris expected his testimony to be irreversible to save his mother and sister. He knew what he meant and had no time left to make sure they were not made a victim of his crime.

He removed his one-piece white jumpsuit with the bold black OC on the back. Sat naked on the cot, except for the thick white sock-slippers, and put the sleeve of his garment in his mouth. He worked up as much saliva as he could and started sucking it down. The years he spent in the sex business seemed to aid him now. He got the whole sleeve down his throat before the body of the jumpsuit became too bulky to swallow. He gagged. Fire burned in his neck. The fabric rubbing up and down in his throat causing ever-increasing violent heaves. The cotton bunched and knotted, building a huge bulge in his neck. His chest expanded painfully, looking for air, collapsing with the feeling of being ripped through his skin. Agonizing realization that this life was coming to an end, tortured his final moments. A red vale of death colored the room and Nathan was free.

"So, what's your opinion of the situation?" Nicky asked.

I sipped my drink and recalled the five guys playing cards. I watched their reactions to Carmella in the mirror behind the bar. They smiled, but not a smile of recognition, one of lustful intentions. "They did not know her. I'm sure of it."

"What about her? Did she hesitate or try to hide her face? You know, look down or anything like that."

"No. She couldn't care less about those guys. She did the job as ordered and that was that." I finished my drink then offered my unbiased opinion knowing it was not what Nicky wanted to hear. "I don't think she had anything to do with the hit on your life. She did not know the players. They didn't know her. And by now she's onto the fact that you were hunting down the hit squad. Especially after you had her kill Benny Brunello. I think she is in the clear."

Nicky sat at the desk rolling his drink around in his glass like he didn't hear a word I said. He stared into the dark liquid, drifting further away from reality. He never looked up from his glass, nor did he drink the last of the rum that fascinated him. After an eternity he said, "Ok. Take her on the last mission."

I WAS DRIVING with Carmella through the heat of the Arizona desert. The argument I had with Nicky played in my head. "Are you fucking crazy? Why make her do this? Yes, Chris has to die, but I can do it."

"No, I want her to do it."

"Look, I can make him suffer. I can make it quick. Hell, I'll even make her watch. But you, making her do this is more than cruel, Nicky. You were never a cruel person, what the fuck happened to you?"

Nicky looked at me, cold and unwavering, "This is not about revenge. Ok, maybe a little revenge is sweet, but it's about loyalty. She wanted something, and I gave it to her. She must prove her loyalty to me and this family. Above all else." Nicky walked from behind the desk in the study. He hooked his hand around my neck and brought me face to face with him. "If my father had ordered me to kill you, as close as we are, like brothers me and you, I would have done it. IF MY FATHER

WOULD HAVE ORDERED ME TO KILL SAL… I would have done it. It's about loyalty."

"No. This, this is about Sal." I pulled away. "Your father might have been losing his mind, but he was still wise enough not to have you kill the only person you truly love. Maybe he thought you loved her enough not to hold this against her. Be careful my friend, you are about to create a hydra. Cutting off one head will only double the threat you face."

"You know the way to kill the hydra is to stab it in the heart."

Carmella broke my trance. "Hey, you passed a gas station just now. Don't you think we ought to fill up?"

"No, we don't have much further to go, according to Peter's directions." I tell her, "we will see the town over the next rise."

"Who is the mark this time?"

I give her a look. Her question confirmed my suspicion, she had no part in the hit on Nicky. This question was going to be hard to answer but I had planned to tell her before we reached the place. "Christopher Carmine."

She laughed. "Come on, stop kidding around. Who does Nicky want me to kill and why?" She waits for an answer. Then stares at me with increasing fear. "No. There has to be some kind of mistake."

"You said so yourself, that Christopher was the most likely choice to try and kill Nicky. All the people you killed so far were all part of that scheme. Now, there is only one more person to go. Well, maybe two. But Christopher is next."

"Stop the car! Pull over. Stop!"

"I can't. And you know that." I keep my foot heavy on the gas pedal as we speed through the desert.

"I know I said Chris would have the best reason for wanting Nicky dead, but he didn't know about us. And those other guys were Benny's men. He doesn't know Benny or his guys. Nicky is wrong. Tell him he's wrong."

"You think I didn't check out the story before we had you

start killing people? I knew Chris was behind the shooting the day I called everyone into the office. What I didn't know was if you were involved. I'm glad you are not."

"And if I was?"

I chose not to answer. I kept speeding along the only road for miles in any direction. Out in the desert the typography looks flat, but the land rises and falls into small valleys hiding entire towns until you are within a few miles. Chris was in such a place, follow this road and we run right into it, turn off the road or take another that crosses it, and you will never find it. The Arizona desert is dotted with ghost towns and as you approach, it's hard to tell which has living ghosts haunting them.

"When he sees you, he will know why you are here. It's best to get it over with quickly," I coach her. "The longer you wait, the harder it will be to pull the trigger. Do it quickly for both your sakes."

Carmella holds the .45 caliber revolver in her lap. She rubs its shiny steel body softly. "What's to stop me from taking this gun, shooting you, and Chris, and I disappearing forever? Happily, ever after, as the story goes."

"One thing, there is less than a quarter tank of gas. If you go back to that gas station without me, or with Chris still alive, you won't get any further. If you continue on, the two of you will be dead in a day or two. There is nothing for a hundred miles around. The desert in the summer is no joke," I warn her. "He is only alive out here because they bring him food and water. Today, that will stop, no matter what happens next. If it's any consolation, I argued with Nicky not to make you do this."

"I know why he wants me to, it's punishment for Sal." She looks at me for confirmation.

I nod.

"I sometimes wonder, what if that shot had killed Nicky, then what?"

"You would be ok," I conclude, "but I would have hunted down Christopher and he would still be a dead man."

"You think you would have found out? You think I'd let you?"

"I'm really good at what I do," I say and stop the car in front of the run-down hotel. "Trust me, do it quickly."

Carmella gets out of the car with the gun in her right hand at her side. She walks into the dusty light of the hotel and looks around; it is like an old western movie.

Chris is standing on the stairs smiling, then comes down quickly and wraps his arms around her tightly. He's excited and happy to see her. "I'm so glad he sent you. I dreaded the thought of never seeing you again."

"Don't be such a fool," she chastises him, "you know he sent me to kill you."

"Of course, he did," Chris holds her at arm's length and looks in her eyes. "And you must."

"What? What's the matter with you? Has the heat fried your brains? I don't want to kill you."

"And I don't want to go on living without you." Chris leads her to a chair. "I was ok with marrying the boss' daughter. Yes, the others made jokes and I knew I'd never get a real crew, but I was ok with that too. I was not good with being married to the BOSS' BITCH!"

"It was never like that," Carmella chokes up, seeing in his eyes a look of disappointment and a hint of hatred towards her. "At least I didn't mean it to be. I wanted us to be more than just my father's children. I wanted us to be taken seriously. For you to be more than just his go-for."

"That was your dream," he counters with a toneless voice, "you wanted to head up a crew. Probably someday to be boss." Chris had died long before being brought to this desert and Carmella knew she had killed him. "That is why you took up with Nicky Nails, and why you eventually took his bed. I am glad Fr. Guido had lived up to his reputation and crippled that bastard."

"You mean, killed him."

"No, I didn't want him dead. I wanted to ruin his life the way he was ruining mine. I wanted to make sure he could never feel what it was like to touch you again. I wanted to leave him an empty shell like he left me. Killing him would have let him off easy. I could have killed him myself if that all I wanted."

"I'm so sorry," Carmella starts crying. "I didn't want to hurt you. I didn't mean for you to find out. I was going to end it…"

"I didn't find out on my own, you were very careful. Somebody else did, told Benny Brunello, and he made it his business to tell me. He wanted me to kill Nicky, but I wasn't going to play his game either. I only wish I had a chance to get even with Benny before today."

Carmella smiled, "I took care of him. I didn't know why Nicky wanted him dead but now I'm glad I got to shoot that prick. We can still get out of this—"

Chris puts his hand to her cheek, "Carmella, my love, I am sure Morris already told you there is no way out of this desert if I'm still alive. Either I die or we both die, that's the way it is. Fr. Guido wasn't sure of the outcome of his shot. Somebody shot Sal and threw off his shot."

"I had Sal shot," confessed Carmella.

"Why?" Chris was taken aback. "What did he do… Oh, Nicky had him killed for killing his parents, didn't he? The poor sick bastard."

"No, it wasn't Nicky. It was the father. He was saving Sal from the hangman." Carmella regretted ever getting involved with the Roccis now. "The Rocci family is a very twisted and tormented bunch of people, and I'm done with them. I won't go down this road with Nicky anymore. If he wants you dead, Morris will have to kill you. He can kill us both, I don't care. I won't be like him. Like them. We can still get out of this. I go upstairs and fire one shot. You hide behind the bar down here until Morris comes in to check on the job. He won't believe I killed you without seeing it for himself. You kill him and we prop his fucking corpse up as I drive us out of here."

"And the men at the gas station?" asked Chris.

"We take them down too," Carmella hands are flying around her as she hastily plans their escape. "It's a convertible, you can start shooting as we pull into the station."

"Ok. So, you fire one shot, I fire one to take out Morris," Chris reasons with her, "and if there are more than four people at the gas station, we are screwed. I have seen at least three different people bring food here. It is too risky."

"It is a risk I am willing to take."

"I know you are. Come upstairs," Chris coaxes his wife. She follows him to a bedroom where he begins to remove her clothes, gently lifting her blouse over her head. She follows his lead and unbuttons his jeans. They fall together on the bed he has been sleeping in for months, dreaming of the day she would be here with him. Hoping to feel her body entwined with his one more time. He runs his hands over her breasts. He kisses every inch of her flesh, licking and savoring her taste. Enraptured by the soft moans from her mouth in his ears as she willingly lets her love flow over him. Hour pass as time stands still in the old west town.

They dress and Carmella picks up the gun from the night table. "I'll delay Morris for a few minutes so you can get into position when I leave. He won't be expecting it, so one shot should be all you need." She looks at the bed wet and disheveled from their passions and fires a shot into the wall. Carmella leaves the gun on the table and walks towards the door.

"Carm," Chris calls to her.

She stops and turns to him.

"Is Nicky crippled? Did Guido hit his mark?"

"Yeah. You got him good."

I AM LEANING on Peter's convertible caddy watching her marching defiantly towards me. I knew Nicky had asked too much of her. I was not surprised when minutes passed and there wasn't a shot. I figured she would have gone upstairs with him for a little while before coming out. She was inside long enough for a goodbye screw. I supposed she was going to try and bargain for his life again.

BOOM.

There was fire in her eyes, her hands were empty, and a sharp shrill to her words, "I killed my husband. You can go and see for yourself. Report back to Nicky, that son of a bitch. Not for him. You can tell him—"

BOOM.

The sound of a single gun blast cut her words off. She spun around but could not move toward the hotel. I held her by the arm as she struggled. "Wait! Sometimes the hand shakes, even if the mind is steady in its intentions. Give him a few minutes."

Christopher was a standup guy; he would not let anything happen to Carmella. He knew when he ordered the hit on Nicky this day was coming. He went out knowing Carmella truly loved him. Loved him more than she wanted to be boss. He knew she would make a great boss and he could not take that away from her. He loved her too.

As night began to creep across the desert, I sat Carmella in the car. I went into the saloon alone, saw exactly what I expected to find, and wanted to spare her from seeing. The flimsy table was flipped over. Chris was laying on his back on the floor, the chair shattered. A pool of blood surrounded his head and shoulders. As I walked around his body, I saw almost the entire top of his head blown open. He had buried the forty-five-caliber revolver under his chin and pulled the trigger. The gun was laying on the floor near the bar, I went and retrieved my favorite gun, I called 'The Crowd Pleaser'.

There was an open grave dug weeks ago behind the hotel. Chris had plenty of time to think about what it would be like to lie down in that hole and forget all about this life. I lowered his body, wrapped in the hotel sheets into that hole, and shoveled in the dirt. I drove Carmella back up the rise. We stopped at the gas station and filled up. The attendant asked if there was anything he needed to do. I told him I took care of things.

He retrieved the shovel from the trunk.

I knew he didn't want the shovel but to make sure I didn't go soft for Carmella. We left for the flight to New York.

I WALKED into the office at the mansion. Nicky was pacing the floor like a caged cat. "Damn it, it's eight o'clock in the morning and you're already hopped up," I said.

"I'm not on anything," he replied with a tone that I knew meant this could come to blows.

We had on occasions traded punches like brothers do, but we were teenagers then, this was different.

He yelled, "You lied to me! Your GODFATHER gave you an order and you disobeyed me!"

"To start, I'm not in the Mafia," I said tapping the back of my left hand with two fingers of my right to draw his attention to my blackness.

"Don't give me that bullshit! You've been a part of this

family for about as long as I have," he came within inches of my face, "you lied. You told me she killed Chris."

I pushed him back gently, "I didn't lie. I said, 'She went in. She came out. I buried him. I never said she killed him. You just assumed she did. Where is Carmella now?"

Nicky was staring me in the eyes, "I sent her to Colombia to reorganize things with Grandma Coco. Now that Chris is out of the business, she will be running things down there."

I decided to back away and ease the tension. "I would not leave her with that crazy old lady too long, she hates you. She might turn Carmella into a real killer. Plus, she is the best cook you have, we need her to do the books, unless you want a visit from the IRS. About the Christopher thing, he did the honorable thing and blew his own goddamned brains out. So, as far as I'm concerned, mission accomplished. Can we fucking move on?"

But he was still staring me down.

"What the fuck is with you today? It's too fucking early for this bullshit."

"You spent too much time with her," Nicky smiled, "did she fuck you? Is that why you went soft on her? It's ok, she is a great piece of meat, that one."

"I'm sure you're besides yourself with conflicting emotions," I rationalized, "but she's your tail. You are going to have to come to terms with the fact that she loved her husband, maybe more than you. Anyway, I told you that was a bad idea. Never put a person in a position where they have to give you an answer you really don't want to know." The tension is still in the air but we both come to the point where we know we need to move on. "Have you heard from Pauley? What's the latest in Chicago?"

"Not directly," Nicky finally sat behind his desk and I took a seat on the corner of it. "I think the DA is trying to find a way out of their deal. But the lawyers tell me it's ironclad. He got immunity for fingering Benny for the Congressman's murder; they'll have to cut him loose."

"What about Benny's men? They are going to find out Pauley set him up. That can't be good."

"Well, he's already in good with a couple of Benny's capos, so he's going to help them take control of the business. For a small piece of the pie, of course." Nicky laughs.

"Ok. That's youse guys thing," I fake an Italian accent, "let me know if you need any muscle."

"I thought you weren't part of the Mafia. Now, you want a piece of the action?" Nicky feigned indignation, "make up your mind. Are you in or out?"

"That all depends, how much am I getting in on," I joked, "and what am I getting out of it?"

"Does it matter? If you're in for a dime, or in for a dollar, they will still kill you if things go bad. Thanks for the offer, but we have this under control. And it would be better if we keep this just us brothers," Nicky taps the back of his hand as I had done. "Meanwhile, I do have another problem we need to handle."

"Yeah, Jackrabbit was Lucas' boy," I knew where we were going next. "This thing isn't over yet. But I don't think you should involve Carmella, after all, she will only complicate the situation."

"I don't know. Maybe we can use her as bait."

I snapped my head around so fast I gave myself a pain in my neck.

"Only kidding, I just wanted to see your reaction. But how did they know to hit me at the cemetery?"

I wasn't quite sure he was kidding. Using her as bait might work, because Lucas probably wanted her dead as much as he wanted Nicky's head on a pole. "You remember how we got to Banoa. The weak link in your chain is?"

"Rocky... Somebody got to him," Nicky's anger started to visibly rise. "I will beat the name out of him. I loved that boy like a son."

"Yeah, well, I'm glad I'm not your son," I said laughing. I took a seat in the hot seat, which at this time of morning is quite comfortable. "No one got to him. He looks up to you as a father. Although, I don't know why. He doesn't live at the mansion, does he?"

"You know he doesn't," Nicky's demeanor changed back to a sympathetic nature. "He lives in Queens, comes when I call him, or he would be here in the morning if I let him know we are going somewhere in advance."

"But it was a regular thing for him to take you and Sal to the cemetery."

"Yeah, but we hadn't gone there in a couple of months while the mausoleum was being built."

"But after it was finished, you would resume your trips there with Sal. Once you went to get Sal, the hit was on. Anyone clocking his trips would have known. Even a speed freak like Jackrabbit, could easily track you. To get to Lucas, we are going to need a real good plan, not some weak idea about dangling Carmella as bait." I threw that last part in just to be on the safe side. "Youse guys should really start looking at the benefits of public transportation."

"Yeah, very funny," Nicky said and then walked over to me. "Hey, don't take this the wrong way, but I think I got this from here. What happens from here has to be family business. I think once you leave town, things will loosen up. You know, make it easier for me to make a move."

That was true. I got on a plane and headed back home. I had been away for too long anyway.

14

SUCH A NICE GUY

Beniamino Brunello's arrest stunned the people of Chicago. He was a well-respected restaurateur affectionately known as Big Benny, for the size of his heart, as one television newscaster remarked. Benny owned a chain of both high-end and fast-food restaurants. He was known for giving out Thanksgiving turkeys and Christmas diners in the poor neighborhoods and throwing hundred-dollar-a-plate fundraisers for charities and political campaigns.

The general comment on the street, which was played on all news channels was, "He's such a nice guy, there must be some kind of mistake." His being accused of murdering a hooker at a party for a Congressman, then being implicated in that Congressman's murder, when it was already deemed a murder-suicide by Representative Webb was too much for Chicagoans to believe. The next comment out of people on the news, "this smell like a police setup," did not get any better for the police when Big Benny was found murdered in his cell the next morning.

His half-eaten plate of food, which naturally came from his restaurant, led investigators to summarize he had been killed sometime between eight o'clock pm when his food arrived and eight am when he was to be arraigned in court. The last person to see him alive, which they did not reveal to the media, was a redheaded policewoman no one could identify. She was not a suspect because it was assumed Benny had time to eat his meal before his three .22 bullets dessert. What the news did learn was that the video cameras in the precinct had been broken for weeks.

With Benny's gang-style killing came stories of his involvement with people of lesser standing in Chicago society. In less than a week, he went from Big Benny Philanthropist to Benny the Butcher, Benny Balls, and Brunello the Brute. He was tied to every organized crime family and unsolved crime committed since the St. Valentine's Day Massacre, even though he was not yet born when it happened. Pictures played nightly of mob-style murders dating back decades. People gunned down on Chicago streets, bodies turning up in the River, one an Irish gangster floating down it during the turning-the-river-green on St. Patrick's Day. Part of the information came from what the police knew about him but could not prove. The information was deliberately leaked since he could no longer defend himself, and to divert criticism that the police, either through neglect or complicity, allowed a person to get murdered in their custody.

By the end of the week, most believed Beniamino Brunello was a nice guy on the surface, but as the saying goes, "scratch a liar find a thief." Chicagoans feared the start of another Mafia war had begun. Those fears were not unfounded as Benny's death and the disappearance of his second-in-command, Deano Belladini, left a power vacuum in their wake. The violence did not start immediately. There was a respectable amount of time for Benny's funeral, which was attended by less people than was expected. Only the biggest politician who could survive the scrutiny, or not avoid it anyway, showed up. Known and unknown mobsters, looking to portray their dominance were in full view of the cameras. One person who was not present, Paul Bochi, not out of fear of reprisal but because he had the ear of all those who were there.

In the underworld, Pauley, no fancy mob name, was still regarded as the number two man in the Rocci family. With Benny Brunello gone, the Rocci family was considered by most as the top crime family in the United States, if not the world, so it was inevitable that the Brunello family would be taken over by the Roccis. There would be the necessary house cleaning, the only question that remained, how brutal would Nicky Nails Rocci be? And the only one who held the answer was Paul Bochi.

PETER LUCAS TOOK notice of Benny's death and was not surprised or shocked by how he died. He warned Benny that Paul Bochi was a loyal soldier of the Rocci family and letting him into his sphere of influence would be a tragic mistake. He had made the mistake of trusting Nicky Nails Rocci before and vowed to never do that again. He also made the mistake of trusting Benny Brunello and now he was preparing for an all-out war with the Rocci family.

He called a meeting with his five capos and twenty lieutenants at his home in Manhattan Beach, Brooklyn overlooking the picturesque Sheepshead Bay. The front bay windows gave the wives a wonderful view between the trees along Shore Boulevard of the golden sand beach and the sailboats on the water. While the men gathered in the pool room at the back barbequing and planning their strategy.

"I want all pickup routes changed and placed on a rotating

basis. Double the men in the cars and have them tailed by a backup assault squad."

"We have already changed the routes twice since Antonio the Jackrabbit died," said Leo, the most senior of the capos, "there haven't been any signs that Nicky Nails had a hand in that drug addict's death. He was my sister's only son, which is why I gave him a job in the first place, but he probably died giving some fag a blowjob for a hit."

"Yeah, and what about Benny?" Lucas fumed, "was he taking it up the ass in that jail cell when he got whacked? And who do you supposed put him in that cell? That goddamn moron!"

Christopher Lucas, Peter's eldest son spoke up, "Don, we were very careful with whom we dealt with in Brunello's family. I made sure nothing led back to us. I agree with Leo, Jackrabbit's death proves nothing. If we start posturing like we are ready for a war, we will draw one to us." At twenty-two, he's the next in line to take control of the family. He prides himself on looking like a younger version of his father but has a reputation for being timid. He whispers to his father as he goes for another drink at the bar, "I heard Nicky sent his black homie away."

"So, the nigger is gone, and we should all breathe a sigh of relief." Peter backhands his son hard for being soft. "I'd rather he was still in town, so I would not have to go hunt him down. And if you think because he isn't around the darkies aren't still going to fight for the Roccis if called on, shows you are as stupid as the rest of youse. Your sister is dead, Nicky was behind it, so this war is going on. Am I CLEAR?"

There was an enthusiastic rumble of Yes and Si. No one else spoke up until Peter Lucas asked for suggestions on how and where to strike Nicky Nails Rocci.

Leo offered, "we hit him at his place in the Bronx, The Sons of Italy. Since he beat his court case, he's bound to show up there for a victory celebration. I'll have a hit team stake out the place starting today. We don't have to do anything fancy, just go in and spray the joint for roaches."

"Yeah, I like that. See, Christopher? That's the thinking that will make you worthy of being the Don one day." Peter grabbed his son by the back of the neck and shakes him. "And I want you to get a team together and watch his house out on the island. We may get a chance to ambush him when he's coming or going. I say we strike first, and we strike hard. That's how you win a war." He smiled at his son. "Now, go get those sausages off the grill and let's feed these kids and ladies before they come storming in here."

NICKY SAT with Rozalina at diner. She was telling him that they should go to Europe for a vacation. "You know, now that all the madness is over. The trial and the funerals, you deserve a break. Summer on the Med is a great idea, what do you think?"

"Yeah, sure, that sound great, sweetheart," Nicky answered absently.

"We can rent a yacht, with a crew," she continued with a look of concern on her face. "We can sail to Italy, France, maybe even Spain."

"Anywhere is a great place."

"And we can outfit the ship with a torpedo or two, maybe a cannon on deck," her face twisted from a smile to a smirk, "maybe a few of the crew will have eye patches and peg legs."

"Yes, that will be fine." Nicky's head was staring past her at the door to the office.

Rozalina threw a spoon at his head.

He caught it out of reflexes.

"Well, at least you are not totally ignoring me."

"Oh, sorry dear. I'm waiting on a call from Pauley. But I did hear you, we can go on vacation very soon. Business is not quite over yet. But soon." He slid the spoon back across the table.

Rozalina got up from the table with a scowl, "I hope you live long enough to enjoy a break. And you are not taking a vacation in the graveyard."

"Don't worry about me, I'm going to live forever. But keep your black dress pressed," he laughs.

She slapped him on the head on her way out of the dinner room, "You died once already."

"Yeah, that's what I'm telling you. I'm already dead, so I can't die again. I'm gonna be with you forever. You are never getting rid of me." He slapped her backside then headed for his office. He smiles at her and closes the door softly. The phone rings. "Yeah."

"The horses are in the starting gate," Pauley told him. "Who's your money on?"

"I don't care. You pick the winner and get back here. Make sure it's someone who is going to play ball and not get a big head."

"I got just the person in mind, but it won't be quick," Pauley informed him. "There are about three people ahead of him. They will have to be dealt with, won't be easy. If you want it done quietly, I'll need some assets to work with."

"Make it loud and noisy," Nicky commanded. "I want everybody to know there is a new boss in town. You know that fat bastard had a lot of people in his pocket, I don't want any of them thinking they can start doing their own thing. I need that place nailed down tight."

Pauley looked at the device he had attached to his phone and hoped the electronic jammer was keeping the call from being recorded. He did not care if the Feds were listening in, as long as they could not produce the conversation in court. Morris had shown them how to use the device, and the recorded tape ended up with a high-pitched whine that made it useless. But he still didn't trust the little black arm attached to the mouthpiece. "Are you ready to make a move?"

"No. I was told I need to take a vacation."

"You're kidding!"

"No. It was almost a command," Nicky smiled as he imagined the look on Pauley's face. "It's a good idea, I'll be out of the country while things heat up over there. And things will cool down here. A wiseman once said, don't fight a war on two fronts."

"Who said that?"

"I did," Nicky laughed, "it didn't work out for Napoleon or Hitler. So, we will fight one battle at a time, and I'll make my wife happy, before I have another battle on my hands."

PAULEY MET with the capos and Lieutenants of the Brunello Family. The meeting was held in Benny's lakeside mansion. He had two of his lieutenants to back him up.

"The passing of Beniamino Brunello saddens us all. I have known him for quite a few years and was grateful when he opened his doors to me when my own Don was stricken ill. Being the cause of his malady notwithstanding, has led us to the situation we are faced with today. Who will take over the Brunello Family?"

"Surely, not you," said John Asconi, the most senior capo in the family. "All cards on the table, I believe you are behind the Don's death. You and that young cur, Nicky Rocci."

"All cards on the table," repeated Pauley, "Benny made no

secret he had a hard-on for Nicky Nails, my boss. I don't pretend to know why. But he bet his life against Nicky's and lost, those are just the facts. Now that things have been settled back in New York, I am going back. I want to be able to assure my Don that Chicago no longer poses a threat to our organization. I like the city, but I don't want to have to come back here. The Don will be agreeable to Anthony Perlman or Michael Spirilla taking control."

With that statement the fuse was lit. The room erupted into a shouting match.

"How dare you offend this body with the audacity of Nicky Nails Rocci to determine who will lead this family. If we had not worked together in the past, and out of respect for your dearly departed Don, Nicolas Rocci, you would be dead where you sit."

"I assure you, John, and all of you, Nicky does not want to interfere in the working of your family. He will simply feel safer with one of those two men, whom he had and still enjoys a pleasant camaraderie with as head of this family. And he only makes this request so there is no further misunderstanding between our two organizations."

"I have been a capo in this family for the last fifteen years," Anthony Perlman said in a soft voice to calm the rising tensions, "whereas Rocci's request is not the first of its kind, in times like these, it's actually quite ordinary. We should take it under consideration when we pick the new Don. Benny's actions have cost this family dearly, monetarily and in reputation. He was bested twice by a young upstart of a boss and his… black friend."

There was loud curses and 'traitor' hurled at the balding middle-aged man in his overstuffed suit. He took it all in stride and waited for the room to return to a semblance of quiet.

"You all know me. I kept my place when Benny ran things. I disagreed with some of the plans and policies, but I was loyal. This proposal seems to be a good way of avoiding and escalating a war, frankly, none of us were behind. I will gladly give the job to Michael… although, no disrespect, Michael, he is too young to hold this family together."

"That is magnanimous of you, Tony," John said, "but the fact remains, neither Nicky nor Pauley runs this family. If they don't want war, Pauley should leave Chicago today and tell Nicky and his friends to stay out of our business. That is the only concession I am willing to make."

"Is that the feeling of the room?" asked Pauley.

Four of the six agreed loudly.

Pauley got up from the table, put his fedora on, and said, "I wish you all luck and the next time we meet, may it be in a celebratory manner."

After he left, the meeting went on for hours. John pushed hard to be the next boss. Three of the capos, Tony, Michael, and James Davino backed Anthony, at least as a temporary boss. The meeting went late into the night and the six capos returned to their cars for the drive home. The mansion was locked up. Tony was the first to drive off, followed by Michael. John's car was third in line and when its engine started, a flash followed by a huge fireball engulfed the car.

The blast knocked the other capos and lieutenants who were outside their vehicles to the ground. The windows shattered up to the second floor on the mansion. The heat kept everyone from reaching John Asconi's car. The car behind it, James Davino's, was also on fire but he managed to escape unharmed.

The bombing was meant to start the war that night. The surviving capos had their own suspects and reasons for killing John Asconi. Pointing the finger at Nicky was easy, but he had the least reason to target anyone and the best opportunity. However, with John's death there was no trust and no vote coming. The leadership of the Brunello Family would be decided by blood.

Sides were not drawn as anyone would have expected. It was a winner-takes-all for the capos and their crews. There was a moment when it looked like they could come together and settle the leadership. James Davino was invited to the law office of Michael Spirilla to support Tony Perlman.

"James, good of you to come. The assassination of our brother two nights ago was uncalled for. I have drawn up an agreement that I'd like to send around and see if we can't get a civilized solution to this matter."

"You want me to sign my name to a RICO admission document?" James laughed, "I thought you went to law school. Did you not graduate?"

"I did," Michael took the statement as a joke, "I drew up a number of agreements for Brunello that would not carry any criminal implications. Consider this a document that covers a shell company with no ties to any entity. It just shows support for Tony and give an avenue to debate his worthiness."

"I don't know…"

"James, parts of the Brunello Family have already been raided. The Rocci Family has looted some South American holdings. We have to get a new leader and transfer holdings before we lose anymore. This will just give us a way to start the process, safely."

"Ok. I'm in."

"Good, wait here and I'll get the documents." Michael left the office.

James and his four men, two lieutenants and two soldiers, sat waiting in the boardroom. The air conditioner began to hum. A couple of minutes later James unbuttoned his shirt collar. He wiped his face, but it was dry. "That goddamn AC must be broken, it's hot as hell in here. I'm getting a headache."

"Let me see if I can turn it up, Boss." As his bodyguard stood up, he doubled over and vomited on the floor.

"What the fuck?" James demanded. He looked across the table at his lieutenant. The man was going limp, and his head was bobbing. Next to him his other bodyguard was holding his chest and struggling to breathe. "Bobby, Booby, Bod… something is up. Where… is Mikey?"

Bobby, James's lieutenant, exclaimed. "It's a trap. We are being gassed. Open the door."

The soldier who had vomited got to the door and found it locked. Bobby drew his pistol and fired two shots at the window. Both bullets stuck in the white ice of the once clear glass. Twelve stories up the windows were made of three-inch-thick ballistic plastic, not regulation building code in Chicago, but the type of precaution a mob lawyer would install. Bobby went into a seizure shaking on the floor before he could get off another shot.

James tried to walk to the door but only got one step from the table before hitting the floor. The five men were motionless on the monitor in Michael's office, three on the floor and two in their chairs at the table.

"Give it another five minutes then vent carbon monoxide," ordered Michael into the intercom on his desk.

"Yes, boss," replied a husky voice from the speaker.

"You need to replace the window in there right away," he commanded, "then bag the trash and wait until tonight to dispose of them. Have you gotten word on what happened to Tony?"

"No, sir. Word is he has gone underground. He hasn't been to his dealership in two days," replied the disembodied voice.

"Too bad, I was hoping to wrap this up quickly. Well, the other two capos are backing me, so he'll come around. Put the word out, I am the new Don of the Brunello Family."

NICKY WAS LYING on a deck chair with a newspaper on his lap. The nine sails of The Princess Virginia were billowing softly in the Mediterranean breeze. The warm early morning sun was momentarily interrupted as a shapely figure walked past. He squinted one eye to see Gisella in a white bikini spreading a towel on the deck chair next to him.

"I haven't had a chance to thank you for inviting me to come along on this trip," she said, noticing him giving her the once over.

"No need to thank me. Thank Cherry, she is the one who put together the guest list."

"I will. I didn't think she was that fond of me. Why do you call her Cherry?"

"That's how she was introduced to me back in her stripper days. I like the name," Nicky told her, "and she likes you just fine. I think they are going to initiate you into the Russian Dolls."

Gisella's face turned red then a kind of shock set in.

"Hey, don't worry. It's nothing serious, not like you have to kill anyone, or spin on a pole. It just means you will be one of the girls, if you're not already."

"In that case, I am honored. I will make sure to doubly thank her. First for the invite on this lovely yacht and then for membership into the club."

"You don't have to be too grateful for the invitation," Nicky swung his legs around and sat up to face her. "This is your yacht. Didn't Morris tell you?"

The look on her face went to amazement. Nicky knew he hadn't yet told Gisella about her inheriting Benny's Venezuelan companies. "You own oil rights, cattle farms, and this one-hundred-and-sixty-foot luxury sailing yacht. Of all the things you inherited from your grandfather in Venezuela, this is the nicest. Wouldn't you say?"

"I don't know what to say."

"Here comes Morris. He'll explain it all to you." Nicky

stretches back out on the lounge chair with a satisfied smile on his face.

"What trouble is Nicky stirring up now?" I ask Gisella. I look down at the newspaper. "The Chicago tribune? I thought we were on vacation, Nicky."

"Just doing a little light reading. You know, trying to stay informed."

"Anything interesting in there?"

"The obituaries…"

I sit next to Gisella on the lounge chair and begin rubbing suntan oil on her back. I feel her tense up as my hands glide over her back. I massage her shoulders, "he told you about the boat, didn't he?"

She nodded her head but did not respond.

DINNER WAS SERVED in the main cabin of The Princess Virginia by the crew of six who then departed back to the lower decks.

The Captain came in briefly, as was his custom before the main meal, to give Gisella a status update. "We are approaching Gibraltar, we will be docking in the mooring in the morning, I can have the crew ready the skiff if you or your party would like to go ashore." He slowly looked from one face to another around the mahogany table to make sure everyone understood his heavy Spanish accent. "It is sometimes good to get your legs back under you after a month at sea."

Maria looked down at her legs and giggled, not under-standing what the captain meant. Then see looked to me and said, "I want to go ashore, Daddy. I can practice my Spanish and we can shop for sombreros, Mommy."

"I don't know how much Spanish you'll get to speak; Gibraltar is a British territory." I point out. "But I think we can go. It will be fun."

Elizabeth nodded. "Captain Diego, perhaps we will all go ashore."

"Very good, Madam. The boat will be ready when you are," the captain then addressed the men at the table, "be assured two of my finest sailors will be with you at all times. They are ex-Venezuelan marines."

After the captain left, Cherry tapped her champagne glass lightly, "I want to welcome Gisella Alejandra Montilla to the Women of Hidden Assets and Real Estate Sorority, known to all of us gathered here as WHARES. Gisella has by far exceeded us with this beautiful ship, lands, and other businesses in her home-land of Venezuela."

"I… I don't know what to say, I mean, I didn't even know I owned any of these things until this morning. When Nicky told me." Gisella stammered.

"Way to ruin a surprise party, Nicky." Yana cut her eyes at him as she shook my hand under the table.

Elizabeth, sitting on the other side of me, said, "I thought you were the Don. I would have expected you to keep a secret better than this."

"Yeah, even I knew we weren't supposed to tell her until tonight, Uncle Nicky."

"What… These women have gotten to you too, Maria?" Nicky shook his head and bowed, "well, Honey, aren't you gonna pile it on?"

Izolda shakes her long blonde hair innocently, "I told Morris not to tell you. It's his fault you boys can't keep a secret. I'm just amazed the two of you have lasted as long as you did in this business. But back to the woman of the hour, Gisella. Be glad you're not the owner of a string of grimy chop shops masquerading as greasy automobile repair shops."

"Yes, or a bunch of sleazy sex joints pretending to be night-clubs," Rozalina adds.

"Or…"

"Don't you say a word," I caution Yana, then smile at the rest of the women at the table. "Need I remind you all that you have a sizable piece of the R & D division of Global Munitions Inc., and various other very legitimate businesses around the world? Although Nicky cannot hold his tongue, everyone here has done alright by him and me." I tap my glass and raise it up, "Salut, drink up because we are probably going to sell those oil shares quickly."

"What! Are you kidding me?" questioned Nicky. "Those wells are gushing liquid gold."

"But the government is questionable at best. I know a man in Saudi Arabia who wants to buy us out. Oil is just another reason for war. I say let them fight over it. We take the money and run."

"Ok, enough shop talk," commands Rozalina, "this is a celebration of WHARES. Besides, Gisella, at least you got a nice boat out of it."

"And cows," Gisella smiles and gulps her champaign, "at least I'll get fresh milk."

The drinking and eating went on from there. The ladies were happy. After a while Nicky and I slipped away to talk. We went to the helipad at the back of the ship.

"So, the papers said Michael Spirilla was found wearing a piano wire necktie. I didn't know he liked music."

"I guess he was more of a music critic than a music lover."

"How does that stand with you? I thought he was your man in Chicago."

"He was my number two man," Nicky smiles, "I learned from you, offer the number two man the moon, and he will do anything. But the number one guy is still going to win. So, it looks like Tony the Pearl will be in charge."

"So, when you get back, you'll wrap up things in New York?"

"Plans are in the works."

Nicky is vague for no reason so I press for details, "If you need help, I can influence some of our island friends in Brooklyn to get involved. Give the word and they will wipe out the whole upper echelon of the family and you can take over. Won't have your fingerprints on it at all. Make it look like a major drug war that Lucas lost."

Nicky rubs the back of his neck while he ponders the situation and its possible outcomes. "Yeah, that's not gonna work for me. I think I need to handle this thing with a little more finesse. I can't take over Lucas' Family."

"Really, because this whole mess stems from your father wanting you to marry and partner up with them. What's the difference?"

"The five families like it to remain the five families. Sure, we partner with each other on occasions, but basically each family is still separate. If we have internal power struggles that's one thing. But trying to eliminate another family will bring the other three into the mix, and then things get really fucked up."

"Sounds a little antiquated to me," I concede, "but you might still want to use the Jamaicans. They make excellent hitmen, and they are not tied to either of us."

"I'll keep that in mind, if I need to give my idea a boost. How long do you plan to sail around out here?"

"I figure we can finish out the season," I look at the white moon reflecting off the black waters of the Mediterranean Sea. "I've never seen Maria so happy. It's good to have you around."

Nicky smiles and punches me in the chest. "She has grown into a fine young lady. Getting her out of New York was a good thing. Taking care of your family is all that matters." Nicky's smile fades.

"One of these days, I might retire to a life like this. Where nobody knows me, just sailing around the world without a care. What about you?"

"I don't know, I think I'm addicted to the noise, dirt, and smell of the city. But a vacation is nice now and again."

"What dirt and smell? You live out on Long Island. It's all trees and lawns out there."

"Hey, I go into the city plenty. You can't get decent cannoli on the island. All the goombahs there are pretending to be hebes."

PETER LUCAS IS SITTING at his bar in his Manhattan Beach home when his son Christopher walks in. He pours a second glass of red wine for him and pats the stool next to him. The other three men, who are playing pool, lay their cues on the table and leave the father and son to their business.

"How old are you now, Chris?" Peter is looking straight ahead at a picture of his father hanging on the wall behind the bar. And right next to it in an ornate silver frame, Angela's.

"I'll be twenty-three in two months." Chris hates when the conversations start this way. It's not like his father forgets his birthday, June 12th, 1970, as he never misses an opportunity to remind him he was the second born.

"I was twenty when I took over the family from my father."

"How many times did you tell me Papa was shot and, in the hospital, when you took over," Chris pushed back on his father's obvious diatribe. He knew where this was going, it had been a constant rant in recent years since his sister's death. This time he would get out in front of the berating, "if you want to turn the family over to me, I am more than ready."

"Ready? Ha! My OWN MEN would eat you alive. I put you in charge of one task, killing Nicky Nails. And is he dead? NO!"

"I have a hit squad watching his club in the Bronx, which was your preferred plan," Chris retorts, "and I have personally been supervising another team in a house on Peconic Bay Boulevard, the main road leading to his Long Island mansion. We are less than a mile away with no way for him to get past me."

"Doing what? Jerking each other off!" Peter slaps the glasses of wine from the bar.

"He hasn't made a move in a month. I have feelers on the street, nobody has seen him." Chris stares down his father. He's not going to let the slight against his manhood go by unchallenged, not this time. "Your attempt to kill him, which FAILED, and the trial have made him more careful now."

"Have your feelers…" Peter lets the last word roll off his tongue with contempt, "inform you that Paul Bochi is back in town. And what about his whore? She has disappeared."

"What about Carmella?" Chris knows she has been the subject of much of his father's anger.

"Have you tried finding her? If you grab her, Nicky Nails will come to her rescue. She's not in Miami, or New York, he has her hidden away somewhere. If you want to get to Nicky, find the whore and put the screws to her." Peter pours himself another glass of wine and drinks it down. "I wouldn't have to tell your sister how to get things done. She had the balls this family needs. If you could have half the backbone of her… If she were alive…"

"If you didn't make her whore herself out to Nicky Nails she would be—" Christopher Lucas never finished his sentence. He woke up on the floor with his father standing over him and the three men holding him back.

They were wrestling a gun from his hand as he shouted, "I'll kill that little faggot. I will blow your fucking head off, you little prick. You don't talk about my Angela like that! I'll shoot you dead!"

"Go put some ice on your eye," said Gio, Lucas' top lieutenant. "Then make yourself scarce. Maybe you come back tomorrow when dad's calmed down."

"He's not my son, that little faggot. He's his mama's boy. You will never take over this family. I will kill you before that happens."

Christopher bolts past his mother as she tries to stop him. His father's stinging condemnation in his head and his right eye, now completely shut. That has always been the problem ever since he was a boy. How many drunken beatings had he taken, how many had his mother, even though he is his father's spitting image. Somewhere in the darkness of Peter's mind, he decided Christopher was not his son. Not man enough to be his flesh and blood. Always second to his elder, better, beautiful sister who could do no wrong. No more! He will kill Nicky Nails Rocci and prove once and for all, he was a Lucas. He will be head of the family, even if it kills his father to make him so.

15

THE COST OF DOING BUSINESS

A package arrived at the house on Peconic Bay Boulevard, Long Island. Mario stopped Christopher from opening it. "Hey, what are you doing? You want to get your hands blown off?" He took the small brown cardboard box and walked carefully to the bathroom. He started filling the bathtub with water.

"What are you doing? That package came from my father, look at the address."

"Oh, yeah," Mario, an older man with gray sideburns, fading dyed hair, and deep lines across his forehead laughed at him, "when was the last time your father gave you anything but grief?"

Chris' hand went to his right temple, then he immediately pulled it down, "So, what are you going to do?"

Mario wrapped the package in two thick bath towels as the other two men of the hit squad arrived at the bathroom door. They were about Christopher's age, dressed in tee shirts and blue jeans. The three men were crowding in the door trying to see what Mario was doing. "I guess you all want to get your fucking asses blown up. Get the fuck out of here! Bunch of stunod kids."

He placed the package gently in the tub and backs away as

the water soaks the towels and rises over it. He waited for five minutes looking at his watch. He turns to Chris and the other, "Ok, if it is a bomb that should have shorted out the electric detonator. Get me a long kitchen knife."

One of the men heads for the kitchen.

Christopher is still looking in the door, "What for, I thought you said that will disarm it."

"Kid, I was in the army, Vietnam, you know how many times what should have worked, didn't? Now, get back." He knelt beside the tub and reached one arm over the side. He took the twelve-inch knife and gently flipped the folded towels off the top of the box. "If this thing does go off, the water will diffuse the explosion. Maybe I'll only get me arm mangled and not blown completely off." He peeked at the box, it was soaked through and dark brown. He ducked back down as he stuck the knife in one corner and peeled the cardboard box open.

A couple of quiet minutes passed, and he peeked in the tub. He reached in and pulled out a plastic baggie with a cell phone inside.

Chris, still peeking around the doorway asked, "is it a bomb?"

"It's a cellphone, kid." Mario tossed it to him.

Christopher nearly dropped it, not knowing if he should catch it or not. "I heard stories of people turning cellphones into bombs."

"No, you heard stories of people using cellphones to detonate bombs. Generally speaking, wouldn't be enough explosive material to fill a device that small to kill a person. However, I would not hold it to my ear to answer it. You think your father sent it?"

"The address on the package was from the house," Christopher said, "so, yeah. He is probably going to check in on me and bust my balls. What do you think? You know him better than I ever will."

Mario finished drying his hands. He looked over the phone

and handed it back to Chris, "it is a new model. And putting in the plastic bag makes sense; he knows I would drown any unsolicited package we received. But the only way to know who sent it is to answer the phone when it rings."

"When it rings?"

"Kid, whoever sent it, knows the number. They plan on calling you but be careful what you say. People think a cellphone can't be traced or recorded; both are untrue. The cops could have sent that thing. Well, that's enough excitement for me today, I'm going to relax in the pool out back. Somebody get back to watching the monitors and one of you go sit in the car. Just in case today is our lucky day."

Christopher went to the kitchen and placed the knife back in the drawer. He put the phone on the table and took a seat. He stared at the phone, waiting for it to ring. The day waned.

Mario came in from the pool, grabbed some cold dish and a beer from the refrigerator, and took a look at Chris. He shook his head and left without a word.

Angelo and Raffie, a nickname for Raffaello, and sometimes called Turtle after the cartoon character, tried to engage him in a conversation and then left him alone to brood.

All three men had heard about his trip to see his father and were surprised when he returned with a black eye that took weeks to heal. The shame on his face lasted much longer, prompting Mario to do a couple of night reconnaissance missions to the mansion. The main house was on the beach but had a six-foot wall separating it from the sand. The guesthouse was nestled in the trees and gave perfect cover fire for the mansion.

Trees surrounded and encased three sides of the property and a wall ran the perimeter. He wasn't able to see much, but he knew the place was down to a skeleton crew of soldiers and lieutenants. There were a few people coming and going a few days during the week, probably making their drops. Nicky's driver, Rocky, came by twice in a month and left alone both times.

Mario surmised Nicky wasn't lying low, he wasn't home.

THE PRINCESS VIRGINIA had hugged the coast of Spain and docked in Barcelona for provisions. The women had gone into the city with three of the marines to sightsee and shop. Nicky and Morris had slept in after their nightly binging of drugs and alcohol. Although, sleeping in didn't work as well with church bells ringing through the soundproof walls.

"I thought you told me I could murder someone in here and no one would know."

"Well, I guess God would know," I said, making my way to the deck chairs. "Are we going to the Old Country?"

"Maybe next time," Nicky said, "I'm going to catch a flight back when we get to Marseille. While I can still afford it. Those damn hookers only know how to do two things, and the thing they do the best is shopping." Nicky checks his watch for a second time as one of the female deckhands brings us Mimosas.

"You got somewhere to go?" I ask.

"No, I got to make a phone call."

"Go ahead, I wanted to ask you about something that has been on my mind, but it can wait."

Nicky shifts in my direction and gives me his full attention. "It can wait. It's going on two O'clock in the morning back home. So, what's up."

"How was Sal able to kill you parents?" I never beat around the bush with Nicky, and he never minced words with me. We were always straightforward no matter the subject. "Didn't your father have some bodyguards to watch his back? Sure, Sal was family and all, but shouldn't someone have stopped him from going into the bedroom and offing them?"

"That's rich, coming from the man who tried to set me on fire," Nicky fell back laughing. He sat back up and turns solemn, "My father retired from the Mob, that meant all his debts and vendettas were turned over to me. He was untouchable to anyone in the business. So, sure he had Pauley and Vinny to run errands for him. And occasionally one or two other guys would help him out, but anything more than that and people would start questioning if he really was retired. So, a fulltime bodyguard? He didn't need or want one. Who knew Sal was going to go off the deep end?"

"Or your father was going to push him over the edge." I lie back and sip my drink. "Go ahead, make your phone call."

"I was waiting for those stupid bells to stop ringing. Hey, you are going to like this." Nicky perks up, "I'm gonna put the screws to Lucas' boy. This is gonna be fun." Nicky dials a long number. We have our own communication company, so we can call anywhere in the world, from anywhere in the world, and it is untraceable. I told him the network had a non-repeating white noise generator built into it to prevent recording. It was better technology than I provided the government.

The bells go silent just as Nicky says, "Hello."

"Hello," the sleepy voice echoes back.

"Christopher Lucas, do you know who this is?" Nicky smiles at me and covers the mike with his hands, "the poor bastard is dead asleep."

"What? Who? I am Christopher, who are you looking for?" Christopher rubs his eyes and looks at the red digits on the clock by his bed. "Do you know what fucking time it is?"

"Yeah, I do. And the weather too." Nicky laughs. He is enjoying this like he's making a prank call. "Listen up you little piece of shit," his tone, and attitude, is all business now.

"Who the FUCK IS THIS?" Christopher sits up in bed, pulls the lamp cord, and lights up the bedroom.

Nicky hears the click and knows he has awakened his target, "it's Nails…" He never gives his name or his full street name on the phone. "I need you to hear me out because people's lives depend on it. Are you with me?"

"Yeah, I hear you. I guess I know who sent me this phone, now." Chris starts to get out of the bed but then lays back, deciding to handle things himself. "So, what the fuck do you want? Are you going to tell me you have a hitman outside my house ready to blow me away? Or maybe your nigger friend…"

"My friend is right here, and he can hear you."

"What! What did he say about me?" I ask.

Nicky shakes his head and goes back to the conversation, "If I wanted you dead, I wouldn't have sent you a phone. You think you can sit your ass a mile away from my house and I wouldn't know about it? Or you can have guys hanging out across the street from my place? But I know this is all your father's doing. So, I'm not mad with you. I sent you the phone so we can talk peace… you still with me?"

"Yeah, I am with you. Why don't you and me set up a sit-down? You know, work this thing out in person."

Nicky looks at me and starts mimicking jerking off. "First off, that should be you and I, and second, if that were to happen, I would kill you. I'd have to because I would be sure you intended to kill me. Look, I'm going to tell you the truth. Your sister, Angela was a real good lay, that being said, I didn't mind marrying her. It was unfortunate she got caught in the crossfire of some hit on me. You know what I think."

"NO, WHAT?"

"Hey, what are you getting all railed up about? I said I was going to tell you the truth. I think that fat bastard Benny the Butcher was behind the whole thing. He tried to kill me, which got your sister killed, killed my mother, father, and tried to have your father kill me. But he only managed to kill my brother."

"You are crazy," Christopher tried to deny what he felt was probably the truth. No one knew how or why Nicky's parents died, but they didn't believe it was an accident, not in this life. "My father had nothing to do with the Brunello family. He…"

"He was hurting because his daughter was killed," Nicky sounded sincere, "I avenged her death tenfold. I had the killer's family whacked. Obviously, I would never say this to anyone else, but I know your family is hurting. I tried to square thing with your father and look where it got me… my family's dead. And your father is ruining your—"

"Seriously, let's have a sit-down, we can work this out."

"I had a friend named Christopher, he tried to fuck me over. I no longer have a friend name Christopher. Your father is too far gone. And because his people no longer respect you on the streets, the Jamaicans are running you out of Brooklyn, and you are barely holding onto what business you have in the city. Christopher, I know it's not your fault. I am throwing you a life-line here, grab it. I have nothing against your family, but your father will not stop. Just give me a time and a place."

"No."

"NO!" Nicky jumps to his feet as the church bells start to ring.

"I mean, I can't do that," Christopher wonders about the strange bells ringing in the background. He begins to think maybe this is a dream.

"Ok. I guess you don't believe how serious I am. I hope you are not close friends with the people your father has watching my place." Nicky ends the call.

"That was quite a performance. Now what?" I ask. I signal the deckhand in the tight white short skirt and she brings a tray with two more mimosas and an ample amount of coke. I pat the chair and slide over to make room for her to sit. The three of us do lines from the tray in her lap and then she departs leaving us the drinks.

Nicky looks at his watch, it's set to New York time. "Now what is already over."

IT WAS a usual quiet Saturday night at the Sons of Italy Social Club and Bar. The summer crowd was not in full gear yet and the place closed promptly at two every night. The people who lived in the apartments above were appreciative of the winter hours as the noise levels rose considerably as the hours of operation increased during the summer. Culminating in bar fights, loud cursing in both Italian and English, and the occasional gunfire around the Fourth of July. This cloudy cool Saturday night was serene.

Across the street, three houses down, lived Carl and Carol Pollock. The Jewish couple lived in the two-story single-family house with a basement for fifty years. They had raised four children on the quiet tree-lined street, all married and living in their own single-family houses now. Carl Pollock retired from the New York City Transit System years ago, and Carol was a retired teacher. They watched the evening news and then *Jeopardy!* And were in bed and asleep before the nightly news. It was more than a ritual; it was a lifestyle from decades of being up at dawn and done by primetime.

A single man dressed in black fatigues and ski mask walked in the shadow of the Pollock's home to the back basement door. He jimmied the slam lock and entered the darkened house. He went upstairs, looked in on the elderly couple and was satisfied they were in a deep sleep. He had picked their house because it had an access ladder attached to the wall leading to the roof hatch. These houses all had roof hatches of a sheet of plywood nailed to a two by four frame and held down by a hook and eye. Some had a layer of tin nailed over them as waterproofing, but most were just covered in a thick coat of tar.

The man in black climbed the ladder and crouch walked to the back of the house. The knotted ball of rope he had thrown up there was a foot from the edge. He carefully pulled the rope which was tied to a ten-foot long two by three plank of wood up to the roof. Then he quietly extended the plank across the driveway to the roof of the house next door. He crossed the plank with catlike movements and as he stepped onto the second roof, vanished into the background of black tar paper. He pulled the wooden plank, backing up on the roof using the edge as leverage against its weight, then just as carefully lowered it down the back of that house. It was a long step, a foot and a half separation between this house and the next.

He was now on the roof of the house directly in front of the Sons of Italy Social Club and Bar. The windows across the third floor were all black. All the lights of the apartments across the street were out. He looked at his watch, pulled a small iron pry bar from his cargo pocket and began removing the plywood cover from the roof hatch. This one was covered in dried and baked on tar, giving a clear line as to where the plywood ended, and the two by four frame began.

Noiselessly, he dropped into the hole onto the landing at the top of the stairs. This house did not have an access ladder. He quickly swung the twelve-gauge pump action shotgun from his back and spun into the hallway between the bedrooms, his sleek frame plastered against the wall. These houses were similarly built, a twenty-five-foot hallway leading to the master bedroom and three bedrooms along the right wall. The bathroom was behind him to the left. The house was completely dark, its occupants had gone to bed a while ago, except one.

The man in black could see him from down the hall sitting at the front window, silhouetted by the streetlights outside. He needed to get closer, beyond the first bedroom door off the master bedroom before he made his move. Otherwise, he could be caught in a crossfire when the others in the assault team awoke. He crept slowly towards the master bedroom on his toes, like a cat stalking its prey. His third footfall caused a creak from the floorboards and he thought ended his element of surprise.

The man in the chair shifted and found a more comfortable position for himself. The man in black sighed in relief and quickened his step. With his right-hand index finger on the trigger and the shotgun nestled snuggly against his shoulder, he reached across with his left hand to open the bedroom door. There were two bodies under the covers, as he expected. He had been watching the team of hitmen for a month from the apartment above the club. On a Saturday night there could be as many as eight people in the house, the four hitmen and their concubines. On this night when the order came to eliminate the team, there were only two women in the house.

He didn't know who they were sleeping with, but when the shooting started, they had to go too. He pumped the first shot into the sleeping man in the chair, shattering the window and the peaceful night in the neighborhood. He swung to his right and a second blast followed immediately on the sound of the first, lighting up the bedroom. The man in black pumped another shot into the bed, creating a second bloody patch on the covers and sending a spray of red across the white walls.

He heard feet hit the floor behind him and a woman screamed. He had already turned about and begun back up the hallway to the back two bedrooms. A rectangle of light appeared before him and a man in boxer shorts stepped into it. He dropped to one knee, expecting a gunshot from the third mark and cut him in half just above the white boxers. More screaming filled the house. It was coming from the last bedroom. Then, it stopped.

The man in black stood for a moment; two more Mississippis. He had been counting them since the first shot fired, no longer before the door. He was up to seven. He calculated, this job should take no more than ten to complete. He heard the squeak of bedsprings and pumped his shotgun three times at the closed door. He spun back away from the door, and quickly shoved two more shells into the empty shotgun. He stuck the tip of the barrel through the bottom most section of the splintered door and cautiously peeked into the dark room. Two figures were crumpled against the wall beside the bed. The woman in front of the man. His arm wrapped around her neck, he used her as a shield. The man in black heard a low moan and fired one shot into the pair of bodies at head level.

He quickly goes down the stairs and out the basement door. First, he retrieved the plank and rope from the backyard next door, then he hopped the fence into the backyard behind the house and comes out on the next street. He slides the wood into the back of his van. When the police arrive, they will have no clue as to how he got onto the roof. He had swept up the shotgun shells from the hallway before he left, so not to leave any evidence behind. He gets into his van, starts it up, and drives away as a few lights in the neighborhood begins to come on.

THE RINGING of a telephone replaced the violent sounds of murder. A dozen cycles of the bells completed then minutes of silence returned. It would not last long as the police sirens could be heard approaching in the distance.

Christopher Lucas hung up the phone in the Long Island house and woke up Mario, "I know who sent the phone, Nicky Nails."

"So, he called you," Mario stretched a hand out for his watch. He looked at it and said, "goddamnit, don't that guy ever sleep? What did he have to say?"

"He sent a warning. We end this now or we are next."

"What do you mean, next?" Mario was out of bed and putting on his pants.

"I called the house in the Bronx, he knew about them," Chris was holding the little black mobile phone in his hand.

"You didn't call them on that phone, did you?"

"No. I used the phone in my bedroom, but no one answered. I think they are all dead." Christopher was sheet white, and his hands started trembling. "He knows we are here. I think we need to get out of this house now."

"You're right." Mario was getting dressed in a hurry now. He looked at Christopher and took the phone from his hand. "Hey, it's going to be ok. Go wake the boys. Tell them to get dressed and leave everything." He had to push Christopher towards the door to get him moving. "If Nicky Nails wanted you dead, he would have sent his hitman here instead of the Bronx. Don't worry, I got a safehouse I am going to take you to, the boys will be fine going back home."

It was one of Mario's girlfriend's place. To be sure his wife did not find out about her, he kept her completely out of the mob world. To her, he was an investment banker, which he was, and she worked at a financial institution. She figured he was married but powerful men liked to set their own rules. So, when he called her early Sunday morning and told her to pack for a trip to Europe, she did just that. She never saw Christopher. It was two weeks later when Christopher felt safe enough to leave the apartment in Queens.

Christopher went home to speak to his father. His mother

told him that his father was spending a lot of time at his sister's gravesite. He would go there on Sunday morning and not return until Sunday night. She had gone with him at first, but he just sat there on the marble bench he had bought, staring at the tombstone and muttering curses. She couldn't take it anymore. It was not how she wanted to remember her daughter. "Chris, go to him. You try and get him back. He is overwhelmed with grief."

As his mother requested, he drove out to the cemetery in Queens. It was a small place, a few blocks long and wide behind a Catholic church. It wasn't much to look at, one side had a tall wall that protected it from the highway traffic. A small black iron bar fence enclosed the rest of it and a few trees dotted the edges. The neighborhood was quiet but rundown, broken bottles and trash piled up along the fence. It was the last place one would come to find peace. "Hey, Dad. Mom said I would find you here."

"She stopped coming. Her heart is broken and is waiting for you to fix it." Peter Lucas spoke without looking back to his son. He was staring at the tombstone, at the eight by ten graduation picture of Angela encased in the granite.

"That's new," Christopher pointed to the picture behind the glass. He sat next to his father and waited for a response. None was given and he decided to tell his father what he knew. "You know we lost four good men in the Bronx? Nicky…"

"Don't you mention his name in her presence. Do not disrespect your sister like that. Why are you here? Did you finally kill him? Can she now rest in peace in this God-awful place?"

"He killed the team in the Bronx. He knew about the house in Long Island—"

"And so, you ran and hid," Peter sighed heavily, "you fucking coward."

Christopher felt the sting, but it was because it was true, he did run and hide. But he also knew he could not hide forever, not from Nicky, and not from his father. He had to make his father see the truth. He was in a war he could not win. "Dad, listen to me for once. We are losing on the streets. Our territories in Brooklyn are being overrun. The other families are chipping away at our gambling houses in the city. Your men are saying you are losing your mind. You have lost their respect. You must put an end to this war."

"Why haven't you?" Peter's voice is low and far away. "Why haven't you got the balls to take some men, a dozen, two dozen, I don't care. Take them all and storm his house and kill that bastard for killing your sister."

"Because he is not in his house on Long Island. He's not even in the country. He's somewhere in Europe." Christopher lowers his head. "He's laughing at you."

"How do you know he's not in his home?" screams Peter Lucas as he turns towards his son.

Christopher catches his father's arm as the hand heads towards his face. The struggle is short lived, and his father lowers his hand. "Because I heard the bells."

"What?"

"Church bells, Dad. He called in the middle of the night to tell me he had sent an assassin to the team in the Bronx. I heard church bells in the background. He had to be somewhere in Europe. It must have been Sunday morning where he was calling from." Chris pulls the little black cellphone from his pocket and places it besides his father. The black digits are displayed in the green window of the mobile phone. He stands in front of his father and pleads, "press the call button, Dad. Talk to him. You can end this thing now, no one else needs to die."

"I AM NOT AFRAID OF NICKY NAILS ROCCI! If he wants me dead, let him come and get me. I don't care if he kills you. If he kills all of you. This thing will not end until I have peace for my Angela."

Christopher Lucas shakes his head sadly. He walks past his father as he goes back to muttering curses and insults at him and

Nicky alike. He turns around, pulls a .22 revolver from his pocket, places the tiny black barrel against the back of his father's head, and squeezes the trigger.

A small pop. A little smoke streams from the red hole in Peter Lucas' head. He falls over on his knees, his forehead inches away from the eight by ten glass encased picture of Angela with bloody teardrops running down her face. The glass spider webbed by the bullet. Christopher puts the little black revolver back in his pocket.

He picks up the black cellphone from the marble bench in front of his sister's grave and looks at his father's body, which has fallen over onto its side, the blood soaking into the ground. Christopher Lucas presses the white button with the handset pictured on it. "Peter Lucas has found peace with his daughter Angela."

It is over

ABOUT THE AUTHOR

A native New Yorker from the South Bronx, Fort Apache, during the 60's, a time when everyone needed a gang.

He worked in finance and later earned a degree in computer programming, his other love. A prolific storyteller, his experiences seasoned his crime novels, unleashing the characters in his head.

This journey led to RockHill Publishing LLC to publish his own work and give others access to the literary world.

Killer With A Heart introduces teenage gangsters and mobsters in the conflicting world of Organized Crime.

Killer With Three Heads has the boys from the Bronx returning as international criminals.

The final book, *Killer With Ice Eyes* is a 2019 NANOW-RIMO winner and is in development.

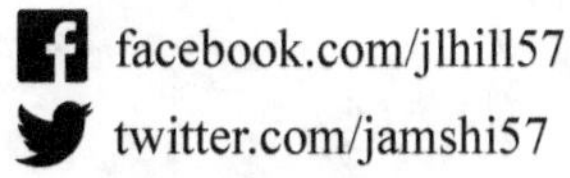

facebook.com/jlhill57

twitter.com/jamshi57

Also by J L Hill (AKA James L Hill)

<u>Fantasy</u>

The Emerald Lady

<u>Science Fiction</u>

Pegasus: A Journey To New Eden

KILLER WITH ICE EYES

Chapter 1 – The Ball Buster

Corine peeks through a crack in the mud-brick wall of her cell. She can hear the voices of men nearby; they are coming from the other side of the compound. She turns to the girls in the other cell across from her "they are coming back. Who do you see?"

"I see the tall one, the fat one, and the boy," whispers Talgi. "Corine, I'm scared. They are coming for us this time." She clutches her dirty blazer tight around her neck. The other girls, ten in all, huddle around her. Talgi is the oldest of the Sudanese captives.

"Don't worry," Corine says calmly, "they are coming for me. Again." She ties the strip of dress she tore from the hem around her waist, knowing it will not stop what was about to happen. Her blue dress was nothing but a rag now, Derreon Gila ripped it down the front the first night he raped her, right after she kneed him in the groin.

She rubbed her cheek; the swelling was almost gone. This will be the third time this week he was coming for her. This time it was different, the big one, as the girl called him, was bringing his brother, the young boy. And they were coming in the morning.

The door to the mud brick shanty swung open with a thud. The girls in the cells on the other side of the room screamed and cowered in the corner of their cell. Derreon loved scaring the young girls. He banged on the bars with the inch-thick rebar he carried as a club, eliciting cries from the frightened girls.

"Don't let that black gorilla scare you, girls," Corine yells as she grabs the bars of her cell. "He can't touch you. You are worth money to his boss if you are unharmed. If he hurts you, I'm sure his master will shove that iron bar up his ass."

Derreon spins around and grabs Corine by the throat before she can retreat. "But you are not worth anything to anyone, you little French whore. You are mine to do with as I wish." He pushes her back with enough force to send her to the ground. He pulls a key from his pocket, unlocks the cell, and stands menacingly in the doorway.

Corine pulls her dress close around her as she scoots away from him. He laughs and says, "I am tired of your little cunt. You no longer amuse me. Today, my little brother will become a real soldier. Katuma, get over here!"

The young boy, skinny and frail, stands in the shadow of his older brother, his eyes glassy with fear. He trembles as Derreon grabs him by the arm and flings him into the cell. He stumbles to the side as he tries to avoid tripping over the woman on the floor.

"What are you waiting for? She is nothing. A worthless piece of meat Allah has placed here for our amusement."

"Can't you see he is just a boy? He should be out kicking a ball around with his friends. Not toting a gun and committing these crimes you are forcing on him. You believe in God; He will punish you both for this."

The fat man laughs, "maybe he does not like whores. Maybe he wants one of his own, closer to his own age. Or maybe we should take him to the other adobe where you are holding the bo…"

Derreon's rebar keeps him from finishing his sentence and sends blood flying from his mouth. "See what I tell you. You dishonor me and yourself. This fool insults your manhood. It is time for you to become a man and a soldier in this army!"

Disgusted with his brother's lack of action, Derreon grabs Corine by the ankle and flips her over. He rips his pants opens and pins her head to the floor. With one arm around her waist, he hauls her up to him and shoves his stiffening penis into her. He humps her furiously for a couple of minutes before dropping her to the floor again. Derreon rips her dress from her body and wipes himself off. Then he throws the garment in his brother's face. "See, that is all there is to it. Just a piece of meat."

He grabs his dick and shakes it at the other girls, laughs, and pulls his pants up. As he walks out of the cell and passes the fat man still unconscious on the floor between the two cells, he kicks him in the groin. He looks back at his brother who is covering the naked Corine sitting with her knees to her chest. "Careful, little brother, she's a kicker. Lock her cell. And when this Mutha Fucka wakes up, take him outside and shoot him. No. Shoot him here. Show these girls you are at least that much of a man."

Katuma locks the cell and leaves the shanty. He returns a few moments later with a pistol in hand. His head is down. He fires one shot into the back of the fat man's head. The head bounces once. Katuma leaves, slamming the door without making eye contact with any of the captives.

There are the sounds of trucks arriving at the camp. Corine peeks through the crack in her wall and sees a white man exiting the first truck. She studies his looks, the way he walks; he is dark-haired, average built. His camo outfit is clean and pressed; he is not a fighter. Perhaps, a businessman who has come to buy the girl.

Talgi asks, "what is going on out there?" It is the first time anyone has spoken since Derreon raped Corine and Katuma killed the other soldier. Two other boy soldiers had pulled the man's body out an hour ago.

"I'm not sure," Corine answers. She cups her hands to make it easier to see through the narrow crack. In the two weeks since they had been kidnapped, she hadn't been able to widen the hole by much. They had to eat their food with their hands, and the tin plates were too big to use. But she could still get a fairly good view across the compound.

"Are they here for us?"

"No. I don't think so." Corine saw about a dozen men, whites and Africans, exit the second truck. They were unloading crates from the last truck. "It looks like these guys are making a delivery. I promise, I won't let them take you."

"Corine, you can't stop them," Talgi says. "They take the boys for soldiers and we are to make wives for them. Or worst, they will sell us as prostitutes. The LRA raided my cousin's village two years ago, I never heard from her again."

"That is not going to happen to you." Corine put up her hand to end the conversation.

"What?"

"It's Commander Raska Diambu."

A fearful squeal came from the other cell.

Corine again waved her hand over her head for silence. The white man in the pressed camouflage and the commander in his beige dress uniform were just out of earshot. Corine was trying to read their lips.

The commander pointed to one of the last boxes unloaded from the truck. An African soldier quickly pried it open. The commander used both hands to pull a long black tub from the crate. He swung the strap over his shoulder and aimed at Corine's hut.

"That is the best rocket launcher on the black market. American made, reloadable, lightweight, and with an advance targeting system. The range is a mile. Fire and go," bragged Otto Boone.

"Yes, it is as you say, a fine weapon. And the guns?"

"AK47s, as you requested. You are going to raise Hell in the capital with these weapons, Commander."

Commander Diambu tosses the rocket launcher to the soldier who opened the crate. "Derreon, why don't you bring out one girl for Mr. Boone? A bonus for you."

"Thanks," Otto says with a smile. "But it will be very hard for me to take her where I'm heading next. You know, a lot of questions."

"What about a nice French woman?" asks Derreon. "We can have her cleaned up in a few minutes."

Otto looks towards the hutment at the other end of the road. He thinks for a moment, "let's just stick to the original deal. I'll take the diamonds and we will be on our way."

"Of course," concedes the commander. Derreon hands Otto a briefcase. After a quick look inside the two men shake hands. The commander returns to his headquarters and Otto Boone climbs back into his truck and leaves.

Corine steps away from the wall. She had seen what she came to see. The commander was in the camp, but she didn't know for how long. She sat on the floor and started clicking her teeth together. The other girls didn't know what she was doing, but she was behaving oddly. She looks up at the girls, goes back to her crack in the wall and watches for a while longer.

She turns back to the girls. "We are getting out of here soon. I need you girls to gather in the corner over there." She points to the corner of the cell behind the entrance to the room. "When the shooting starts, stay low and keep silent."

"Who's coming to rescue us? And how can you know this? You are a UN teacher."

"Actually, Talgi, I'm not with the United Nations," Corine sees no trouble in sharing her secret now. "I work with a group of soldiers hired by your government to track down Commander Diambu, and he is in the camp now. I just sent a message to my troops; they will be here in a few minutes. My men are a couple of miles from here hiding in the jungle."

Talgi comes to the bars, she looks horrified and angry, "are you saying you could have freed us at any time and yet you did nothing. You let those men…"

"I had to. I had to wait for the commander to show up," she is unapologetic, "I get Diambu and the kidnappings stop. We can break the LRA in this part of the Sudan."

"You put your life in danger. I guess that is your actual job. But what about our lives? Do you not care what happens to us?"

"Of course, I care." Corine left the corner of her cell and came to the bars. "At the first sign of danger to you, or any of you girls, I would have called in my strike force. I would never let them take you out of this camp, not for any reason. Now, quickly, take cover, there is going to be a lot of shooting."

The words just left Corine's lips when the yelling and gunfire started. The gunfire sounded close; she knew it was return fire from the LRA soldiers. Her men probably started the assault with snipers. She used the transmitter imbedded in her cheek to give the location of the commander's headquarters and her own. Although, she figured in the two weeks she been held captive, they must have scouted out the camp.

A loud explosion, quickly followed by a second, meant they blew up the two trucks in front of the headquarters. Something heavy impacted the wall of her cell loudly. A cloud of dust and small bits of the ceiling fell in. The girls were screaming and crying now. She wanted to tell them to remain calm. That cries would draw the attention of the LRA soldiers, who might decide to execute them, over letting them be freed. But there was no time for that.

The gun battle was getting louder and closer. Her men were moving in on the camp. Corine felt sorry for the young boys that were undoubtably being killed. She watched drills in the mornings and again at night; she calculated about ninety percent of the soldiers, if you could call them that, were boys less than fifteen years old. She counted about a dozen men in the camp and a hundred boys. Like the girls in the cell across from her, the LRA had exhausted the older boys and girls in this war and was now gathering the pre-teens and teenagers.

The Sudanese government was desperate to stop the recruitment and building of these kid armies. That was when she got the call. The Sudanese army was reluctant to go after Diambu and others like him. It meant killing children, their children. There was no way around it. So, the government secretly hired mercenaries to hunt down the commanders of the children armies and do what was necessary.

Corine took the assignment for very personal reasons. She gave orders not to kill the children. Her men used nonlethal rubber bullets against the kids. The snipers and the A-Team, A for assault not the popular TV show of a decade ago, although they often played the theme song during a battle on a boom box, fired live rounds at the adult LRA members. There was no requirement to capture Diambu or his commandoes alive. The Sudanese government would welcome a confirmed kill over a trial and hanging, less to explain.

As suddenly as it started, it was over. Deathly silence took hold of the camp. The girls sobbed nervously in the corner of their cell. Corine looked up to see beams of sunlight criss-crossing the shanty. When she stood up a few spots of sunlight dotted her chest. The thick mud walls did little to stop the bullets that someone had taken the time to spray the shanty with. The door swung open, and the full brightness of the sun lit up the room. Dust particles, millions of them, twinkled in the shaft of light.

"Maria, you in here?" A thick deep man's voice entered the house.

"Yeah, don't shoot! We are alone," Corine, whose true identity was Maria Delitanni, informed him.

"Jesus! You look like shit."

"Thank you, Barry. You always know how to make a girl feel special," Maria says, holding her tattered dress as closed as possible. "Can you have someone bring me some fatigues? And stop gawking. There are no mirrors in here, but I can't look that bad. Or that good either."

Maria came out of the shanty dressed in camo. The girls stayed close to her, their eyes squinting and darting around at the soldiers, afraid of them but relieved they were there. There were small groups of boys sitting on the ground around the camps, hands on their heads, heads down. They had been warned not to look up, not to move.

Maria approached Barry Thomas. "I want these girls taken back to their village before nightfall. What about the boys?"

"The government is sending transportation for the girls and the boys. But it is going to be a little different for the boys. Those they can reunite with their family will go home. But they are all going to, ah… debriefing center first. It may be awhile before they can go home… those that still have homes."

"Fumu, come here!" Maria waved a gun toting young African soldier over. "Girls, stay with Fumu Akombi. He will get you back to your families. I've known him for years, he's from Niger." She leaves with Barry as the soldier flashes the girls a big smile. They head for the headquarters, "tell me you took that bastard alive."

"Shot himself in the head when we surrounded his headquarters. But we got a couple of his friends. A big black African, tough motherfucker, when he ran out of bullets, he tried to fight his way out. Took half a dozen guys to take him down. Hey, there is a shitload of weapons in that building over there. Looks like they just got dropped off. Some high-grade American stuff. Why didn't you call us in when the weapons were being delivered? We could have nailed the arms dealer too."

Maria shot him a look of disgust. "Really? Is that what you think? You could have gotten a two for one here?"

Barry stopped abruptly. "It is what we in the US government call a target of opportunity. We would like to know how he got his hands on some of our top equipment. And keep him from getting any more."

"You can pick him up on the road," Maria resumes walking towards the headquarter.

Barry is still holding his position. "Oh, you think so. I sent a squad after him. They found his truck two miles down the road. He ditched it and took to the jungle. He's in the wind now."

"Well, if you would have shown up while his men and he were still here, it would have been a much different fight. It wouldn't have been boys and rubber bullets. It would have been men and lead. I'm not subjecting my guys to that. The commander was the target. We got him, and that's what count. Now, let's go see my friends."

Maria sees Derreon and Katuma are hanging by their wrists a foot off the floor from a beam in the ceiling. She passes between and pulls on the rope that is tied to the bars in the window. Derreon is lifted another foot higher before she lets go and he drops. The handcuffs dig painfully into his wrist.

She spins him around and stops him with his rebar she took from the desk behind him. "I told you God was going to punish you. I guess I should have told you I am your God!"

Derreon spits in her face. She lets it run down her cheek. She cracks the rebar across his knee. "Oh, we are going to have some fun now." She drops the rebar on the dirt floor where a large pool of blood has soaked in. "You should have been smart and followed your commander to Hell."

"I guess you know this guy?" Barry says.

"He had the pleasure. And the other one is his brother. Why isn't he with the other boys?"

"Wouldn't leave the big guy's side," one of the men standing guard said, "said he wanted to die like a man."

"Well, Barry, this piece of meat hanging here probably knows all there is to know about your arms dealer. And I'd like to know who he is and who he works for? Somebody, give me my helping hand."

The same guard snickers and hands her a velvet sack. Maria rubs the bag gently on her right cheek, the side that didn't get spat on. She slowly slides her hand into the black bag. "Know what I have in this bag? No, don't guess! Let me tell you. It is something I picked up in a castle in Spain. It is ancient, but just as effective as the day they created it. They used it during the Inquisition. I call it, The Ball Buster!"

Maria rips the bag off and holds up her hand, encased in a shining silver glove with short spikes on the knuckles. She nods at Katuma and the guard who gave her the bag pulls on his rope, raising him another two feet off the ground. Just high enough for Maria to give him a solid uppercut to his genitals.

Katuma screams. The guard lets him drop. His wrist snaps and screams again. Katuma's camo pants are quickly turning red. Maria rips his pants down to expose the young man's shredded penis and balls. They hang down from his body. "That's why I call it the ball buster. Now, Derreon, I'm going to tenderize this piece of meat here while you think of that gentleman's name. Let me know when I can stop, OK."

Maria is throwing blow after blow into the young man's chest, abdomen, and ribs, as he twirls around like a punching bag. Wherever her steel spiked glove lands blood spurts and occasionally the sound of a bone cracking is heard. After a few minutes, Katuma hangs lifeless. His chest completely collapsed. His abdomen swollen with blood.

She rears back and takes one last swing. Her fist imbeds into his guts, which explodes a sea of blood that flows up her arm to the elbow. "Really, you let your baby brother literally get the crap beat out of him and you have nothing to say?" She shakes the blood from her hand in Derreon's face. "Talk about your strong silent types."

"Hey, have you thought maybe he doesn't know the guy?"

"Barry, he's the number two guy in this place. Nothing goes on that he doesn't know about. Hey, who got the camera? I want to make sure we send his mother a nice family portrait. Let the folks back home know how well he took care of his little brother." Maria pulls a sketch from her pocket and holds it up to Derreon face. "Hey, tough guy, you know this man? Has he ever been here? Perhaps with your gun dealing friend."

Maria rips the clothes from Derreon's body.

Barry throws up his hands and walks out the room.

She watches him go, then waves her bloody hand upwards a couple of times. The guard obliges and raises Derreon another few feet higher. She throws wild overhands punches, concentrating on his groin. He bites his lips until blood is running down his face.

The guard can no longer hold Derreon's weight, and he drops back down. Maria is in a blind rage. Punching the man until he hangs like a bloody piece of meat. She walks out of the office and unstraps the glove.

Barry looks at her with sadness in his eyes. "Satisfied?"

"No. But it will have to do."